Dillon's
DARE

Dillon's
DARE

BY

LEXI POST

Dillon's Dare

Last Chance Series Book #5

Cover design by Bella Media Management
Formatting by Bella Media Management
Cover photo: Killion Group, Inc.

Print ISBN: 978-1-949007-02 2

DILLON'S DARE
Last Chance Series, Book 5

By Lexi Post

Does he dare to love her?

After his mother goes too far in her attempts to marry him off to a woman of social standing, Dillon Hatcher follows in his brother's footsteps and escapes to his grandparents' house. Though he misses breeding the American Quarter horses at home, he's happy to help the horse rescues at Last Chance Ranch. What he's not happy about is Hailey Pennington literally dropping in. Do his mother's schemes know no bounds?

Hailey, "the Hellion" as her brothers fondly call her, has been crushing on Dillon for over a year. So when she discovers he's moved to Last Chance, she takes the opportunity to meet up with him without his mother's interference. It doesn't take long for her to see the man is open to a relationship…as long as it isn't with one of his mother's favorites. Just her luck, that's exactly what she is.

Determined not to fall for Hailey, Dillon finds himself becoming far too interested in her. But before he can decide which is more important, denying his mother or pursuing his own happiness, fate steps in, leaving him no choice at all.

Acknowledgments

For Bob Fabich, Sr., my own protector and biggest supporter. And for my sister Paige Wood, who is always available even when no one else is.

A huge thank you to Kayce Lassiter for her explanations of odd horse behavior that I didn't know about. She always makes me smile.

Thank you to Tammy Windsor for Naming Dillon's horse and to Gayle Lazur for naming Phoenix's mom.

A special thank you to my friends Eric and Gwen for sharing their story of their RANS Coyote, which kept me riveted, and inspired the chilling scene for Hailey.

As usual, I owe a lot to my amazing friend and critique partner, Marie Patrick, who read my pages as quickly as I wrote them. You are a true treasure!

Author's Note

Dillon's Dare was inspired by Bret Harte's short story, "The Indiscretion of Elsbeth," first published in the late 1800s. In Harte's story, an American is visiting a small town in Germany. He goes exploring and finds a beautiful park, but no one is in it. Eventually, he becomes lost and hearing voices, cuts through a hedge to ask directions. Instead, he finds a large family in military uniforms and white dresses with their backs to him, obviously posing for a picture. Ducking back through so as not to disturb them, he wanders around until he finds his way back to his hotel. When he arrives, he asks about the beautiful public park, only to be told there is none, only the private residence of a Duchess.

Two days later he receives an invitation to come to the estate which opens its small farm operation to the public a few times a year. There he is toured by a woman dressed as a dairy maid who says her name is Elsbeth. It is clear the area for the public is just for show, and taken with her, he asks to just sit and talk. Eventually, he kisses her which scares her, and she quickly ends the tour. He goes to a live theatre production the next night and sees the beautiful lady in a box. He inquires who she is. He is told it is the Princess. He reiterates his question by explaining the one in the blue dress, to which he is told that she is "the

Princess Alexandrine Elsbeth Marie Stephanie, the daughter of the Grand Duke."

He soon leaves Germany but at the border he is delayed. When he arrives home, in his luggage, he finds a photograph of himself and the princess standing next to each other against a hedge. He comes to the realization he must have been caught in one of the family photographs, Elsbeth saw him in it, and had arranged to meet him to get to know him. Though she liked him, she knew her place, and feared anyone finding out. He hangs the photo on his wall and when his friends comment on it, he simply smiles silently.

But what if the Princess decided to learn more about the man she's seen, only to discover he didn't want anything to do with her? How could she get him to see beyond her being a princess? And is there a way for their lives to come together or are the differences between them too large to overcome?

Chapter One

"What the hell?" Dillon Hatcher stepped out of the barn at Last Chance Ranch to find a hot air balloon sinking fast just beyond the house.

"What is it?" His grandmother joined him, wiping her brow with the back of her gloved hand. "Well, I'll be a burro's butt. Are they supposed to come down that quickly?"

At her question, the fear in his gut was confirmed. "Shit, no." Running for the corral where Eclipse was trying to impress Macy, he whistled. The black stallion turned at his call and broke into a run. Dillon swung the gate wide, and as the horse came to a halt before him, he grabbed his mane, jumped on his back, and kicked him toward the soon-to-crash balloon.

Galloping through the desert, as opposed to the new dirt road put in for Cole and Lacey's house, made it a shorter ride, but he still wasn't going to get there before touchdown. "Come on, boy."

Unfortunately, his position gave him the perfect view of the catastrophe about to unfold. Two people stood in the basket, one working on something while the other was clearly yelling. He hoped his grandmother had called 911.

"Holy shit." The balloon dropped fast, closer to the prickly pear cacti covering the area. Just as the basket was about to meet its shadow on the ground, it jerked upward about twelve feet.

1

His heart in his throat, he squeezed his thighs to get Eclipse to slow down and jumped to the ground.

The balloon floated slowly down to Earth, somehow finding an empty spot between the plant life.

Running up, he grabbed the rope lying on the ground, not sure he'd be able to keep the balloon from moving, but it had to be worth a try.

Laughter, light and happy, came from the basket, causing him to move his gaze to the occupants. The contrast between them couldn't have been greater. A dark-haired man scowled and shook his head at the woman with golden blonde hair, who was clearly thrilled by the experience. Somewhere in the back of his head he was thinking that she should be screaming or crying at the operator of the balloon.

"Hector, that was awesome!" She threw her hands up before giving Hector a squeeze he clearly didn't appreciate.

"You almost destroyed my balloon."

She pulled back, keeping her hand on his arm. "You know if that happened, I'd take care of it. How am I supposed to learn? I have to do it myself. I have to make my own mistakes and learn from them. And look, I did! Here we are safe and sound."

From the man's shaking head, Dillon was pretty sure he wasn't convinced. That's when the man saw him and nodded in his direction.

The blonde turned around and he froze, irritation sizzling up his spine. "You."

"Dillon Hatcher, right?" She hopped up on the edge of the basket and jumped down onto the desert floor. "I didn't expect you to be out here."

"Hailey Pennington, are you crazy?" He stared at the woman his mother had been trying to get his brother and now him to marry. Or rather, one of the women she wanted them to marry.

Hailey paused, cocking her head to the side. "I don't think so. You are Dillon, right?"

He barely controlled the low growl wanting to come out and threw his free hand up toward the balloon. "I mean the balloon. What the hell were you doing driving that thing, or flying or whatever you call it?"

She grinned. "Oh, I was learning how to fly it. It's an amazing feeling." Her green eyes lit with the thrill of her adventure. "Have you ever been in one?"

His stomach lurched at the thought. "If man was intended to fly, he would have been given wings. I keep my feet firmly planted on mother Earth."

"Well, it's exhilarating to reach beyond our limitations. You should try it some time." She spun toward the balloon. "You can go, Hector. I'll just catch a ride back to my car."

Hector looked him over as if deciding if he was safe to be in Hailey's company then scowled.

He let the man off the hook. "Go ahead, Hector. I'm sure someone at the ranch house can give Ms. Pennington a ride. It's probably safer than letting her back in your balloon."

Hector's lip quirked up before he nodded.

Hailey turned back to him, giving him a brilliant smile. "That's very gracious of you."

"This way." He handed the rope to Hector and turned on his heel toward Eclipse. As much as he wanted to jump on his horse's back and return to the house without Hailey Pennington, his mother had raised him right, despite her machinations to marry him off, and he'd walk her back. Besides, he'd catch hell from his grandmother if he left Hailey out here.

He stepped up to Eclipse and patted the stallion on his neck. "Come on boy, we're heading back."

"Is this your horse?" Hailey walked to Eclipse's other

3

side and started to pet him, cooing as if he were a baby. "You handsome boy. I bet you make all the fillies giddy."

Dillon rolled his eyes and clicked his tongue. Eclipse turned toward him and moved forward toward the ranch. "Yes, he's my horse."

Hailey let Eclipse walk by her then fell into step next to him. "He has no saddle or bridle. You must have been in a hurry."

He ground his teeth as anger surged anew at the almost mishap. "It *did* look as if you were going to crash. I wouldn't be surprised if Gram didn't call 911."

"Oh, Annette is here? That's wonderful."

At her obviously happy mood, he grew more irritated. "Which begs the question, why are you here? You're a long way from Ironwood or was the balloon crash just a coincidence." He let his sarcasm be obvious.

She gave him a disgruntled look. "That's a nice welcome for a guest. As a matter of fact, I've been taking lessons up here for a little privacy. Too many people know me closer to Tucson, and since I'm in the market for a rescue horse, I thought I'd kill two birds with one stone, so to speak."

And almost kill herself while she was at it. Still, a twinge of guilt crept into his conscience for assuming the worst, which was that his mother had sent her to stalk him. If Hailey was really at Last Chance to buy a horse, he needed to retrieve his manners. His brother, Cole, was always looking for kind owners for his rescue horses.

He had no idea if Hailey was kind to her animals, but he did know the Ironwood Ranch had a luxurious stable for its working horses. "Cole will be pleased to hear that. He's at the fire station today, but I'm sure Trace would be happy to show you the horses that are ready to leave or almost ready to leave."

"That would be great. I think what Cole has done here at your grandparents' ranch is wonderful."

"Yeah." It *was* wonderful, and it never would have happened if his mother hadn't refused to allow Cole to do it at Morning Creek. Despite missing his home, he was happy with his decision to move to his brother's and grandparents' horse rescue ranch. His mother had to learn that he wasn't her puppet.

"Did you get Eclipse from here?" She sounded so impressed, it made him want to say yes.

"No, I bought him." Much to his mother's displeasure, which had been exactly what he wanted, though it hadn't been his primary motivation for purchasing the Frisian stallion.

"He's beautiful."

He glanced over at her. She was admiring his horse who had his ass to them. For some reason, that lightened his mood. "Your family has a lot of horses. Why do you need another?" Shit, that sounded accusatory, though he hadn't meant it to be.

She moved her gaze from his horse to him. "I know, but I thought it would be a nice thing to do to give a rescued horse a home for the rest of his or her life."

Though she appeared sincere, his bullshit meter woke up. "Did my mother send you out here?"

Her head jerked back as if he'd slapped her and her brows lowered. "No, why would your mom have anything to do with my decision to buy a horse from Cole?"

Now he'd gone and stepped in it. He shook his head. "No reason." Though he didn't look at her, he could feel her gaze on him.

"Dillon, why are you here at Last Chance? Last I saw you, you were living at Morning Creek breeding American Quarter horses."

Yup, he'd stepped in it and now he was up to his waist in shit. "Hanging out with my cousins." That was true…in a sense.

"It's your mother, isn't it?"

He snapped his head around to look at her. At the sympathy in her eyes, he dropped his gaze.

Hailey sighed. "I can't imagine what it must be like to have Beverly as your mom. She's been less than subtle about getting me or one of my friends interested in you and Cole. At Cole's wedding, she must have been getting desperate because she even introduced me to Trace."

At the sound of Hailey's chuckle, he glanced at her. Her cheeks were pink with the sun or the heat, he wasn't sure.

"I thought Whisper was going to lose it and hit your mother a good one to the jaw."

He wouldn't put it past his cousin's girlfriend. She didn't exactly act like most people in social situations. "I'm sorry my mother has been so obvious about her wishes."

She waved away his apology. "Oh, don't be. She's not the first and she won't be the last to try to bring a Pennington into her family. When you're part of the oldest family in Arizona, you get used to it."

He'd never thought about it from her perspective. While Morning Creek Ranch was a thriving Quarter horse operation, Ironwood Ranch was the largest cattle ranch in the state. "And the wealthiest." Shit, that was rude.

Hailey laughed. "Yes, that, too. My poor middle brother, Cord, really takes issue with it and hides on the ranch most of the time, but the rest of us are fine with it."

He couldn't help looking over at her. She was so comfortable in her own skin. He liked that.

She turned her head toward him. "How long have you been hiding out here?"

He shrugged. "A couple months."

"Ah, that explains the long hair. The last time I saw you, I think it was at Cole's wedding, you had it very short."

He rubbed one side of his face with his hand, partly from habit, partly from the realization he also hadn't shaved in a couple days. He probably looked like he'd been out on the range for a week. "I think Last Chance is just as good a place as Morning Creek." Even if he did miss his work at home. Had Salud foaled yet?

Hailey shook her head. "Beverly must have really—ack!"

Luckily, he was looking at her when she tripped and started to fall. He grabbed her arms, just before she hit the ground.

Pulling her back up, he was unprepared for her to fall against him, and his body immediately responded to her soft breasts as they pressed against his chest.

Just as quickly, she tried to step back. "Ow."

Once again, she lost her balance.

He helped her stay upright, careful to hold her away from him.

"Shit. Excuse my language. I think I twisted my ankle."

He looked toward the ranch house. They were still a ways off. He clicked his tongue and Eclipse stopped. "Here, you can ride on Eclipse."

"Hold on, let me see if I can walk it out. It might just be sore." She held onto his arm and hobbled forward a couple steps before conceding. "I think you're right. Damn, I'm supposed to go out with my friends tonight."

"To the movies?" If that was the case, she could get a pair of crutches and hobble in.

She shook her head. "No, dancing."

He helped her over to Eclipse. "Grab his mane and step into my hands with your good foot."

She did as he asked, and he lifted her up high enough for her to swing her leg over. That she did it with ease wasn't lost on him.

He walked around to the other side. "Your ankle could be swelling. Let's get you to the house and get it packed in ice."

She grinned down at him. "Yes, doctor."

He ignored her comment, instead patting Eclipse to get him walking again.

"He's a large one. I thought you bred American Quarter horses."

He didn't look at her. "We do."

"Um, this big guy is no Quarter horse."

"As I said, I bought him. I wasn't planning to breed him. Just ride him."

At the sound of Hailey's laughter, he finally looked up. Her chin tilted up, and her cheeks were rosy as her lips lifted in a wide smile. Was she always so happy? Then again, she was a Pennington, so there wasn't much to cause her trouble. "Did I say something funny?"

She shook her head. "I guess not. It just struck me as funny. Here I was thinking you had some grand plan to start a new breed or something and you simply bought him to ride. I like that."

He looked forward again, avoiding the cacti as they came closer to the house. His grand plan had been to buy a reliable horse and piss off his mother, and he'd succeeded. Unfortunately, it hadn't stopped her from trying to marry him off. If she even thought he was talking to Hailey right now, the wedding invitations would be in the mail.

The last thing he had any intention of doing was marrying someone his mother had chosen. One of the great things about living at Last Chance was that the local women had no idea he was connected to Morning Creek, so he'd been having fun dating everyone from a cocktail waitress at the Black Mustang to Dr. Jenna's closest neighbor.

He only had two criteria for the women he saw. They couldn't be someone his mother picked out and they couldn't be wealthy. Anyone else was possible relationship material, and if they liked his long hair even better.

Hailey admired Dillon as he strode through the desert in his tight blue jeans and sleeveless button-down shirt. Every step he took was sure and confident. She'd liked that about him the first time they'd met at his home when Beverly was trying to interest her in Cole.

He'd come in from outside while they were in the kitchen, his face covered in sweat as he'd walked in. Taking off his hat, he nodded to her as his mother gave a half-hearted introduction. Then he'd pulled a cooler out of a lower cabinet, filled it with bottled water from the fridge and lifted it into one strong arm as he grabbed up his hat with the other.

"It was nice to meet you, Miss Pennington." Were his final words before striding out the door.

She couldn't help looking at his ass as he exited. Even then, she'd thought him much more attractive than his brother. It was one reason why she'd always accepted Beverly's invitations. Her hope was that she might see Dillon again. It happened less often than she'd wished.

Despite her best efforts to forget about him, when she'd come to his brother's New Year's Eve party only to discover it was a surprise wedding, she'd finally accepted that she had a crush on Dillon, who just happened to look hot in his tuxedo since he was the best man…in so many ways.

At first, she thought fate was on her side as Beverly went out of her way after that to throw the two of them together as often as possible, but the more his mother pushed, the less he'd participated.

She wasn't sure, but she had a feeling the final straw was the Bachelor Auction for a children's charity. She'd seen that Dillon was on the roster of men to be auctioned off, presumably to take the lucky lady, who was willing to bid the highest for charity, on a date of her choice. There was no way she'd let anyone else have him if he'd volunteered, but if his mother had somehow forced him, she had planned to bid the highest and let him off the hook. His mother was more of a hindrance than a help in this instance.

Her excitement had grown as she caught a glimpse of him getting out of his truck in a black shirt covered in rhinestones. On any other man it would have looked feminine, but Dillon filled it out perfectly and that stride of his just made her sigh.

Yet when they called his name to come out on stage, her heart beating so hard she could barely breathe, he never appeared. The announcer covered it up, joking that men were a dime a dozen that night and moved on to the next bachelor. Since no matter what Beverly had conjured up, Dillon had always been polite, she had a feeling something big must have occurred between them.

It had taken her a while to figure out where he might have gone. When she finally did, she'd hatched her own plan. Maybe without Beverly, they could get to know each other like normal people. "So, bring me up to speed on how everyone is. I haven't been here since the wedding, though I heard that Beverly told your grandmother about Whisper's parents. I knew I knew her from somewhere."

"Yeah, that didn't go over so well. Things got hairy there for a while, but her and Trace are living in a couple trailers up on the north ridge."

"A couple trailers? You mean they aren't together?"

He shook his head but didn't look up at her. "Oh, they're together. Whisper and Trace in the new one and Old Billy and Uncle Joey in the other."

"I don't think I met those two men."

He chuckled, something she'd yet to hear him do. "Those two were meant to be friends. Uncle Joey can't talk due to a stroke, but he understands everything, and Billy never shuts up. It's a perfect pair."

That sounded precious. "I would love to meet them."

He looked up at her at that. "You would?"

She smiled. "Of course, they sound interesting."

He looked forward again shaking his head, but he didn't comment.

They were almost to the house, which meant soon she would have to share him with everyone else. "What about your cousin Logan?" Beverly had tried to get her interested in him as well, but the man barely spoke two words to her, which was just fine with her. "He didn't seem very happy at the wedding."

"He's happy now. He and Charlotte moved in with Dr. Jenna, the vet who checks out the horses here at Last Chance."

"That's great to hear. I mean, about Logan and that the vet checks out the horses. I have a feeling I'm not going to be able to look at any today though. I really hope this ankle isn't a sprain. I've had one of those and they take forever to heal."

Dillon led the horse right up to the front porch. "Don't worry. If you have to come back, the same horses will probably still be here along with some new ones." He shook his head. "I don't understand it."

"Understand what?"

He looked at her then. "I don't understand how people can be so inhumane to these outstanding animals." His blue eyes blazed with anger under his dark brows, proving him to be a man of strong emotions, which she'd always suspected.

"I don't either. I've always felt their punishment should be equal to what they inflict."

He nodded curtly before reaching his arms up. "Let's get you down from there and into the house."

More than happy to slip into his arms, she placed both her hands on his shoulders, glad he'd come to the side with her good ankle, though she fervently wished they were both good.

He grasped her waist and pulled her toward him until her leg cleared the horse's back. He was a big man, so his strength didn't surprise her, but it did cause the faeries in her stomach to dance around. As she landed on her good foot, she made sure to keep her other from touching the ground. She couldn't afford to have it ruin all her plans.

Dillon kept her at arms-length, not really where she wanted to be.

"Can you walk?" He appeared concerned.

That had to be a good thing. "I don't know. Let me have your arm, just in case."

He let go of her waist and held out his arm. She was more than happy to grasp his bare forearm, the muscle beneath her hand like a rock. Their warmer than usual November had its advantages after all, like Dillon wearing a sleeveless shirt that revealed his masculine arms.

Taking a step on her sore ankle, she felt a sharp twinge and quickly compensated with her other foot. "Crap. It figures I could land a hot air balloon safely but can't seem to walk through the desert without injuring myself."

Dillon shook his head. "No use complaining about it now. Let's get you up these stairs."

She was pretty sure her ankle wasn't sprained, but the

thought of testing it on the steps had her pulling back. "I guess I could hop up?"

He gave a heavy sigh. "No. You'd probably break your neck." Peeling her hand from his arm, he scooped her up and strode up the three steps.

She'd barely had time to enjoy the thrill of being in his arms before he set her down on the wrap-around porch. Luckily, he kept one arm around her back because sore ankle or not, she was sure she'd lose her balance after that excitement.

"Gram, we have a guest," Dillon yelled into the house, the screen door the only obstacle to his voice.

In no time, footsteps sounded on the hardwood floors. "Is it the idiot who almost crash-landed?"

Hailey felt her cheeks heat, but at Dillon's mortified look, she sucked it up. "Yes, it's the idiot who almost crashed in your backyard, though I need to emphasize the *almost*."

The screen door opened, and Annette Benson stood in the doorway.

"Hello, Mrs. Benson."

"Hailey Pennington. What are you doing here?"

She chuckled. "Crash-landing in your backyard."

Annette waved her comment aside. "But as you said, you didn't. Come in."

Dillon held out his arm again. "If you could hold the door Gram, I can help her in."

Annette's brows lowered in concern before she stepped out, keeping the door open. "What happened?"

She grasped Dillon's forearm again and used it to hobble into the farmhouse kitchen. It was a lot like the one at Ironwood, with a few more windows which made it a lot brighter. She waited as he pulled a chair out for her then sat, grateful to be off her foot.

Annette bustled in after them. "Dillon, pull out another chair and grab a couch pillow from the family room, so she can put her foot up." Annette turned to her. "I'm assuming you hurt your foot in the landing?"

She shook her head. "No. I brought that baby down with barely a bump, but I couldn't seem to put one foot in front of the other without tripping on the ground."

"*You* brought the balloon down?"

At Annette's surprise, she grinned. "I did. Made a couple mistakes at first but figured it out in time. It was the walking that did me in." She pouted before she grinned.

"But why here?" Annette pulled a pitcher from the refrigerator and took out two glasses.

She was about to answer when Dillon came back in and set up the chair next to her with a pillow.

"Try that." He stood back and let her put her foot on the chair.

"Dillon, you need to take off her boot so we can see if it's swollen. Actually, I think we should ice it down anyway."

"Really, Mrs. Benson I don't—"

"Don't even try." Dillon shook his head. "It will go a lot better for you to just do as she says." He sat on another chair and gently pulled the boot off and studied her sock.

Shit. She'd never thought he'd be looking at her socks when she'd dressed herself that morning.

"Hailey." His voice was deep, but there was a hint of humor in it. "Why do you have on purple socks with black bats on them?"

"Dillon."

At Annette's scolding tone, he smirked. "It doesn't look swollen."

As he sat back, she peered down at her ankle. Thank her

lucky stars because she needed her foot if she was going to catch his attention. "No, it doesn't. I'm so glad."

He met her gaze. "But I think your dance plans for tonight are still off."

That was fine with her.

"Dance plans?" Annette bustled over with a dishtowel full of ice. "Absolutely not. You're not going anywhere, young woman."

Huh? She widened her eyes and snapped her gaze to Dillon, who just shrugged.

"You're going to stay right here." Annette carefully placed the knotted dishtowel on her ankle. "Until you can walk again, it's our responsibility to see you are well since it was our land that tripped you up."

Hailey laid her hand on the woman's arm. "Really, Mrs. Benson. It was my fault."

Dillon shook his head as he stood.

"Balderdash." Annette shrugged off her hand and brought over a glass of lemonade. "Here you go, and you can stop calling me Mrs. Benson. Haven't heard that in so long, I almost forgot it was my name. Just call me Annette." The older woman sat down opposite her, though to call the strong and lean grandmother of the Williams and Hatcher men "old" would be an insult.

Annette Benson looked no more than fifty though she had to be seventy or more. Her long hair was pure white and she had the wrinkles of most who lived in the desert, but in a pair of blue jeans, a pale blue button-down shirt and cowboy boots, she appeared strong and determined.

"Thank you, Annette."

Dillon moved to the counter and poured himself a glass of lemonade, too.

"What are you doing, Dillon?" Annette's voice turned stern

again. "You have two stalls to get ready. Trace should be back with those horses within the hour."

"I was just on my way." He lifted the glass as if in a toast and taking it with him, he exited the room.

"So, young lady, why did you decide to drop in on Last Chance?"

She laughed at the pun on 'dropping' in. "Good one, Mrs. Ben—" At the woman's stern look, she quickly corrected herself, "Annette. I actually came to talk to Cole about a horse."

Chapter Two

Dillon strode toward the barn, but seeing Eclipse back over by Macy, he switched direction, clicking his tongue. "Will you stop flirting? It's not like she's even noticed you. She's a new mom and has more important things on her mind."

The horse trotted over to him, showing off his high step.

He rolled his eyes as he led the stallion to another corral. "You need to get control of yourself. You're as bad as a cat in heat." His horse ignored him as he closed the gate, simply trotting to the far fence which was closer to the mare.

Dillon shook his head and headed for the barn. His grandmother knew the two stalls were almost ready. Obviously, she just wanted to have some girl talk with Hailey. That was fine with him.

He stopped just inside the barn, swallowed the last of his lemonade, and perched the glass on a beam. He spent so much time avoiding Hailey and the numerous other wealthy and prestigious women his mother threw at him that he couldn't remember having a single conversation with her beyond the weather or some social event his mother was trying to get him to go to. It was nice to see the woman had a brain in her head, though he questioned her choice of hobbies.

He pulled a bag of shavings from the stack and proceeded

to spread them across the clean stall. Who in their right mind went for a hot air balloon ride? Never mind a ride, but decided to learn how to pilot it, or whatever it might be called?

Sure, there had to be some people out there, but he hadn't expected it from the daughter of a wealthy rancher. She was supposed to be perfecting her shopping skills and keeping up on the latest fashion or whatever women of that group did.

He much preferred a woman who wasn't afraid to get her hands dirty, like his grandmother. His cousin Trace had one of those in Whisper, but she was a bit too odd for his tastes. His brother's wife, Lacey, was nice and at least she could ride a horse, but she was all about the numbers. He just didn't want to have to think that hard.

Grabbing another bag of shavings, he opened it and dumped it. His plan was to do what Cole did. He would find a woman that fit him, not his mother's expectations. He'd always assumed he could handle his mother better than Cole had. Having been taught to respect his mother, he thought he could keep her at bay, and he had…until Cole married last New Year's Eve.

That was when she turned her total focus on him.

He closed the door to the stall and moved to the one next door. Opening another bag of shavings, he worked them across the floor. Even after his mother proved to him how little she respected him by throwing socialites at him, he still stayed at Morning Creek because of the horses.

He was damn proud of his work there, and his father had said he had a keen eye when they went to look at new mares. Yet his father allowed his mother to do whatever she wanted. He didn't understand that. Sometimes he thought his dad was happy to have his mom focused on someone besides himself, but he hated to think that could be true. Though he'd lost respect for his mother and her warped values, he still respected the man that taught him everything he knew.

Finishing up with the second stall, he gathered the empty bags and stuffed them in the trash. He wouldn't put any food out until he knew what they were dealing with when the new horses arrived. Coming to Last Chance had certainly opened his eyes to the cruelty of man.

It had also helped him to understand his brother's passion. At first, he thought Cole was nuts to leave Morning Creek, but now he understood. Cole's ranch was truly the last chance for many of the horses that came to him. Just since moving to Last Chance two months ago, he's seen starved, abused horses, psychologically scarred, sick, and neglected horses.

True, some were able to find new, caring homes, but if they couldn't, Cole kept them. Some of the Last Chance horses had been adopted by the family. He strode to the exit of the barn and looked at the two corrals of horses. In the cooler weather, they loved being outside.

Macy and her colt, Lucky, shared a corral with Tiny Dancer, the paint with the crooked legs, who Cyclone was obsessed with. Watching the Clydesdale moon over the little paint was hilarious, until the day he smashed the fence to be with her. Today, Cyclone was at Cole's house pulling an old tiller Cole picked up at an estate auction. They'd figured out the more work they gave the big horse to do, the happier he was.

His own horse had a thing for Macy, which shouldn't be too much of an issue this time of year. Then his cousin Logan had adopted Black Jack who was in the corral with Eclipse and Lightyear, Trace's horse.

He'd learned a lot about the horses' backgrounds and phobias. Black Jack was claustrophobic due to a mine cave-in. Lightyear couldn't be touched around his face, thanks to an episode with bees, and Cyclone had been badly burned in a barn fire after his owner had dropped him off at a rescue shelter for pets because the big horse liked to smash things, fences in particular.

They rarely got a heads-up as to what the problem was until they picked up the horse or it arrived at the ranch. That was because when Animal Welfare or the police called Cole, he always said yes. His brother's heart was bigger than he'd ever given him credit for…until now. He just hoped the new horses were being taken away because of their markings, like Macy, or deformities, like Tiny Dancer rather than due to abuse. The last horse they'd taken in from abuse didn't make it.

His gut twisted at the memory. No use borrowing trouble when it may not show up. They were told to expect two horses and they were ready.

The sound of a truck pulling into the yard had him stepping outside the barn, but it wasn't Trace. It was Trace's girlfriend, Whisper. His mouth went dry. Maybe she was just stopping by.

Jumping out of her shiny new double cab pick-up, Whisper slammed the door. "Trace isn't back yet?"

He shook his head. "Should be here any minute. Did he call you?" He sincerely hoped the answer was no.

"Yes. He said it's bad but couldn't talk."

"Fuck. I hate these." He swallowed the apology for his language. Last time he'd apologized to Whisper for swearing, she'd argued with him about it.

She strode over. The woman wore a pair of dirt-covered jeans and a red-checked button-down shirt that looked suspiciously like the one Trace wore a couple days ago.

"You and me both." She stopped next to him and scowled as she impatiently threw her long, straight black hair over her shoulder. "He had me call Dr. Jenna and tell her it was an emergency. Connie said she'd let the Doc know as soon as she finished her surgery. I hope that's damn soon. I don't want to lose another one."

Whisper's gaze swiveled across the dirt front yard toward the grove of Palo Verde trees where the last rescue now slept in peace. "Last time this happened, I told Trace I was grabbing Sal and going after the bastard, but he wouldn't tell me who the owner was. This time, I'm not going to tell him."

Dillon stifled a grin. He had no doubt Trace would keep the owner of these rescues from Whisper as well, especially since Sal was her Glock. His cousin knew Whisper better than anyone, which meant he had no doubt she'd kill whoever harmed a horse. Hell, she'd probably shoot someone for hurting a rattler.

The tension inside him while waiting started to eat at his gut. "I'm going to pull out the table for Dr. Jenna's medical bag. It sounds like she's going to need it."

"I hope that's all she needs."

At Whisper's statement he turned away, part of him wishing she didn't have such keen insight into animals while the other part of him wanted to grab his own gun and force his cousin to tell him who'd abused the horses.

Pulling out the sturdy folding table from the shed near Black Jack's outdoor stall, he set it up next to the two stalls where the horses would be housed. Having done all he could to get ready for their new residents, he picked up his forgotten glass and strode back toward the house.

Whisper had moved to the porch and sat in one of the straight back chairs. Her gaze was riveted on the road behind him. He'd just made the steps when the tell-tale sound of a trailer hitch rocking as a truck hit a divot in the dirt road had him turning around. Sure enough, Trace's truck kicked up dust on the dry desert floor as it moved toward him.

"Shit. I was hoping Dr. Jenna would get here first." Whisper jumped out of her chair and ran down the steps.

Setting his glass on a table next to one of the porch chairs, he jogged down the stairs after her, every step tightening his chest.

Trace pulled to a stop and immediately the trailer started rocking. The frightened whinny of a horse and the sound of hooves scraping on metal rent the air.

All of them ran to the back of the two-horse trailer.

"We need to get mama out first." Trace grabbed the lock on one side.

Dillon pulled the one on his side and at Trace's nod, they dropped the back ramp. The sudden noise halted all movement for a few seconds. In that time, two things hit him. First, the big black horse causing the noise looked big enough to be a Frisian. The second thing that hit him was the horse was ready to trample anyone in her path.

Sure enough, the mare started up again.

Traced yelled over the noise. "I'll get her out first!"

"No!" Whisper spun toward him. "Bring her colt out. She's petrified for her baby!"

He'd learned the first time he helped settle in a new horse that Whisper could communicate with the animals in an eerie way, so without a thought, he unhooked the halter from the trailer and walked the young colt down the ramp. As the baby came out into the sun, Dillon drew in his breath, unable to let it out. His hand on the rope tightened as if he could break it, punish it for what someone had done.

Whisper smacked his arm to get his attention. "Don't."

He stopped, thinking she'd changed her mind and wanted him to stop.

"Keep going, but don't get angry. Mama can feel it and she'll hate you. That won't help this colt," Whisper nodded toward the little brown Frisian.

He forced himself to calm by looking into the eyes of the young horse who wobbled with fear. Whisper was right. He needed to relax. Forcing himself to breathe, he smiled at the shaking horse, talking softly to it as he slowly led it out and around for its mother to see.

The mare stopped her movements as she caught her son's scent. When she finally could see him, she whinnied.

"Okay, Trace, bring her out."

At Whisper's command, Trace brought mama out and let the two have a moment.

Dillon looked at Trace, not able to look at the colt's body and the foot-long bleeding cuts on him without completely losing it. He kept his voice low. "I don't think Dr. Jenna is going to want this guy to be lying in shavings."

Trace lifted his hat from his forehead before setting it down again. "I think you're right. Whisper, can you grab the rope from Dillon?"

She shook her head and grasped Trace's rope. "No. I'll stay with mama."

Trace shrugged. "Guess I'll be clearing out the stall then."

He watched Trace stride away.

"He doesn't always listen so well. Only when it comes to animals." Whisper frowned. "Now if I could just get him to think of Uncle Joey as an animal, maybe he'd listen to me when it comes to not spoiling that man."

His lips twitched, but he kept his smile to himself. That Trace and Whisper argued over—

"Oh, my God."

At the sound of the feminine voice, he moved his gaze to

the porch. Hailey stood there, leaning against the post at the top of the steps.

"Come on, Hailey." Gram patted Hailey's shoulder. "Now you've seen them. Let's go back inside and leave Whisper and the men to their work."

He couldn't look away as tears started to cascade down her cheeks though her brows were lowered in a scowl. With her golden hair loose about her shoulders, she looked like an avenging Arch Angel, or what he'd like one to look like, beautiful and angry. Too bad she couldn't come down and wreck vengeance on the animals' former owner.

Her hands clenched into fists. "We need to bring whoever did that up on charges. No one should get away with that kind of abuse."

Her anger helped some of his own dissipate. Having someone from outside of Last Chance understand what was happening in Maricopa County and beyond, gave him a false sense of accomplishment, as if he was responsible for showing her. If she told a few people here and there, maybe it could help.

"Okay, it's ready." Trace strode toward them. "I cleaned out the shavings in one stall. We'll need to wrap those wounds, so the mare doesn't lick them while we wait for Jenna."

Whisper led the way to the barn. "We'll do it outside the stall. You can't separate them now."

Dillon looked at his cousin as they walked the horses toward the barn. "What do you want to do?"

Trace shook his head. "It's not about what I want, or what we think is right. Whisper has a direct line of communication with these animals, and I'm not sure about you, but..." He looked at the horse he led for a moment then continued. "I don't feel like getting kicked by an angry horse today, so we do what Whisper says and hope Dr. Jenna gets here damn fast."

It didn't take long to get the bandages around the colt. Luckily, they kept a large supply on hand. The only thing that slowed them down was getting the halter off the baby without touching a nasty cut on the side of his face.

He finally solved the problem by cutting the leather nose and crown straps on the top, which allowed it to drop to the ground. He wasn't going to cause the animal any more pain than it had already suffered.

When they had finished and had the two horses settled into the clean stall, Trace insisted that Whisper stay with them until Dr. Jenna arrived. Whisper didn't agree or disagree, and Dillon had a feeling that she'd do whatever she wanted.

As he and his cousin left the barn, his anger surged anew. "What the fuck happened? What kind of monster does that to a newborn? How old is he? A week? Ten days?"

Trace stopped and pulled his hat off. He swiped the sweat from his forehead with the bandana from his back pocket before setting his hat back on his head. "I've got the paperwork in the truck. I didn't even look at it. I was in too much a hurry to get those two away from the bastard."

He followed his cousin to the truck. "You saw who did this and didn't kill him?"

Trace grimaced. "See. That's why Cole only trusts me to do pick-ups, but I have to tell you, if the police weren't standing there surrounding the guy as he sat on the ground moaning, I would have done him more bodily harm."

To see his easy-going cousin scowl as he spoke made him feel a little better. "So, what's the story?"

Trace opened the passenger door. "Believe it or not the owner is a rich bastard, or he was. I think his bank account hit the skids. The stable manager called the police on him. She's one gutsy lady."

"She called the authorities on her boss?"

Trace nodded as he pulled a pile of paperwork from the truck and slammed the door. "Yeah. Not only was she fired, but she was negotiating with the owner to buy his last horse since the police said they didn't have enough cause to take it from him."

Dillon nodded. "That's a good stable manager. If I was still at Morning Creek, I'd offer her a job."

Trace leaned up against the truck and grinned. "I already did."

"What? Where?"

"Here. All she said she needed was room and board, so I figured Cole would be open to it."

Dillon widened his eyes. "You obviously hold more sway over my brother than I do."

Trace laughed as he pushed away from the truck. "Of course I do. I'm not his little brother." He headed for the house.

"I may be Cole's *younger* brother, but you are literally Logan's *little* brother."

Trace laughed again, not an uncommon occurrence. "Touché. Let's go inside and grab an iced tea. I think my throat is dry from keeping my mouth shut about what I thought of that idiot." Trace pointed over his shoulder with his thumb as he walked up the steps.

"What about the horses? Will Whisper stay with them?"

Trace pulled open the screen door. "I don't know, but I do know she'll do whatever is best for the horses."

He followed his cousin into the house. He'd like to find a woman who cared about horses like Whisper, but preferably one who had a few more social skills. Even as the word "social" popped into his head, he grimaced. Society was all his mother cared about. Maybe he should find a woman just like his cousin's girlfriend only with a lot less money.

Hailey wiped at her eyes one more time. At Annette's urging, she'd hobbled back inside the ranch house but her stomach was still upset at seeing the little horse's wounds. How could the people here deal with that on a regular basis? She was ready to prosecute the owner herself.

When the men walked into the kitchen, Trace smiled at her, but Dillon hesitated as if he'd forgotten she was there. She couldn't blame him for that. If she'd just helped that poor horse into the barn, she'd be a bit distracted as well.

"Hi, Hailey. I didn't see a car out front. What are you doing here?" Trace looked at Dillon for an explanation.

She beat him to it. "I just dropped in."

Dillon went straight to the refrigerator. "Literally, as in she almost crashed her balloon behind the house."

Trace took a seat. "Are you okay?"

She nodded. "The key word in that statement was *almost*." She gave Dillon her best "get it right look," and was pleased and surprised to see him smirk.

Annette pointed to the stack of papers Trace held. "Is that on the two new horses?"

He nodded. "Yes, but I haven't looked at it yet."

Dillon put a glass of lemonade down in front of Trace.

"I thought we were having iced tea."

Annette frowned at him. "Go right ahead, but you'll have to make it first."

Trace looked appropriately contrite. "Thanks, Dillon." As if to prove he was happy to drink anything in front of his grandmother, he chugged half the glass, much to Dillon's amusement.

It reminded Hailey of how it was on Sundays when all her brothers, or most of them came out to Ironwood for dinner. As much as she enjoyed the banter, her heart was still with the poor baby in the barn. "Do you know anything?"

Both men looked at her before Trace spoke. "Actually, I do. The stable manager was very forthcoming. The owner, who shall remain nameless, is a wealthy investor here in the valley whose luck hasn't been so good lately."

Her stomach clenched. "He's not wealthy anymore?" She had a sinking feeling where the story was headed.

"I don't know for sure, but from what I gathered, he once had about twenty horses, all for pleasure riding. After a land project east of Cave Creek was denied by the county, he sold most of them, but kept the Frisian mare and his own personal ride. He had the Frisian bred, hoping to sell her offspring."

Dillon swore under his breath. "But she obviously had the red gene and the baby was born brown."

Her family owned a cattle ranch, so she wasn't that familiar with the Frisian horses. "And that's not good?"

He shook his head. "No. That breed is supposed to be black, but once in a while a recessive red gene shows up and then the mare is no longer used for breeding because the chance of having another brown foal is high."

At the unfairness of that, she couldn't stop herself. "So he beat on the baby? That's beyond cruel. I want his name. He needs to go to jail for life. Though I'd prefer to beat him in the same way he did that poor little guy." She inhaled, her breaths having grown short with her anger.

"Hold on there, Hailey." Annette grasped her shoulder. "Let's hear the whole story."

She blinked before looking at Dillon, who eyed her

with curiosity, but as she moved her gaze to Trace, she found affirmation from his nod.

"The man actually refrained from taking his frustration out on the horse until he got word this morning that another land project he invested in went belly-up. That's when he lost it. According to the stable manager, she had just tied the colt outside and had gone back into the stables for the mare. The owner came outside, grabbed a rasp she'd set out for the farrier and he started wailing on the colt."

Dillon's brows were so low he looked ready to kill someone. "Who stopped him? The stable manager?"

Trace grinned. "Nope. Oh, she tried, but he threatened her, so she opened the mare's stall door. The mare raced to the rescue. She kicked the owner then took him by the arm and dragged him away. She wasn't gentle about it either. The guy has a dislocated shoulder and a number of broken ribs."

Hailey couldn't help stating the obvious. "He deserves so much worse."

"I agree." Dillon's voice came out in almost a growl.

Trace nodded as he dropped the paper work on the table and shuffled through it. "I'm just glad the stable manager called the police. Now if Dr. Jenna would just get here."

"Does it tell you the horses' names? Names are important." She leaned over the table to peer at the papers, trying to see what they said.

Dillon snorted. "You mean like Pennington?"

She frowned at him. "No, not like that. Knowing someone's name is a sign of respect. These animals deserve our respect. We need to refer to them by name."

When he lost his smirk, she returned her attention to Trace. She was disappointed that Dillon had such an attitude about her family's name. Then again, with his mother pushing rich young women at him all the time, she'd make an allowance… this time.

"Here it is." Trace frowned at one of the pages but didn't say anything.

"What's wrong?" She was dying to know.

He passed the paper over to her. "How do you pronounce that?"

She found the line that described the three-year-old Frisian mare. "It's Nizhoni. It's a Navaho word, I believe, for beautiful."

"That asshole didn't name the horse that. A man who beats a foal doesn't have the sensitivity to give a horse such a fitting name. Excuse my language." Dillon looked at her, so she nodded.

Annette however frowned at him. "I'll let it go this time."

She handed the paper back to Trace. "What about the colt?"

He shook his head. "He doesn't have a name."

"What? That poor baby. To have been alive all these days with no name. That's awful."

Dillon shook his head. "What's awful is what that bast— base lowlife owner did to him, not his lack of a name."

"I disagree. His wounds will heal and don't tell me they won't. I refuse to believe that. But he needs to have a name, because he's going to grow to be a beautiful handsome stallion."

Dillon's eyebrows rose. "Okay, so give him a name."

"Me?" She looked at Trace. This wasn't her horse. She was just visiting.

"Sure." Trace nodded to her. "All the horses that come to us already have names. Since you feel so strongly about it, I suggest you give the colt his name."

Naming an animal was a big responsibility in her eyes. "What about Whisper? Wouldn't she want to name it?"

Dillon chuckled, grabbing her attention, but it was Trace that spoke. "Actually, she'd love to, but the last animal she named ran away."

She looked from one man to the other. Finally, Dillon spoke. "It was an antelope jack rabbit and she named it Hopalongcassidy. I think the animal was so embarrassed, it left the area." He chuckled again.

She couldn't blame him. That was not a particularly auspicious name.

"So, what will you call him?" Annette's question made her think.

It had to be something he could be proud of. He'd been through a lot and would probably have the scars to prove it, but he would be built like his mother, only probably bigger, and he'd be unique. As if she'd called for it on the wind, the name came to her and she smiled. "Phoenix."

"Phoenix?" Trace shook his head. "But he was born in Scottsdale."

She barely kept from rolling her eyes and glanced at Dillon to see his reaction.

He shook his head at his cousin. "Not the city, the mythical bird the city was named after."

Trace chuckled. "Forgot about that."

Though he seemed to agree, she wasn't sure he understood. "Phoenix is the bird that rises from the ashes of destruction. I believe this colt is going to overcome his beginning and grow into a handsome horse."

"Except for his scars if he makes it through this." Trace gathered the papers on the table back together.

"No, because of his scars and because he *will* make it through this, he will be majestic. If your vet can't help him, I'll find one who can."

Annette stood. "Don't worry, Hailey. Dr. Jenna is the best. She's seen everything Cole has had brought here and only lost one."

Hailey's stomach twisted into a pretzel at that pronouncement. Glancing at Dillon, she saw the truth of that pain in his eyes. How did they do this every day?

"I'm going to get dinner started." Annette looked meaningfully at the men.

Trace immediately rose. "I'll bring a glass of lemonade out to Whisper and see how the horses are doing."

"I should bring the other horses in unless you think I should wait until after Phoenix has been treated."

At Dillon's use of the new colt's name, she smiled. It was as if she was a part of the little one's new life.

"Hailey, you will be staying for dinner, right?"

At Annette's question, she glanced at the kitchen clock. "Oh, I don't want to impose." She started to rise, completely forgetting about her ankle, and a sharp pain went up the side. "Ouch."

"I'll take that as a yes." Annette gave her a stern look. "How were you planning to get home?"

Dillon moved around the table behind her. "I told her one of us would bring her to her car."

Annette shook her head. "Well, you're not driving anywhere with that ankle. Dillon, why don't you and Trace go get Hailey's car and bring it back here? I'm sure Dr. Jenna would prefer not having you two hanging around while she helps that colt."

He froze on his way out the door and looked at her. "Where's your car?"

Now didn't she seem like a damsel in distress? Stupid ankle. "It's at All Hot Air on Lake Pleasant Parkway."

Trace responded. "I know where that is. It's right across from the Wild Hog Saloon."

Dillon raised an eyebrow. "Go there often?"

Trace laughed. "Get off your high horse and let's go. It's already getting dark and that place is in the middle of nowhere. It's just ripe for burglaries."

As Trace headed down the hall, Dillon shook his head. "I'm hoping you have the keys?"

"Oh, of course." She put her hand into her back pocket and pulled out a single key. "Here. It's red and the license plate reads DARE."

He took the key from her, his hand warm against hers, and a tiny shiver of excitement raced up her arm. "DARE?"

She grinned. "Yes. It's my motto. You know, dare to try. Dare to live. Dare to learn. I fell in love with that word when I was little and haven't grown tired of it yet."

"Okay." He shook his head as if she was crazy, then headed out the door.

The sound of his confident stride as his cowboy boots hit the hard wood floor almost had her sighing, but she held it in. She didn't want anyone to know she was interested in Dillon, and Annette was a smart woman.

She looked at the older woman who was studying her. "What?"

"There's a twinkle in your eye, young lady."

She chuckled. "I'm sure there is." She listened for the screen door to shut to make sure he was out of ear-shot. "Dillon never asked what kind of car I drive. He may be driving Trace's truck home."

Annette smiled. "Something tells me, he's not going to be happy." Then she turned back to the counter to start the meal.

Hailey sat back, content. Except for her ankle, things were going well. Already Dillon had stopped looking at her like she was a pariah that he needed to get away from as fast as possible.

Now to figure out how to get him to fall for her without him knowing she liked him.

Chapter Three

Dillon frowned at the small red car while his cousin laughed his fool head off.

"You better drive my truck." Trace's words barely made it out, his amusement knowing no bounds. "I thought she'd at least have a sporty convertible, then you could have driven with the top down so your head wouldn't hit the roof."

He gritted his teeth. He should let Trace drive it, but he felt it was his responsibility, which was dumb. Just because he was the one who spotted her balloon about to crash didn't make him her keeper. Yet, despite his sound reasoning, he *would* drive her car back to the ranch. "Just because I'm not a scrawny thing like you, doesn't mean I can't fit."

"Sure. After all, they used to pile twenty people at once into those babies...in the sixties." Another round of laughter followed.

He stared at what had to be a fifty-year-old Beetle. There had to have been six-feet-four-inch-tall people back then. Of course there were, but did they drive a Bug? He had a sinking feeling tall people in the sixties were more likely to drive a van.

"You want me to try it out first? If I can't fit, you won't." Trace continued to chuckle. He was far too happy since he'd hooked up with Whisper.

"No, I'll drive it. Let's get back. If we're late for dinner, Gram will have our hides."

"You mean yours. Whisper and I have to feed Uncle Joey. If Dr. Jenna isn't at the ranch by the time we get there, you'll have to stay with Phoenix and his mom."

He was about to remark on how Trace refrained from mentioning Nizhoni because he was afraid to pronounce it, then skipped it. The sooner he got into the midget of a car, the sooner he'd get dinner. Unlocking it with the key, he opened the door using one finger on the small handle.

"Since she's so good with names, do you think she calls it Herbie?"

He glared at his cousin. "Enough. Unless you want me to start into your horse's name, lay off."

Trace held up his hands, though his smile never left his face. "Okay, okay. If you're sure you can drive that thing, I'll head back and pick-up my woman."

He waved him off and brought his attention back to the car. How bad could it be? He was only ten miles from the ranch. If he had his knees in his chest for fifteen minutes, he should still be able to walk when he arrived.

Adjusting the seat as much as he could, he crawled inside, his knees crammed between him and the steering wheel. Immediately, the scent of Hailey assailed him. He hadn't realized she had a scent, but inside the small vehicle it surrounded him. It was some kind of citrus with a tang. He liked it.

There was something very personal about a person's car. He'd never thought about it before since his brother, cousins and himself all drove trucks and weren't particular about who drove them but being in Hailey's vehicle was a whole different experience.

In addition to the scent, there were small things that

said something about her, something different than his first impression when his mother had first invited her over to meet Cole.

She had a small dream catcher hanging from the minuscule rearview mirror. On the passenger seat were pamphlets from hot air balloon operations and small Arizona airports. On the floor of the passenger seat was a small waste basket, which told him she was neat and she didn't often have passengers.

Unable to resist, he glanced at the back seat. Then he took a double take. A helmet? Did she own a motorcycle? That didn't fit with the image he had of her. Then again, he probably didn't fit the image she had of him either. He rubbed the stubble on his jaw. There were definite advantages to living at his grandparents' instead of at home.

There were other items underneath the helmet as well as something black and silky. Was that the black dress she'd planned to wear when she met her friends to go dancing tonight? Was it short? Did it have a low neckline? Did it hug her figure?

In her jeans, it was clear she had a nice ass, but her button-down shirt fit her loosely, hiding the shape of her torso. Though he was pretty sure he'd seen her in a dress before, he hadn't paid attention.

So why was he now? Shaking his head, he turned the key and searched for the headlight switch. He was just doing a favor for one of Cole's soon-to-be customers. The last woman he'd be interested in was someone his mother had chosen.

As the headlights illuminated the empty desert beyond the dirt parking lot, he found the shift. He rubbed one hand down the side of his face. Great. A standard. He had no problem driving standard…in a truck. Trace's truck had a standard transmission. But to shift, he needed room to move his left foot.

"Fuck."

~~*~~

Hailey listened as footsteps ran up the front steps and the screen door slammed shut. She loved that the Benson's had never changed out the old-fashioned, wood-framed, screen door. As cowboy boots sounded down the hall, her excitement waned. The steps were too light to be male.

Whisper walked into the kitchen and stopped when she spotted her. "What are you doing here?"

She'd accidentally caused trouble for Whisper back in January. The last thing she wanted was for the woman to think she was causing more now. She held up her hands. "I just came to buy a horse."

Annette wiped her hands on a dish towel. "Don't mind her, Hailey."

Whisper moved to the refrigerator and took out a bottle of water. "Cole's outside talking to Logan. We need to get home to Uncle Joey."

Annette dropped the dish towel. "Logan's here? That means my great grand-baby is here. Excuse me, Hailey, but they only let me babysit her three days a week now and today was not one of them."

Without another word, the woman strode out of the kitchen and the screen door slammed behind her.

Whisper twisted off the cap from her bottle. "I don't like babies. I'm waiting until Charlotte is old enough for me to teach her to shoot." She took a swallow then stared. "You're here to buy a horse?"

Whisper's keen perception at the New Year's Eve wedding came to mind at her look. Hailey nodded. "Yes, that was the plan until I twisted my ankle. I can't stand so I'm stuck sitting here." She gestured toward her foot resting on the chair next to her.

The other woman finally took another swallow that clearly said her mind was not made up yet. Then she recapped the bottle. "I have to get the four-wheeler into the truck for tomorrow."

She walked toward the door.

"Four-wheeler? Like in ATV? You own one?" She couldn't keep the excitement out of her voice. She loved four-wheeling.

Whisper stopped. "Cole owns it. We all use it."

An idea began to form, though it was risky, especially with Whisper. She was the most unpredictable. "Don't you just love riding it?"

The woman shrugged. "I never thought about it. I use it to haul stuff."

"Haul stuff? That's it? You've never raced across the desert or ridden over jumps?"

Whisper leaned against the kitchen counter to face her and uncapped her water bottle again. "I thought ATVs were used for work. Why would I jump it?"

Hailey laughed. "Oh my, you definitely need a lesson in sport riding. If you want, after my ankle has healed, I'd be happy to come by and show you how much fun they can be. I could bring mine and show you. After all, you are looking at the ATV Motocross champion in the female teen division for the state of Arizona."

Whisper's grey eyes widened. "ATV riding is a sport?"

Hailey nodded, but didn't say anything. She could see Whisper's mind working. Then the woman smiled. "Yes. I want to learn how to ride the ATV for sport."

"Great!" It would be so much fun to ride with someone besides Austin, her best friend. Plus, it would give her another excuse to come to Last Chance. "If you give me your phone number, I'll call you as soon as my ankle is working again."

Whisper capped her water and turned around to pull a pen

from the magnet on the fridge. Ripping off part of what looked like a grocery list, she wrote. "Here. Call me when you can ride. "Whisper's eyes danced with interest.

"I will. Just as soon as my ankle can take it."

Whisper gave a curt nodded and continued out of the room. Her footsteps were halfway down the hall when she stopped.

Curious, Hailey stared at the kitchen entrance.

Whisper returned, her brow furrowed. "You're not after Cole, are you?"

She laughed. "I promise. I'm not after Cole. He is well taken and I'm happy for him. And I'm not after Trace either." She thought she'd relieve Whisper's fears but at the mention of Trace, the woman's face grew hard.

"Good. I'd hate to have to use Sal." Then without another word, Whisper headed down the hall and out the screen door.

Sal? Who was Sal? Hailey shrugged. As long as she had more than one reason to come back to Last Chance, she was happy. For now, she'd have to go home and let her stupid ankle heal, but she'd be back. Austin's boat was moored on Lake Pleasant, so she could stay there and be at the ranch every day without the over two-hour drive back home.

Maybe her ankle problem was a good omen. Now she could pack a bag and move onto the boat while finishing her hot air balloon lessons and getting to know Dillon better. It wasn't as if Austin used the boat much anymore since he was given sole custody of his child.

It would probably be a little awkward—

Voices on the front porch interrupted her plans. Was Dillon back?

Again, cowboy boots sounded in the hall and they were definitely male. Her heartbeat raced. It was a big man for sure.

She smiled at the doorway into the kitchen and then froze as Cole Hatcher walked in dressed in a blue fire department polo shirt.

He stopped, his eyebrows rising in surprise. Obviously, Annette had failed to mention her presence.

"Hi, Cole."

"You make a better door than a window, honey. Keep moving." The female voice behind him had to be his wife, Lacey.

Cole's lips twitched as he stepped aside and let Lacey pass. She didn't get two steps into the kitchen before she, too, stopped.

Great. Looked like she'd have to explain it to everyone separately now. "Hi Lacey. Before you ask, no I'm not here for Cole. No, Mrs. Hatcher did not send me. And no, my car isn't here because I came in by hot air balloon. I'm taking lessons in how to control one, so I thought I'd drop in to talk to Cole about buying a Last Chance horse." That should cover everything.

Lacey grinned. "I hope you'll stay for dinner." She continued into the kitchen and began pulling plates from the cabinets. Her pretty white blouse and flowered skirt was a little too fancy for serving dinner.

Cole watched his wife, that half smile still sitting on his lips. Maybe someday, a man would look at her the same way.

Cole finally moved into the kitchen and sat across the table from her. "Did Trace or Dillon show you the horses we have? Not many are ready to leave yet, and some can't leave."

Curious, she couldn't help asking, "Why can't they leave? I promise, whatever care they need, I can make it happen."

He shook his head. "It's not so much about care as about behaviors, phobias, and…" he seemed to be searching for the right word, "attachments."

"Attachments? Between horses?"

"No, though we've had that before, but I was able to find a

home for all three. No, some of my family members have grown attached to particular horses. Which ones were you thinking about?"

She'd only seen two and…at her new idea she smiled. "I'd like to purchase Nizhoni and Phoenix."

Cole frowned. "I still need to assess the damage done to them. Dr. Jenna is out there now, but even after the wounds are healed, if everything goes well, we still need to determine behaviors."

She shrugged. "That's fine with me. I'm in no hurry. I can wait. Besides, I can't even get on a horse right now." She pointed to her foot as she leaned back to allow Lacey to set a dish in front of her.

"Oh, what happened?"

Lacey's concern made her feel more comfortable. She was lucky the woman held no hard feelings over the fact that Beverly had preferred Hailey over Lacey as her son's wife. Personally, she thought Lacey and Cole were perfect together.

"When we were walking from where I set the balloon down to the house, I twisted my ankle. Stupid, I know. I can land a balloon, but I can't walk a quarter mile in the desert without getting hurt." She rolled her eyes, still disgusted with herself.

Lacey smiled sympathetically. "Look on the bright side. You'll get to have some of Gram's taco bake."

"You're right. I can't complain about that."

Cole returned to the horse subject. "Why do you want to buy those two horses? Actually, why would you want to buy any of our horses? Your family owns a cattle ranch. I'm sure you have all you need."

"Because I want to help. I know it's not much, but if I can give a couple horses a forever home, then I want to."

Cole sat back and crossed his arms. "Just like that? Out of the blue?"

She knew she'd have an uphill battle separating herself from Cole and Dillon's mother, but she hadn't realized exactly how much damage the woman had done.

She wasn't Beverly. Not even close.

She stared Cole in the eye. "Listen. You don't know me. Don't presume to think I'm like your high society, desperate mother. I already have everything she craves. I felt sorry for her and accepted a few of her invitations out of courtesy and kindness. That's all. You obviously have some psychological hang-ups because of her, but I'm not her. Is that clear?"

Cole's shocked expression was completely opposite of Lacey's, who gave the thumbs up behind his back, nodding her agreement. He finally unfolded his arm and acquiesced. "Yes."

"Good. Now that we have dumped that baggage, we can move on. Every month I like to do something to make the world better. Yes, my family donates to wonderful causes through our foundation and each of us has our pet projects, but money distances a person from the actual cause. I know it's what these organizations need to do good work and I know they have far better expertise than myself. But that doesn't keep me from wanting to do something myself."

Lacey set the salt and pepper on the table, before taking the seat next to Cole. "What are some of the other things, you've done?"

Now this was something she loved talking about. "Since I don't technically work, I like to volunteer. You know, like at the food kitchen, the shelter, the schools, the animal rescue and the hiking trails. My favorite activity is building houses for low-income families, but I had a blast helping a girl scout troop sell cookies outside a mall this year. I'd like to do that again."

When she finished, both of them just continued to stare at her.

"Oh no, don't give me that look."

"What look?" Dillon walked in, his eyebrows raised.

She hadn't even heard his footsteps, she'd been so into her explanation. She faced him. He really was the better looking of the two brothers, in her opinion. "Like I'm either crazy or an angel. I get that a lot, even from my own family."

Dillon chuckled before bending over to open the oven and peek inside. Then he closed the door and leaned his tight butt against the counter. "I'm going with crazy."

She shrugged. "That just proves how little you know me."

"I know that you almost crashed a hot air balloon and you drive a deathtrap of a car."

"A what?" Lacey rose with the sound of the oven timer and pulled two oven mitts from a drawer.

"A deathtrap, the thing she drives." Dillon pointed toward her. "It's so small, if she was ever in a crash, she'd be a pancake."

"It's not that small." She let her gaze travel from the thick, black hair on top of his head, down his massive chest, past his slim waist and over his blue jeans to his dusty brown cowboy boots and back up. She appreciated every inch of him but kept that to herself. "Not everyone is built like a truck. I find my Bug quite roomy."

"Bug?" Cole barked a laugh as he faced his brother. "You drove in a Beetle? How the f—did you get yourself into that?"

Dillon frowned. "It wasn't easy and it wasn't funny. The thing has a stick."

Cole let out a full-blown laugh.

Lacey set the baking dish on the table and swatted her husband. "Stop that. Go tell your grandmother dinner is ready."

He rose from the table, still chuckling, and strode out of the kitchen.

Lacey walked back to the counter and pointed at Dillon's hands. "You're going to wash those, right?"

"Yes, Ma'am." He nodded at Lacey behind her back before moving to the sink.

Everything about the scene had Hailey relaxing. It was so much like dinner at her house when her brothers were home. The only thing missing at her house was sisters-in-law, but she doubted that would happen for a while yet and for her oldest brother, probably never.

Lacey sat down at the table and peeled back the tinfoil on the large baking pan. "You're going to love Annette's taco bake. I just hope it doesn't make you too sleepy to drive—" Lacey looked at her then back at Dillon, who was drying his hands. "Did you say her car was a standard?"

He nodded. "Yeah." He walked behind her chair and took the seat next to her. "Why?"

"Because," Lacey stared right at her, "there's no way she's going to be able to maneuver the clutch with a twisted ankle."

Suddenly, her comfort fled like the sun from a haboob.

Lacey grinned. "Guess you'll have to stay the night." She switched her gaze to Dillon. "Logan's old room is empty, right?"

Hailey started to shake her head. This wasn't what she'd planned. It was too close, too soon. She didn't dare look at Dillon.

As if he didn't have a care in the world, he lifted his plate and stuck the spatula into the steaming food. "Sure, if you want to call it that. It was also Trace's and Billy's room at one point. I swear you never know who you'll find in that bedroom next."

"And you're now in Cole's old room. I wonder who will have that one next."

Dillon finished piling his plate with food, then set it down and handed her the serving utensil. "Don't expect anyone but me. The only way I'll go back to Morning Creek is if my mother stops trying to marry me off, or I get married myself, which I suspect will happen a lot sooner than my mother changing her behavior."

Hailey took the spatula from him, managing a polite smile as she scooped the cheesy beef concoction onto her plate. She'd never been one to back down from a challenge, but she had a sinking feeling that getting Dillon to look at her without his mother's shadow behind her would be an uphill battle.

Dillon led Tiny Dancer into the barn for the night. The desert temperatures would be too cold for the fragile horse, but he'd leave Eclipse and Cyclone outside. The last thing they needed was to scare Phoenix and his mother.

Closing the stall, he moved to the one housing their newest residents. Dr. Jenna had bandaged Phoenix up. He looked like a little mummy horse. At least his face and legs were mostly undamaged, except for the one cut. He nursed off his mother who at least had the tetanus vaccine.

Dr. Jenna gave the colt his shot, though she hadn't wanted to. Usually the vets waited until the horse was almost six months old, but the chances of tetanus developing were too great.

He leaned on the stall door. Phoenix seemed oblivious to his wounds as he hungrily drank from his mom's teat. Nizhoni, however, watched him like a hawk watched a hare. He didn't blame her. She was a beautiful Frisian. There was no way to tell she had a recessive gene by looking at her. She was midnight black like Eclipse.

He stepped away and headed out of the barn. Before Cole left, he'd told him what Hailey had said about their mother. He wouldn't put it past his mom to talk Hailey into crash landing onto Last Chance. His mother acted as if he was incapable of finding his own wife. He snorted. To hear his mother, you'd think he was incapable of wiping his own ass. She treated him like he was still five.

When he reached the corral with Eclipse, he set one foot on the bottom rail and leaned his arms on the top one, watching the Arizona sky spit its last purple streaks across the sky above the mountains of the valley. Hailey was another matter. Part of him could see her planning with his mother, but the other part of him said she was an honest person.

That part of him recognized a woman with a backbone. To put his brother in his place was no easy task. He wished he could have seen that. Cole was a by-the-book man, one reason why he'd caved to their mother for so long, before he'd finally reached his breaking point.

Like himself.

Eclipse nudged his shoulder. "What do you want? I don't have anything for you. You already had your dinner." He stroked the animal's neck. Eclipse had been one of the best things he'd ever done to spite his mother. Most of the other things had been just plain stupid.

Giving his horse a last pat, he straightened and headed back toward the house. As he passed the little red car, he shook his head. Who in their right mind would drive one of those today? Then again, who in their right mind would pilot a hot air balloon?

Skipping a couple steps, he jogged up to the porch and opened the front door only to find that very someone hobbling down the hall toward him. "What are you doing?"

Hailey stopped. "I'm heading upstairs, what does it look like I'm doing?"

She was in the hallway and had one hand on each wall. She'd been lifting her good foot by bracing herself between the walls and swinging it forward. Something told him she'd get to the bottom of the stairs just fine, but he wasn't brought up to ignore a person in need. "Here, let me help you."

"I'm fine."

"I know but humor me." He took the few steps to reach her. "I'll carry you upstairs."

Her eyes widened. "I don't think so."

His ego reared its head. "Trust me. I can carry you without a problem."

Hailey rolled her eyes. "Believe me, I have no doubt about that. But those stairs are narrow. *Trust me.* I can get up them just fine."

He glanced at the stairs. He hated that she was right. It gnawed at him that he couldn't help.

"Dillon, if you don't mind? You're in my way." She looked at him expectantly.

He stepped back, and she took another swinging step, bringing her closer to him. He took two more steps back and glanced at the narrow stairway to his right. "Piggyback." The word came out as the thought emerged. He returned his gaze to her. "My father used to give Cole and me piggyback rides up these stairs."

Instead of looking at him as if he'd completely lost his mind, a slow smile curved her lips. "I love piggyback rides. Haven't had one in a dog's age though."

"Then it's time you did, especially if it will save your ankle." Feeling proud of himself, he turned his back.

"Uh, Dillon?"

He looked over his shoulder. "Yeah."

"I'm not going to be able to jump on your back from one

foot. Let me get up on the first stair." She looked him over again like she had in the kitchen, and he forced himself not to react. "Maybe the second stair."

He swallowed hard before proceeding to the bottom of the stairs. The last thing he wanted her to realize was that her perusal of him had parts of his body thinking things it shouldn't. As one of his mother's chosen few, Hailey was strictly off limits.

He waited for her to make it to him, then insisted on helping her gain the first step. Even there, she wasn't as tall as he was.

"I'll go up one more." She immediately sat down, pulled her good foot up one stair and rose again. "You know, I could just go up on my butt."

He shook his head. "Gram would kill me if she saw you doing that while I stood here and watched." Not to mention it would grate on his cowboy code. She was hurt, and a female, which meant he needed to assist.

Hailey looked around. "I don't see her anywhere."

He smirked. "Those were my exact words when I stole a peanut butter chip chocolate cookie from the kitchen counter before dinner when I was eleven. My ass still hurts from the paddling I got."

Hailey's laugh warmed his insides, and he forced a fake frown. "You laugh at my injury?"

She nodded. "Of course, because your Gram was right. Shame on you."

He shrugged. "It was worth it. Her cookies would give the Cookie Monster a heart attack, they're so filled with good stuff." He looked behind him then back at her. "Just to be safe, let's do the stairs my way."

"Fine. Turn around."

He did as she requested. He was ready for her weight, but the scent of lemon as she wrapped her arms around his neck immediately had his body reacting to her. He forced himself to concentrate and grabbed her legs as she hopped on.

This was a stupid idea. He could feel her breasts pressing against his back and her thighs were resting in his hands.

"Am I too heavy?" As her breath brushed by his ear, longing shot straight to his groin.

He growled. "Of course not." As if to prove it, he spun around and headed up the stairs, but every step bounced her against him until his breaths shortened from his growing need. At the top of the stairs, he turned toward Logan's old room. The door stood open and he walked in.

"Gram keeps these made up in case we have company." He stopped in front of one of the two twin beds. "It's probably not what you're used to."

"Oh, it's perfect. I slept in a twin bed when I was little. This reminds me of my princess bed."

He glanced at the green quilt then looked at the rest of the room. It was nothing but browns and greens. "Princess bed?" That had to be pinks and whites for a little girl. That's what Logan had used for Charlotte.

Hailey whispered, "Oh, I wasn't the typical princess."

Her soft voice in his ear caused a riot in his jeans, and he quickly bent his knees and lowered his arms, so she could slip off. Having her close was like flirting with a rattle snake. As soon as she let go, he stepped away quickly.

She started to fall back, so he grabbed her arm, but her good foot slipped out, and they both landed on the bed.

Hailey laughed. "Really, Dillon. If you wanted to get me into bed, all you had to do was ask."

He scowled at her as he rolled off the bed and onto his

feet. He wasn't oblivious to her soft curves or the harsh need tightening his gut.

She shook her head as she sat up. "That was a joke. You're strung way too tight for me."

Her statement both relieved him and insulted him at the same time. He hooked his thumbs in his front pockets. "Well, we can't all be as easy going as Trace."

"Huh?"

Shit, now he looked like an idiot. "What kind of princess were you? I assume some kind of fairy princess. Your blonde hair would be very typical."

She grinned. "Not even close. Ever hear of Robin Hood, prince of thieves?"

"Sure." She didn't need to know that he'd taken archery in school because he'd wanted to be Robin Hood.

She placed her hands on her hips, lifted her curvy chest and looked off to the right. "I was Hailey Hood, princess of thieves." She glanced over at him without moving her head. "My loyal followers called me HH or Big H for short. Of course, my followers were George, the dog, three chickens and a jack rabbit when he showed up. They made up my merry men." She looked very serious, until she broke out laughing again. "My poor mom. She'd finally had a daughter, and all I wanted was to be one of the boys."

He had a hard time picturing her as a girl with a bow and arrow, so he didn't even bother. "You obviously outgrew that."

She didn't agree, but she didn't disagree either, and there was a mischievous look in her eyes.

Not wanting to know any more about her than he did already, he moved toward the door. "There's clean towels in the cabinet in the bathroom down the hall, and under the sink Gram keeps extra soap and shampoo. If you need anything else, it's probably in there. Just look in the drawers."

"Great. Thank you."

He hesitated in the doorway, glancing at the darkness outside the window. It wasn't that late yet. "The remote for the television should be on the table there between the beds."

"Got it."

What if she needed something downstairs? "Can I get you a bottle of water or anything?"

"Dillon, go. I'm a big girl. If I need something, I'll yell. Just close the door on your way out. I'm going to get undressed and settle into bed."

At the thought of her undressing, he clenched his jaw and nodded. Without another word, he pulled the door shut and bounded down the stairs faster than a rabbit from a hawk. The last thing he wanted to be thinking about was Miss Hailey Pennington without clothes on. As far as he was concerned, the sooner she left, the better.

Chapter Four

Hailey stepped out of the shower gingerly. Her ankle was still sore, but it was definitely better than is was last evening. That was a relief. It meant she could come back to Last Chance sooner rather than later.

After toweling her hair dry, she looked for a brush. Annette had everything a guest could want. She'd even put clean clothes Lacey had left behind in the spare bedroom. There must be a brush somewhere. Opening the top right drawer of the vanity, Hailey stilled.

The scent of juniper assailed her. It was the same smell she noticed when she'd walked into the bathroom, but she hadn't been sure what it was. The lemon grass soap she'd found under the sink had been perfect for her and had filled the bathroom during her shower.

She lifted the unopened bar and smelled it. It was so familiar but she couldn't place— "Oh." It was what she'd noticed when Dillon had given her a piggyback ride up the stairs, only it had been very faint. There hadn't been any soap in the shower, so he must have used it up.

She took another sniff. It was a pleasant scent, though a bit strong in its bar form. Unable to resist, she scanned the contents of the drawer. It had everything a man would use, including a comb, but no more. She liked that, but she wouldn't be using Dillon's toiletries. That was far too personal…for now.

After setting the bar on the counter to remind Dillon he'd need a new bar in the shower, she closed the drawer and proceeded through two more before finding what she needed. She quickly ran the pink comb through her wet hair, then pulled the strands out of it and placed it back in the drawer.

She double checked that the towel was tightly about her body before opening the door.

"Oh, I forgot you were here." Dillon stood just on the other side, his arm outstretched as if he were about to try the doorknob.

She would have been thoroughly insulted if she hadn't been so distracted by him. He stood there with his dark hair messed, his chin darkened by his growing beard and shirtless. She couldn't seem to take her eyes off his chest.

The mounded muscle was covered with a soft sprinkling of black hair that congregated in a line leading over a rippled stomach to disappear beneath a pair of loose sweats that looked in danger of falling down. As she raised her gaze upward, she was able to appreciate the flair from his narrow waist to his broad back. She finally looked into his blue eyes and recognized interest in their depths.

She swallowed hard to slow her breathing and tamp down the faeries in her stomach, who were doing summersaults that were making certain female parts come alive. "I was just leaving." Her voice came out in barely a whisper, and she cleared her throat. "I mean you probably guessed that. I left a new bar of soap out for you. I found it by accident when I was…never mind." She swallowed again and grabbed hold of the doorframe. "It's all yours."

She took a slightly wobbly step forward, hoping he'd back out of the way, but he didn't.

"Here, take my arm. I'll help you back to your room."

Rather than argue and prolong the encounter, she did as he suggested and hobbled out of the bathroom. Luckily, it was right next to the room she had slept in. She grabbed the door handle with her free hand but didn't look at him. "Thanks. I've got it from here."

"Are you sure?"

She nodded, her throat having closed up at the realization that they were both almost naked. Why hadn't she brought her borrowed clothes into the bathroom with her? She had no problem having sex with a man she knew, but she didn't know Dillon. Not yet.

"Alright." He slipped his arm out from under her hand and strode back to the bathroom.

She still didn't look at him, though she heard his bare feet on the wood floor. Turning the knob to her room, she stepped inside and closed the door, leaning against it. Holy fire in the churchyard well. She hadn't been prepared for that.

Closing her eyes, she relived the sight of him. No wonder she'd had a crush on him for over a year. She knew he was built, but the naked truth of it was far more than she'd expected. More than she'd ever had in a boyfriend. For the first time, she doubted her plan.

Was Dillon too much man for her? The surprising thought had her popping her eyes open. Of course not. She'd been around men all her life. Growing up with three brothers and having a guy as her best friend meant she was comfortable around men. It was just that Dillon's sex appeal was far stronger than any boyfriend's she'd had.

Pushing away from the door, she made her way to the bed where Lacey's old clothes waited for her. She'd only had two serious relationships with men, both long term. She thought back on them fondly, not with regret. They had been comfortable partnerships, equal in all ways.

There was nothing comfortable about Dillon Hatcher though. Something about him gave her the same rush she had when she cleared a jump in competition or when she'd made her first solo flight hang-gliding. He caused her adrenaline to rev and made her double think everything she did—a rarity for her.

Shaking off her surprising thoughts, she got herself dressed. Maybe her twisted ankle was a good thing. She needed a little time to re-evaluate. Her gut told her a relationship with Dillon wouldn't be a temporary thing. She had no doubt he could be addictive and as with every new adventure she tackled, she needed to think long and hard about that before moving forward...*if* she moved forward.

Dillon held the beam up as Logan settled the sawhorse under it. "Don't take all day, old man."

His cousin ignored him, readjusting the wooden brace to just the right position.

He completely agreed with his brother's decision to build a small barn near his own house, and the only part left was the large doors, but working with Logan was getting on his nerves. Then again, everything seemed to be bothering him lately. Ever since Hailey had left over a week ago, he'd felt antsy.

Probably because he was haunted by how natural she looked coming out of the bathroom. Her lemony scent filled his nostrils and her smooth bare shoulders were a feast for his eyes. Knowing she had nothing on beneath her towel, hit him like a monsoon storm. He'd noticed how attractive she was before, but in that moment, it was more than that. He had wanted to follow her into her bedroom, remove the pale green towel and forget he was a gentleman.

"Are you going to put that down or are you hoping for a Guinness Book of World Records shot?"

Logan's remark had him dropping the beam. "Listen, if you want someone else to help you, I'm fine with that."

Logan stared at him. "What's wrong with you?"

He sighed, rubbing one hand down the side of his face. "I don't know."

His cousin picked up the circular saw. "It can't be a lack of female company. From what I saw last night, you were like sugar to ants."

Yeah, it had been a fun night at the Black Mustang, but despite the three women he'd danced and drank with, he'd left alone. That he hadn't even asked for one phone number bothered him. "They were nice, but I'm not like you were. I don't love 'em and leave 'em. I'm a more long-term kind of man, and I didn't see any long-term there."

Logan turned the saw on and cut the beam then lifted his goggles from his face. "Just remember I got two of the best long-term relationships from those crazy nights. But I was out there just to bury the pain of losing my dad. Are you saying you're out there to find a wife?"

At the incredulity in his cousin's voice, he shrugged. "I didn't say that. I'm just interested in something longer than one night."

Logan studied him. "Don't let Aunt Beverly push you into doing something you don't have to do."

He scowled. "If I were going to cave to my mother, I wouldn't be living on Last Chance. I can handle her."

"Not if you're looking to settle down, before you're ready, just to spite her." Logan shook his head. "That's worse than caving."

He lifted the beam. "You don't know what you're talking about. Let's get this mounted before lunchtime."

His cousin put down the saw, and they set the beam above the opening.

He wasn't looking for a wife, but when he found one, he'd definitely make sure his mom came to his wedding just like his older brother had done. He'd never forget the look on her face when she realized Cole was marrying Lacey right then and there. He grinned at the memory.

"So all it takes is getting this up to put you back in a good mood?" His cousin stepped back to view their handiwork.

"Yeah. That and lunch. Let's take a break."

Logan smiled. "That's fine with me. Charlotte should be just about done with her lunch. I'll put her down for her nap."

He slapped his cousin on the back as he walked by. "That is if Gram will let you." He chuckled before whistling for Eclipse, who had wandered to where Lacey's horse Angel was staked, far from them. Angel had a fear of men, thanks to her former owner.

He was determined not to let that happen with Phoenix. The little guy was doing far better than his worried mother on that issue.

Eclipse trotted over, passing Logan as he walked toward his horse, Black Jack.

Dillon patted his mount. "Good boy. Let's go get you some lunch." He hooked his foot in the stirrup and swung his leg over. "See you at the house."

"Let's go, big guy." His horse took off at a run down the dirt road between his brother's new home and the hundred-year-old ranch house. If anyone had said he'd enjoy living on Last Chance three months ago, he would have told them they were crazy.

In fact, he'd tried to handle his mother longer than he should have because he couldn't imagine working for a horse rescue operation instead of breeding his pride and joys. But it had only taken one rescue horse to arrive for him to change his mind.

That's what he and Cole should do, insist his mother live here for a month. Maybe then she'd get some perspective on what was important. He shook his head. Then again, probably not. As far as he was concerned, Beverly Hatcher was a lost cause.

He slowed Eclipse as they came into the dirt area that served as both a front yard and a parking area. There was a truck there that he didn't recognize, and he heard ATVs running on the other side of the barn. Curious, he directed Eclipse over there. As they cleared the side, he pulled on the reins.

A woman was bent over, looking at something on a red ATV, her head covered in a helmet. The view of her ass in the tight-fitting jeans aroused his interest…among other things, but a noise that sounded like someone talking pulled his gaze away and he found another woman wearing a helmet sitting on the ranch's ATV.

That woman lifted her visor, revealing herself to be Whisper, and yelled, "We're busted!"

The woman at the red ATV straightened and looked at her. Whisper pointed to him and the woman turned. Lifting the helmet off, her golden blonde hair fell about her shoulders as she smiled. "Hey, Dillon!" Reaching over her machine, she turned it off.

"Hailey? What are you doing here? Again?"

She motioned to Whisper to cut the engine before walking toward him. "Whisper wanted to learn how to race and jump ATVs, so I told her I'd teach her."

"You?" He could see Hailey Pennington hosting some big

champagne reception and *maybe* piloting a hot air balloon. But the woman was far too delicate to be racing ATVs.

She put one hand on her hip. "Yes, me. You're looking at the women's sixteen to eighteen-year-old class, Motocross champion of Arizona."

"Sure I am. And I'm the state's best line dancer. Be serious, Hailey. Racing ATV's isn't a good idea out here. There are a lot of unforgiving holes." He swung his leg over his horse and jumped down, determined to keep her from risking hers and Whisper's neck.

She cocked her head. "Thank you for your unexpected concern." She paused as she studied him. "You really don't believe me. I'm surprised. I knew you were old-fashioned, but I didn't think you were sexist."

He halted halfway to her. Sexist?

She waved her hand as if to dismiss him. "Go look it up, if you don't believe me. Whisper and I have some riding to do before it gets dark. I want to make sure she understands all the rules that will keep us safe."

Before he could respond, she strode back to her ATV.

He followed, still off balance, but determined to stop them from killing themselves. He might not have any influence over Hailey, but his cousin Trace would kill him if something happened to Whisper. He strode straight for her. "Does Trace know you're doing this?"

She lowered her brows in confusion. "No. I'll tell him about it when I get home."

Finally, a soapbox he could stand on. "You don't think Trace might have some concerns about you doing this? Don't you think you should call him and make sure he's okay with this?"

Whisper shook her head. "No."

Shit, he forgot who he was talking to. He turned toward Hailey, who stared at him in absolute disbelief. "What?"

"Do you hear yourself? You sound like a caveman. Even my father wouldn't expect my mother to clear everything she did with him first. What century are you living in?"

His right cheek, just under his eye, began to tick with his frustration. He hated that. Rubbing that side of his face, he glared at her. "I'm from the century that protects women and worries about their safety. Do you have a problem with that?"

She smiled. "Not at all. Thank you for your concern, but I've got this. Now, I'm sure you didn't come out here just to talk to us. Don't let me keep you from whatever you were doing."

Surprised, he stood in silence as she pulled her hair up behind her head with one hand and donned her helmet with the other.

Straddling the red four-wheeler, she looked back. "Ready, Whisper?"

Trace's girlfriend gave a thumbs-up and turned on her machine. Within seconds, Hailey had snapped her visor down and started her own.

Dillon fisted his palms. She was right. He had no say in what the women did, but every instinct was screaming at him to make sure they were safe. He took a step toward Hailey. She at least understood normal social interactions, but just then she turned toward him, waved and hit the gas, throwing up sand higher than his head.

He stepped back as she yelled and the ATV whipped around the corner. Whisper laughed as she followed at her own fast pace, though without the kick-up of desert to herald her departure.

Dillon swallowed. The word painted on the back of

Hailey's ATV caused his throat to go dry. HELLION. The fucking machine said Hellion.

Dusting off his arms, he started for the corner of the barn. Eclipse had wandered off, and he had no doubt where the horse had gone. Sure enough, as he stepped around the barn, Eclipse was nickering over the fence of the north corral. Luckily, Macy was clueless, too engrossed with her colt, Lucky, to give the stallion any of her time.

Dillon caught Eclipse's reins and tied him to the post. "Big guy, you're lucky your lady is all rounded up. I pity the guy who has to worry about that woman." He pointed toward the dust clouds rising behind the ranch house. Luckily, she wasn't *his* problem.

He walked to the house, then took the steps two at a time as he jogged up onto the porch. He'd have to find out if Hailey had a boyfriend. She may not be his woman, but she was on his grandparents and Cole's property, risking Whisper's life as well as her own. If there was someone who could rein her in, he needed to know.

And that was the only reason he wanted to know if there was a man in her life.

Opening the door, he strode into the house.

Hailey wiped the sweat from her brow as she and Whisper finished loading her ATV onto her rented truck, glad she left her Beetle at home and had been storing her ATV at Austin's. She'd had a blast showing Whisper how much fun they could have on ATVs. She was pretty sure the woman would want to do it again, which was fine with her. She liked having the company. Most of her friends weren't into it, and Austin had just unexpectedly received full custody of his kid, so he wasn't available like he used to be.

Austin Leighthall had been her best friend since grammar school. He was always up for a new adventure, until he married. Then his wife was adamant he play it safe and stay home. Hailey didn't understand why people wouldn't believe that they were always safe.

His divorce had happened fast and soon his ex was off to California with their only child, so Austin had gone back to exploring new adventures with Hailey. But that ended when his ex dumped the child on him with the paperwork saying he was daddy and scooted.

Over the past month, she'd actually started to feel lonely, which was ridiculous. She had plenty of friends, three brothers, and she and her mom loved going shopping together.

"That was freakin' awesome!" Whisper's exclamation broke into her thoughts.

She smiled. "I know. Next time, if you want, I can show you how to ride a jump. We'd have to do some preliminary work first though."

"I'm in." Whisper's grin was wide. "I'm also thirsty and hungry. Let's go up to my trailer. It's Trace's turn to make dinner tonight."

"I'd love that." Whisper fascinated her and to have been accepted as a friend after what she'd done to the poor woman by revealing who she was made her grateful. "Do you think Annette would mind if we grabbed a water? I don't think I'd even make it to your place without it."

Whisper nodded. "Why would she care? Next time we need to bring water with us." Whisper headed for the house.

Hailey slammed the tailgate closed. She might not have had the chance to see much of Dillon today, but she'd still had a great time. She'd wanted to stop where he and his cousin were working on Cole's new barn, but she'd refrained. Dillon was a bit of a stick in the mud. The last thing she wanted was for him to spoil the day.

She started to walk toward the house when the sound of a car had her turning around. Since all the men associated with the ranch drove trucks, it made her curious. The vehicle pulled to a stop next to Whisper's truck, which was on the other side of hers, so she walked over.

"Hey, Hailey, what are you doing here?" Lacey closed the door of her car and strode forward in a western skirt, pink, puffed short-sleeved blouse and a pale pink cowboy hat.

"I taught Whisper how to ride." She pointed over her shoulder at her ATV, since the one Whisper had ridden was in the barn because it was being used tomorrow for work.

Lacey's eyes widened. "I've seen Whisper ride our ATV. Why would she need lessons?"

She chuckled. "I don't mean ride as in drive. I mean ride as in race and jump."

Lacey shivered delicately. "That sounds dangerous."

She barely kept from rolling her eyes. "Not if you're taught how to do it safely."

"Ah, I see. Who taught you?"

"My father's good friend. He had sons in Motocross racing and my brothers weren't interested, so I got to learn."

Lacey studied the red ATV, walking around the back of the truck. "Hellion?"

This time she did roll her eyes. "That's my brothers' nickname for me. Hailey the Hellion. All because they're a bunch of sticks in the mud."

Lacey laughed. "I'd tell you my nickname, but then I'd have to—"

Whisper came out of the house and strode toward them.

"I'd have to have Whisper shoot you."

Hailey shook her head. "You don't shoot?"

"I can when I've had to." She exchanged a look with Whisper. "But I don't like it. It's too loud."

Whisper handed her a bottle of water. "Thanks." Opening it, she turned back to Lacey, curious now about her nickname. "Do you do anything for fun?"

The woman blushed as Whisper spit out a stream of water.

Well, shit. She'd just walked into something with that question.

Whisper laughed. "Oh, you bet she does. They don't call her Racy-Lacey for nothing."

"Whisper! That's supposed to be a family secret." Lacey was bright red now.

Feeling bad, Hailey tried to redirect the conversation. "Besides that. I mean is there anything you like to do like trick riding or hang-gliding or jet skiing?"

"Lacey doesn't do anything dangerous." Whisper lifted her bottle toward the road where a truck was headed their way. "Dr. Jenna's the one that likes water."

Lacey seemed put out by Whisper's judgment. "I don't have much time for anything now, but when I was younger I wanted to be a trapeze artist. I know that's old fashioned, but I've always loved the idea of flying through the air."

Hailey smiled. "Have you gone to the Flying High place just south of Phoenix?"

"What is that?"

"It's a trapeze school. They'll teach you how to do it. It's very safe."

Lacey's light brown eyes widened. "Really? Can anyone go?"

She nodded. "Yes. I have." Now Lacey's eyes were not only

wide but filled with awe. Shit, it was that 'you're crazy or an angel' look again. "And you can, too."

Dr. Jenna parked her truck next to Lacey's car, cutting off their conversation. The truck door opened, and the veterinarian jumped out. "Come on, Butterball." The woman set something on the ground. "You need to stretch those legs."

Butterball? Curious, Hailey took a few steps past the tailgate and stopped. "Oh, what a cutie!" She hunched down. "Come here, Butterball."

The tan bull dog waddled as fast as his short legs could move before he tried to jump in her lap, knocking her to the ground. She laughed, trying to keep the wet tongue from actually touching her face.

"Butterball!" Dr. Jenna clipped a leash on the heavy bulldog and pulled him back. "I'm sorry. He's usually not that energetic, but we had a long drive from Cave Creek and the traffic was at a crawl thanks to an accident."

"It's fine." She rose and started to dust off her jeans before realizing they were already dusty from her ATV ride. She gave up on that and offered her hand. "I'm Hailey Pennington. I don't think we've met."

The petite veterinarian with the dark hair and sea-green eyes smiled as she reached out her hand. "It's nice to meet you. Are you one of *the* Penningtons?"

She leaned in closer. "I am, but let's keep it to ourselves."

Dr. Jenna's eyes widened. "I was kidding."

She cocked her head, raising one eyebrow. "I'm not."

The vet looked at the other two women who nodded. "I'm Dr. Jenna Atkins. Most people call me Dr. Jenna but here I'm just Jenna."

"Are you here to check on my horses?"

"Your horses?" Again, Jenna looked at the other two women.

She brought her shoulders up to her ears and spread her hands. "At least, I'm hoping Cole will sell them to me. It's why I came here last week. I looked in on Phoenix today and he seems to have forgotten he's been hurt."

Jenna opened the back door of the truck and pulled out a big black bag, which considering how small she was, made it clear she was strong. She slammed the door. "He might think he's fine, but he's still healing." The knowledge in the woman's eyes and her air of confidence demanded respect.

"I'm so glad you are here to help him. That poor thing has already seen the ugly side of life. I want to make sure he only knows joy from now on."

Jenna's serious face softened a tad. "First, I have to get him well without any infection setting in."

"Can I come with you?"

"No." The answer came from Whisper. "We have to leave. I'm hungry."

Ashamed she'd already forgotten her plans in her concern for Phoenix, she quickly put her hand on her stomach and glanced at Whisper. "That's right. My stomach just reminded me." She faced Jenna again. "I'm sure I'll see you again."

Jenna nodded before she looked past her and smiled.

Hailey turned to see Logan and Dillon ride into the yard. As Logan grinned at Jenna, Hailey stared. That was not the same Logan Williams she'd met at Lacey's wedding. That Logan hadn't smiled that entire night.

No, now it was Dillon who frowned as he jumped from his horse and strode directly for her. "Are you alright?" His gaze swept over her.

She was both flattered that he cared and irritated that he had no faith in her. Then again, the man didn't know her. Damn, but he looked downright yummy with his pale blue t-shirt plastered to his body with sweat, showing off exactly how much strength he was hiding under there.

She grinned. "Of course, I'm okay. So is Whisper. In fact, we're headed over to her place right now for dinner."

As if on cue, Whisper opened Hailey's passenger door. "We're leaving now."

Hailey shrugged at Dillon and walked to the driver's door. Before she could open it, he reached around her and did so. Surprised, she looked at him. "Thank you."

He didn't say anything, just continued to frown, but he did give her half a nod. Biting her lip to keep from laughing at him, she stepped into the cab and took her seat. With exaggerated motions, she pulled her seatbelt across her and buckled it, then looked to make sure Whisper had put hers on as well.

If Dillon Hatcher was going to be in her life, which she'd decided she wanted, he needed to understand that she always took safety precautions, even when driving. Carefully backing out, glad that Butterball had waddled over to the barn to lay down next to a horse housed outside, she slowed to a stop and put the truck into drive.

She smiled as she glanced in her rearview mirror. Dillon watched her leave. In her imagination, she dreamed he was missing her already, but her logical side said he was breathing a sigh of relief that she hadn't been injured on the ranch.

She caught Whisper staring at her. "What? That man is just too funny. I swear he should have been born a few generations earlier."

Whisper didn't reply but turned her gaze to the road.

"I thought you'd drive your own truck home. How will you

get it now?" She glanced at Whisper as she slowed to a stop on the dirt road at the entrance onto Carefree Highway.

"I'll ride Spirit down if I need it. Besides, I always have Trace's truck if I need to go anywhere."

That had to mean Whisper and Trace's trailer wasn't too far. They continued in silence until reaching the middle of town.

"Stop there. I need to get eggs for Uncle Joey."

At Whisper's command, she pulled into the parking lot of a small grocery store. She barely had the truck in park before Whisper was out the door.

Hailey stayed where she was and kept the truck running. Whisper fascinated her. Actually, the whole Hatcher-Williams family interested her, mainly because of Dillon. The family dynamics were similar yet so different from her own family.

The Penningtons, as people referred to them, had all grown up on Ironwood Ranch, the largest cattle ranch in Arizona, their land and family having been around since before there was such a thing as the state of Arizona.

But her mom was an only child and her dad's brother died young, so there was no extended family for her. No cousins to play with growing up and no grandparents to visit as the last one died when she was just two.

That the cousins on Last Chance got along didn't surprise her, but it seemed like the women liked each other, too. Could she fit in with them? At Lacey's wedding, she'd learned Lacey was an accountant and worked at a nudist resort! Not something she would have expected Cole to be okay with, but he must be. Whisper was, well Whisper, and didn't appear to have a job, and Jenna was a vet. How would Hailey Pennington fit into that mix?

Maybe the more important question was why she was so interested in Dillon. When she first met him, she was charmed by his smile and polite ways. Now she'd discovered he was a bit old-fashioned.

The memory of him outside the bathroom door last time she was there claimed her mind, and her breath caught. Then there was the fact that he was incredibly attractive. She needed to find a way to spend more time with him. If this was just infatuation, she needed to know. Maybe she could find out from Trace where Dillon liked to go to have fun.

Of course, that was assuming he had fun. From what she saw at Lacey's wedding, he could dance, which was definitely a plus.

The back door on the passenger side opened, interrupting her musings, and Whisper dumped a bag on the back seat.

"That looks like a little more than eggs."

Whisper closed the back door and climbed in the front, buckling her seatbelt before responding. "Yeah, I forgot I was low on meat scraps for Mani and I needed more molasses and apples for Motley."

Hailey backed out of the parking space and slowed at the entrance to the road. Part of her said to let it go, but it was too much fun learning about people. "Who are Mani and Motley? I thought you said you live with Trace and that your Uncle Joey and old Billie live in the other trailer."

She'd turned onto the main road again and continued west before her passenger answered. "Mani is the mountain lion that stops by occasionally to see what we're up to and Motley is the wild burro who decided he wanted to live with us because we are nicer than his family."

Hailey wanted to laugh, but she kept it contained. The way Whisper spoke was so matter of fact that it sounded as if she knew for certain why the wild animals came around. There was rumor that Whisper actually did understand animals. She found that hard to believe, but she'd happened upon stranger things.

Having answered the question, Whisper didn't offer any further conversation, which was fine with Hailey. She was too busy trying to figure out another way to see Dillon.

She drove through the small town and continued on the road that would eventually take a person all the way to California if they wanted to drive there. She much preferred flying. She was open to commercial flight, but Greyson, her oldest brother, had a private jet, which was definitely the more comfortable way to go. Her own plane, sitting at Deer Valley air park right now was just for fun.

"Turn here." Whisper pointed to what looked like an ATV run in the desert.

She made the turn and continued a lot slower down the dirt path. After a few miles, when there was no trailer park in sight, she had to ask. "I thought you lived on nearby Last Chance land. I didn't realize Cole owned so many acres."

"This isn't Cole's land. This is state conservation land. We just use it to get to the trailer. Vehicles can't get up the cliffside. Only ATVs and horses can do that." Again, Whisper lapsed into silence.

Hailey wasn't sure how she felt about driving on conservation land, but since she seen two other ATV paths off of the one they were on, she could only assume ATV riding was allowed.

"That way." Again, Whisper pointed and at the split in the path she veered right.

The "road" followed a small mesa then took a hard right. She relaxed as she saw trailers in the distance. Still, it took another ten minutes to finally pull up next to what looked like a well lived in campsite with only two trailers.

As Hailey got out of the truck, she looked around. There were no electrical lines or water connections. What did they do for sewer?

"We have company." Whisper, with the bag of groceries in her arms, nodded toward the horse beneath a carport type structure separate from the newest looking trailer.

The horse wasn't Dillon's, but it could be Logan's.

"Door."

At Whisper's command, she quickly opened the door for her and followed her inside the state-of-the-art trailer. As soon as she stepped up to the main level, she halted.

Two impressions hit her at once. One was that the cooled living space was much larger and more comfortable than she expected. The second is what had her heartbeat speeding up. Dillon, who stood in the kitchen next to his cousin, made the large space appear very small.

Chapter Five

Despite the fact that Trace and Dillon filled the trailer's kitchen space, Whisper pushed her away around the two men and started to empty the grocery bag.

"Hi, Hailey." Trace glanced her way before returning his attention to the pot he stirred.

"Hi. I hope I'm not intruding. Whisper told me I should join you."

Trace pulled the pot off a gas burner and set down the serving spoon. "You're in luck. I made enough to feed an army." He turned toward Whisper. "Let Uncle Joey and Billy know it will still be about fifteen minutes and ask them if they want baked beans, corn, or both.

Hailey looked out the window at the trailer no more than twenty yards away. "Aren't they right there?"

Whisper picked up what looked like a two-way radio. "Yes, but this is easier than calling on a phone or walking over there. Uncle Joey always thinks of things he needs after you're done talking to him. I think it's a stroke thing."

"Or he just likes playing with you." Trace's grin said he might know a bit more about it.

Whisper called over and waited for a response. When none came, Hailey got nervous. "Is everything all right over there?"

Whisper gave her a puzzled look. "It takes time for Uncle Joey to get across what he wants. He can't talk, so Billie has to ask a bunch of questions and watch for responses. We'll hear in a few minutes."

"Your Uncle Joey sounds like a fascinating man."

Whisper looked at her as if she was crazy. Boy, she was getting tired of that.

But Trace laughed out loud. "That's one way of putting it."

"No, it isn't." Whisper now looked at Trace as if he'd lost his mind, which made Hailey feel a lot better.

Trace took pity on his girlfriend. "Grab the radio and come help me with the ribs."

She looked at him, her face clearly portraying she was about to decline his request, but Trace's eyebrow rose and Whisper nodded. Within seconds, Hailey found herself alone with Dillon. She didn't mind that at all.

Moving toward the main area which boasted both a living room and dining area, thanks to the pull-out sides, she sat on the couch. "What are you doing here and how did you get here so fast?"

Dillon moved out of the kitchen and pulled out a chair from the dining area across from her. Spinning it around, he straddled it. "Trace called and asked me to give Whisper the nail gun, but she had already left. So I rode Black Jack up here. It's a much shorter distance through the desert."

She wasn't immune to the total maleness he exuded. He'd change into a checked cotton button-down shirt, the open collar calling her attention to the dark skin on his chest, almost making her forget her question. "Why didn't you ride Eclipse?"

"I'm not sure about taking him up the cliffside. The other horses are used to it, except Cyclone. I don't think the

Clydesdale has been up it either. I left Eclipse mooning after Macy, as usual."

She chuckled. "Mooning?"

He shook his head. "Ever since I brought him, once I had Cole's and Gram's permission, the d—um, horse spends every free moment flirting with the mare."

She liked the idea of a horse romance. "And what does Macy think about that?"

He shrugged. "She's so busy watching out for Lucky that she hasn't even noticed."

The devil in her couldn't resist. "Maybe she's just pretending not to notice. You know, making him cool his heels so he doesn't think she's an easy conquest."

Dillon's blue gaze stared at her as if he'd never considered such a thing. "I think you're giving these animals too much credit."

"Oh, really. I'd bet you that's exactly what's she's doing. No one, horse or human, could not notice Eclipse. He's magnificent." She paused to hold back her smile as Dillon lifted his head in acknowledgement, as if he had anything to do with the horse's stature. "But it's not like I can ask her, so we won't know for sure."

His look turned shrewd. "There's always Whisper."

"Whisper? What does she have to do with the horse romance?"

"A lot." Dillon nodded toward the window. "That woman can tell you exactly what a horse is thinking."

He had to be kidding. "You mean like a horse whisperer? Really?" She raised her eyebrows as she lowered her chin, making her disbelief clear.

He shook his head. "Not just horses." Dillon's face turned completely serious. "She can tell what any animal is thinking. I've seen it."

She wanted to laugh, but he obviously believed what he was saying. "So, you're saying that if we made a bet about what Macy was thinking about Eclipse, Whisper could tell us who's right?"

Dillon leaned his back against the table behind him. "Yes."

"How do I know Whisper won't simply say whatever you want her to say?"

Dillon laughed at that and the butterflies in her belly woke up at the rich sound. "Me tell Whisper what to say? Even Trace can't do that. That woman says whatever she wants." He lowered his voice. "You do know she was raised off the grid with little to no social interaction, right?"

She'd heard that rumor at Lacey's wedding, but hadn't realized it was true. Then again, as she thought back on her day spent with Whisper, there was a simple honesty about her. "Fine. Then if I'm right you have to go on one of my adventures with me and see how amazing it can be."

He gave her the side-eye. "With you?"

Oh, she could tell what the man was thinking even if she was in Flagstaff. He thought she was looking for a date. In this case, not exactly. "Yes. I'll show you that a hot air balloon or a race track or rock-climbing isn't as scary or unsafe as you have judged it to be without having tried it."

He leaned forward studying her. "And if I'm right?"

She crossed her arms in front of her. "You decide."

He lowered his brows for a moment as if puzzled by her remark. What did he think, that she would make all the rules of the bet? Wouldn't happen. She was a fifty-fifty girl. Any relationship with her would have to be a relationship of equals.

Dillon let his chin rest on his arm as it lay in front of him on the back of the chair. He was deep in thought, allowing her the opportunity to enjoy the scenery. He didn't have his hat on so his black hair showed exactly how thick it really was. She'd love to feel it between her fingers.

Her gaze moved upward to the view out the window where it looked like Trace and Whisper were having a serious conversation. She didn't want to intrude, even if it was just visually. As she was about to look away, Whisper stepped up to Trace and started a deep kiss.

Hailey quickly brought her eyes back to Dillon, who was smiling like a coyote that just ate a jack rabbit.

"What?"

He grinned. "If I win, you don't come back to Last Chance until Phoenix and Nizhoni are ready to leave."

Her heart froze in her chest. He really didn't want her around. She ignored the hurt in her chest and held onto her irritation. "That's not only rude, but unfair. I want to see how Phoenix is doing."

He leaned back, a smug smile on his face. "That's my side of the bet. Take it or leave it."

Oh, he thought he was so clever. He couldn't even see his mother was still influencing his actions. She shook her head. "Then I'll leave it. It's enough for me to know I'm right." She rose from the couch. "I think I'll see how the ribs look myself. It's suddenly feeling rather stuffy in here."

Before he could say a word, she strode to the door and left.

Dillon rubbed his hand down his face. What an ass he was. He'd accused her of trying to get him interested in her when she hadn't bothered with him all day. It was his own knee-jerk reaction to her side of the bet. Could she really just want to prove that what she liked to do was safe and fun?

He shook his head. He didn't know enough about her to be sure one way or the other, but to have said he didn't want her to be at Last Chance was like he'd forgotten everything his parents taught him. Why did he have such a hard time around this woman?

The answer came loud and clear. His mother. His mother wanted a well-known society miss in their family and she didn't care which son would make that happen. It was as if he and Cole were no more than a commodity to be sold to the highest bidder and that's exactly what Hailey was, at least in his mother's eyes. Of all the woman his mother paraded before them, Hailey Pennington was at the top of the list.

He stood and turned around to look out the window. Hailey laughed at something Trace said and gave Whisper a sympathetic grin. If his mother had never introduced them, he could have looked at her differently. He would have seen her as she was, a beautiful, intelligent, confident and kind person who took too many risks.

But he couldn't look at her like that. Two years of brainwashing by his mother had ruined any objectivity he could have around her. No matter how attractive he found her, he could never be fair to her. His mind was warped and he needed to admit that and move on. There was a great woman out there somewhere for him. Someone just as attractive, just as smart, and not nearly as adventurous.

Walking to the counter where he left his hat, he picked it up and shoved it on his head. He needed to get as far away from Hailey as he could and stay away. Opening the door to the trailer, he stepped outside. "I'll be heading back to the ranch."

He nodded and turned on his heel.

"I thought you were staying for some of my amazing ribs?" Trace's voice halted him.

"I was, but I forgot I had promised Gram I'd take those curtain rods down for her before dinner. I have to get back before she realizes I forgot." He quirked a smile. "I'd rather starve than get in trouble with Gram."

Trace laughed. "I'm with you."

Dillon forced himself not to look at Hailey. Mounting Black Jack, he turned the horse and gave a quick wave before heading for the hillside. He was proud of himself for having the backbone to stick to his resolve and leave, but a part of his conscience was calling him a wimp and he didn't even know why and he sure as hell didn't like it.

Hailey watched as yet another customer said hello to an elderly man sitting at the bar before moving on to find their own seat. He must be a regular, though he'd been nursing the same beer since she'd walked into the Black Mustang bar over half an hour ago.

"So how's the boat? Settled in yet?" Austin, her best friend since grammar school, pulled her attention back.

He was as clean cut as her older brother Cordell, as smart as her oldest brother Greyson, and more open to new experiences than her younger brother Wesley. He could have been her fraternal twin in temperament. "It's great. You didn't have to empty your closet. I could have just laid my clothes out on the couch. It's not like I'll be entertaining or anything."

He shrugged. "Now that I'm renting the apartment up here, I have plenty of room. Our trips to the boat are day outings."

Though many people thought women couldn't have male friends, they were downright wrong. She'd grown up with Austin and her brothers, and that's all she felt for him. Brotherly love. His unexpected twenty-four seven fatherhood had affected their regular adventures, but that was all. "So how are things going?"

He lifted his beer as if to toast her. "They're going. I didn't see your red Bug in the parking lot."

In other words, don't ask. He'd tell her when he was ready to talk. That was the great thing about their friendship. They understood each other.

"I rented a truck because I flew my plane up here."

Austin shook his head. "I didn't realize that little thing could make it so far."

She squinched up her nose. "Very funny."

"I thought so." He grinned, totally unapologetic.

She didn't mind. From Austin, it was just in fun. They'd been best friends since grammar school and had confided in each other as they matured. He was the person she'd turned to when she had questions during her teen years and she started going on dates.

After asking her oldest brother for advice, she'd realized very quickly that her brothers were overly protective and their answers were skewed. Austin had always been honest, even as a horny teenager, he told it like it was. And she'd been able to return the favor as he dated, married, then divorced his wife, or rather was divorced by the Wicked Witch, as Hailey referred to her.

Two more patrons walked into the bar, one of them greeting the elderly man with a "Hey Joe," before moving along to the pool table. The regular at the bar had to be in his late eighties. In his short sleeved-button down shirt, his forearms were exposed and they were wrinkled and thinner than her own. He wore a ball cap, probably with one of his favorite teams on it, his eyes on the basketball game on the television screen above the bar.

"So why did you want to meet? Problems with this Hatcher guy, the hot air balloon instructor, or have you found a new best friend in this Whisper woman and want to kick me to the curb."

She grinned at Austin. "The curb wouldn't be far enough

to get away from you. I'd have to send you to the Space Station or that new Mars colony I hear they want to start."

Austin laughed. "I'm all for the Space Station. That would be a real thrill ride, but I'm not stepping foot on another planet until they're sure there's not some bug that will burrow under my skin and use my body as a baby hive."

She shuddered. "You need to stop watching those sci-fi TV shows."

"And you're avoiding the question." He raised one eyebrow, a common occurrence with him.

She nodded. "It's the Hatcher guy as you put it."

"And?"

It'd been two days since Dillion had made it clear he didn't want her around and she'd been wrestling with her decision to walk away. Her gut kept telling her if she walked away then his mother would win, but if she stayed for that reason then she was being manipulated by his mother as well. "I'm struggling with whether I should keep trying or give it up."

Austin put down his beer and swallowed quickly. "What? Last I heard you were absolutely sure he was the one and all you had to do was open his eyes to that fact."

She squirmed at his reminder of her naïveté where Dillon was concerned. "I was, but I've discovered it's more complicated than that."

"How so?"

"It's the damage his mother has done. By trying to get one of her sons to marry into what she believes is a prestigious family, she's alienated them. Cole is married, but Dillon looks at all women his mother would approve of as suspect and strictly off limits."

"And you, of course, were one of the mother's golden girls."

She rolled her eyes. "Please, you make me sound like an old lady."

Austin laughed. "Well, you *do* have gold hair."

"It's called blonde, and you're not helping."

Austin lost his smile. "You're right. So, you're the pariah in this Hatcher guy's eyes."

She sighed. "Yes. In fact, last time I saw him, he proposed a friendly bet, but when he told me that if he won, my payment would be to not return to Last Chance until my two horses were ready to leave, I realized exactly how deep his animosity goes. My guess is that since he can't hate his mother, he transfers his anger to the women his mother tries to set him up with."

Austin took a sip of beer then set the bottle on the table and continued to stare at it. "You may not like this question, but if the guy is that dead set against you, and there's no way for him to get beyond the category he's put you in, why bother?"

It was a perfectly logical question and coming from anyone else, she would have snapped back, but Austin had always made her face reality without his own agenda.

"That's what I'm struggling with. I've seen glimpses of him that cause my heart to skip a beat."

Austin raised both eyebrows this time.

"Don't give me that look. I'm not talking about him physically." Though she was very impressed in that department. "I'm talking about his personality, like his caring, his manners, his love for his family. There is a lot there and I think if I weren't—" She lowered her voice—"Hailey Pennington, then I'd get to see a lot more. But he not only keeps me at arm's length, but frowns on simple things I do like piloting the hot air balloon and riding ATVs."

"Sounds like a stick in the mud to me." Austin shook his head. "My entire life, I've never known you to walk away from a challenge, yet you're contemplating that. So why? Why are you thinking he may not be worth the effort?"

She took a sip of wine to get her thoughts together. Austin was right, she'd never backed down from a challenge, but she also knew when she was looking at a lost cause and her gut was telling her Dillon was exactly that, his psychological scars were too deep. "It was his request that I stay away. If he actually despises me, then why put myself through that. You yourself know that if you aren't loved back in return, there's nothing you can do to change that."

Austin gave a harsh chuckle. "Damn right I know it." He shook his head. "But I don't think Dillon wanting you to stay away is a sign that he wants nothing to do with you."

"Oh, really? Do you think it's his way of playing hard to get or something?"

"No, I think it's his way of running away from someone he's interested in."

She stared at her friend, her mouth open because she was completely stupefied. She could not find any logic to his statement, yet he was the one that said men were always logical and linear. Closing her mouth, she licked her lips. "Explain."

"Hatcher's mother has suggested you; therefore, in his brain, you're completely off limits. But something must have happened while you were around him that showed him who you are as a person and he liked what he saw."

She embraced the glimmer of hope Austin threw her way. "Okay. So that's good, right?"

"No, that scares the hell out of him because, again, you are a *persona non-grata*. Now he has to fight his own interest, so he needs you to stay away. If you're near, he might give in, which according to you, would not only be capitulating to you but to his mother, the she-demon, as well."

"She's not a she-demon." She gave him the side eye. "Have you been watching fantasy movies, too?"

"Focus here, Hailey. The fact the man wants you gone is a clear signal he's interested. If he was disinterested, he wouldn't care if you were at Last Chance every day or not because he wouldn't be in danger of falling for you."

At Austin's words, her heart leapt. "Do you think that's a possibility? I mean, that he could fall for me?"

Her friend studied her. "Of course he could, if he's smart. But I take no responsibility for cowboy stupidity." He grimaced. "We're all born with our fair share."

"No kidding. Sometimes I wonder how the west was really won."

Austin shrugged. "Luck and carpet baggers."

She grinned at him before she noticed the older man at the bar getting off his stool, his body obviously stiff from sitting. As he waved at the bartender and turned toward her, she recognized the VFW insignia on his cap.

"Excuse me a moment." Slipping out of her chair, she intercepted the veteran halfway to the door. "Excuse me, I couldn't help but notice your hat and I wanted to thank you for your service."

The startled look on the man's face changed to a smile as he looked up at her. "You're welcome, young lady. Korean War, 1952. Long before you were born."

"I know, but time doesn't minimize your bravery and sacrifice."

"Bravery is easier when you have someone with you. My comrades, most of them gone now, helped me make it through. There's something to be said for solidarity." A pensive look came over the older man's face. "It's when you're alone that you have to worry. That's when you come face to face with yourself and find out exactly how brave you are...or aren't."

She couldn't even begin to imagine what he'd been through. Bending over she gave the man a kiss on the cheek. "Thank you."

Even in the dim lighting of the bar, she could see a blush creep up his neck. Damn, she didn't mean to embarrass him.

"Roll me over like a tumbleweed and kick me into the wash, old Josiah's still got it with the ladies."

At the voice of one of the men on the stools, Josiah turned away. "Of course. That's not something you lose. Then again, with you, Harry, you never had it to begin with." As laughter erupted at the bar, he faced her again, the blush gone. "Just ignore them."

She smiled, offering her hand. "I'm Hailey. It was very nice to meet you, Joe."

"Believe me, Miss Hailey, the pleasure was all mine." He gave her a quick wink then walked out the door, his step quicker and lighter.

She returned to her seat, happy to have been able to make Joe's night. As she sat, Austin put his empty beer bottle down. "Playing angel again?"

"Oh, stuff it." She took the last swallow of her wine and handed him the glass. "I think it's your turn to buy."

"Probably." Austin rose and walked to the bar.

She turned her attention to the parking lot, which was bathed in a reddish neon glow from the Black Mustang's sign. There was only one row of spaces that had pavement. The rest of the customers parked in the dirt. That's where Josiah headed. A truck pulled in and lowered its high beams as they swept over Joe.

It sounded as if Austin thought she should continue her pursuit, but how could she do that without Dillon pushing her away? And what if Austin was wrong and Dillon really didn't want her around? He'd been quite rude, even smiling.

Absently, she watched as Josiah stopped by a sedan and stood there looking at the side of his car. She tensed. Did he happen upon a rattler? About to get up and brave the snake herself, the older man turned and spoke to the newcomer, so she stayed where she was.

She looked to where Josiah faced and sucked in her breath as Dillon strode into the muted light.

Chapter Six

Dillon wore jeans, a checkered shirt rolled up to his elbows, and his black cowboy hat. As Joe motioned to his car, Dillon spoke and pointed toward the trunk. It wasn't hard to figure out that Josiah had a flat tire.

Dillon lifted the jack out and squatted next to the vehicle.

Hailey smiled, happy to see him helping the veteran because not only did Joe deserve the help, but it showed her the real Dillon, when he didn't know she watched him. Her instincts had been right. He was one of the good ones. She just had to figure out how to get over the walls he built to keep his mother's favorites out.

"Here you go." Austin set down another glass of Chardonnay. "What are you looking at?"

She grinned. "You'll never guess who's here."

"Cord."

His answer was so immediate that she laughed. "True, that *would* be a surprise to find my brother more than ten miles from the ranch, but you're wrong. It's Dillon."

Austin peered out the window. "All I see is the veteran."

She pointed. "Dillon's changing Joe's tire." Even from where she sat, she swore she could see Dillon's muscular forearms as he pumped the jack to lift Josiah's car.

"I can't even tell what he looks like. You'll have to point him out when he comes inside."

She stared at him as if he'd gone blind. How could he not see the large man with the strong profile? She was about to say so when Austin spoke.

"At least in here there's more light. I could better judge if he deserves you."

She frowned at him. "Seriously? Don't turn into one of my brothers now."

Austin shook his head. "Not a chance of that happening. Just want to get a feel for him myself."

"That's fine. Just don't be getting all protective on me."

He held up one hand. "I swear I won't."

She relaxed. "Good." She turned back toward the window to see Dillon lifting the spare tire from the trunk. He acted like it weighed no more than a beer. And soon, he'd be coming into the bar. What would he think about her being there? Would he be angry? Happy? Her stomach tightened in anticipation.

She faced Austin to calm her nerves. "Actually, I'd like your read on him as he realizes I'm here. I'm guessing he'll be mad and think I'm stalking him."

"Aren't you?"

She squinched up her face. "I hardly think seeing him three times in as many weeks would be considered stalking."

"Come on, Hellion. We could have easily met at the marina bar. Tell me you didn't think he would be here."

She rounded her eyes. "I didn't. I just wanted to see what other places were out here. It's not like this is part of the city. We are in the middle of the desert and our choices are limited."

"Sure." Austin took a swallow of his new beer.

"Okay, so maybe I hoped that I might run into him. For all

I know, he's as much a regular here as Joe, which to tell you the truth would not be a positive."

"You can't tell me you want a 'stay on the ranch' kind of man like Cord."

She shook her head. "Absolutely not. But I don't want to get involved with a barfly."

"And you think he could be?"

She shook her head. "No, I don't, but I haven't exactly had a lot of time to get to know him." She picked up her wine and took a sip, her gaze moving toward the window again as if drawn there.

Dillon was tapping Joe's shoulder and nodding. Then he stood back as Joe got into his car and drove away. Dillon turned toward the bar. She swallowed. "He's coming."

"Shit, Hailey, are you nervous?"

"Of course not." She quickly took a larger than normal swallow of wine.

"You are. I don't remember the last time you were nervous. Oh, wait. I do." A mischievous grin spread across Austin's face.

She pierced him with her gaze. "Oh no, you are not bringing that up again. You need new material."

He laughed. "Why, when the old material is so good. Now let's see. I think it was the seventh-grade talent show if I remember correctly."

She rolled her eyes. "The problem is you never forget." At Austin's innocent face, she laughed.

The door to the bar opened and Dillon strode in.

Her face froze in a smile as he turned and spotted her.

He halted.

The faeries in her stomach started a Congo dance that made her blood pound.

Finally, he moved toward her. "Hello Hailey. I'm glad you're here."

Those were the last words she expected to hear. "You are?"

He looked away, as if uncomfortable. "Yes, I owe you an apology." His gaze returned to her. "I was rude last week. I didn't mean to be."

Her whole body relaxed with relief. "Apology accepted." After all, it wasn't easy for a man to say he was wrong, never mind apologize. She'd seen her brothers dance around it every which way until her mother pinned them down.

"Good." He moved closer. Suddenly, his whole demeanor changed and his face went stoic on her.

At first, she didn't understand why until he turned his head to look directly at Austin. He must have been surprised because the building's configuration made it impossible to see Austin from the entrance until one had come far enough into the open room.

Remembering her manners, she gestured toward her friend. "Dillon Hatcher, this is a friend of mine, Austin Leighthall."

Austin didn't grin. In fact, he remained as stoic as Dillon. What the hell? Both men simply nodded at each other.

Trying to make up for Austin's unusual coldness, she pointed to the seat next to her. "Would you like to join us?"

"No. I just came to play a couple games of pool."

"Oh, I love playing pool."

He glanced at Austin again. "Well, have a good night." Tipping his hat, he turned, striding toward the corner area like he was on a mission.

Austin laughed. "That didn't take long."

She turned on him. "What are you talking about? And why were so cold?" Usually, her friend would rise and offer his hand. Now he was the one acting rude.

"Don't you see? He was jealous." Austin grinned.

"What? He can't be. He doesn't know me. To be jealous he'd have to have feelings…" She looked over to where Dillon was chalking a cue. Did he have feelings for her? She looked back at Austin. "You think he has feelings for me?" She was almost afraid to hope.

Austin shrugged. "I'm no expert, but the minute he discovered me sitting here with you, he was pissed. It radiated off him in waves."

She sat back and crossed her arms. "It wasn't as if you were very welcoming. What was that about?"

"It's a guy thing. I reacted to his surprise and irritation. I didn't want him to know we were just friends quite yet as it would make you too available. Trust me. If he thinks you may be interested in me, he just might be more open to you."

She frowned. "You know I don't play games like that, Austin."

"I know and it wouldn't have occurred to me if the man's irritation wasn't so strong. He's definitely interested."

She glanced over toward the pool table only to find Dillon bending over to make a shot. All her female parts woke up with a start at the sight of his cowboy butt. Quickly, she took a sip of wine then glared at Austin. "Still, you could have shaken his hand and I could have told him we're just friends. I don't want him to think I'm unavailable."

Austin laughed again. "You mean like the time I introduced you to Madonna and told her we were just friends?"

She dropped her arms. "That doesn't count. Your ex is the Wicked Witch of the West. I refuse to believe that Dillon would react the same way."

"You can refuse all you want, but the fact is, that man feels something for you. If you are serious about this guy, I suggest you move on that sooner rather than later because jealousy is a fickle emotion and it can cause him to push you away even more if he stews about it."

Why did it have to be so complicated? The answer came fast and furious. Beverly Hatcher had made it complicated. "So I should go play pool with him?"

"No."

Austin's answer was immediate.

She snapped her gaze back to him. "But you just said—"

"Yes, I did. But I also know if you waltz over there now, you'll piss him off."

"Excuse me?"

Austin sighed. "Hailey, when was the last time you lost a game to any man to avoid hurting his ego?"

She slumped back in her chair. "Never."

"I rest my case."

He was right. She refused to be someone she wasn't for anyone. If she beat him at pool when he was so irritated, she'd probably never see him again. If she ever got that man to give her a chance, it would be one of the hardest things she'd ever done in her entire life…and she'd conquered quite a few difficult challenges.

"Finish your wine and I'll drop you off at the marina. Trust me, you've given him enough to think about tonight, but I suggest a visit to Last Chance tomorrow."

She lifted her glass and toasted the air. "To tomorrow."

Dillon popped the last piece of homemade coffee cake into his mouth and set the dirty pan into the sink. Washing that down with the last gulp of coffee in his mug, he was ready to tackle the new fencing. It would be good to work with his brother. He had a few questions about their mother that he hoped Cole could shed light on.

The sound of hurried footsteps down the hall had him stepping to the doorway of the kitchen.

"Where's my great grandbaby? I know she's around here somewhere."

He shook his head. His hard-as-nails grandmother turned into a marshmallow the minute his cousin's daughter arrived, though why she was here on a Thursday was a question. Luckily, he came downstairs dressed. Logan didn't like if he was around Charlotte without a shirt. Considering the forecasted temperatures today, he hoped Charlotte planned to stay inside. Digging fence holds was hard work.

"She's right here, Gram. We won't bring her over tomorrow since I'll be home."

At the sound of Logan's voice, Dillon stepped into the hall. He was just in time to catch a giggling eighteen-month-old Charlotte as she ran toward him and away from his grandmother who was making choo-choo train noises.

He scooped her up and lifted her high above his head.

Her squeals of delight had him smiling in response. She was a cute little thing.

"Put her down this instant. You're going to make her sick." What Gram was really saying was that only she was allowed to hold her granddaughter and he better acquiesce to her rights.

"If you say so." He pretended to drop the little girl, though he had her the whole time, which just sent her into peels of laughter. But at Gram's scowl, he set Charlotte on the floor, where she promptly ran into the kitchen, a teddy bear with a cowboy hat on, clutched in her hand.

As Gram followed, he greeted his cousin. "What are you

doing here? I thought you were coming tomorrow when Cole goes back on shift."

Logan shrugged. "He said he was taking Lacey to learn how to fly on a trapeze."

"What?" His brother was all about following rules. He couldn't quite see him watching his wife flying through the air. "That doesn't sound like Cole."

"I didn't think so either, but I guess she's always dreamed of doing this and when she heard from Hailey Pennington that they had lessons just south of Phoenix, she was going no matter what Cole said."

Hailey Pennington. Were all the women on the ranch enamored of the woman?

"Let me just grab a water and I'll be out." Logan smacked him on the arm. "Lucky for you, I'm an expert fence-hole digger. Just finished a new corral at Jenna's place last month."

He nodded. "Great." So much for some alone time with his older brother. He shrugged as he strode down the hall. It could wait.

Opening the door, he stepped out onto the porch, the above average temperature already making itself known. Why did he have a feeling Cole chose this particular day to give into Lacey?

Jogging down the steps, he headed for the barn. He still couldn't imagine his brother standing idly by while his wife swung through the air. As the new Captain of the local fire department and the only arson investigator for miles, Cole was all about safety. Even at home, he used to move their mother's candles off of shelves and be the one to make sure the campfires were completely out. He'd often made fun of Cole, but in this case, he would have advised him to keep Lacey firmly on the ground.

Grabbing the trailer, he hooked it to the ATV so he and

Logan could haul all the tools they would need to the new corral site near Cole's finished barn. His brother wanted to be able to take more horses if needed. Cole was always thinking ahead.

He loaded the trailer then walked over to the stall with Nizhoni and Phoenix. The colt was asleep on the floor, his mom standing guard. The little guy seemed to be healing pretty well, most of the bandages having come off already. Would Hailey be taking the horses back to Ironwood soon? That would be a good thing for his own piece of mind. Seeing her at the Black Mustang with her "friend" had pissed him off. He preferred to have his life back to the way it was since coming to Last Chance.

Actually, what he preferred was to find a good woman that his mother wouldn't approve of and move back to Morning Creek. He turned back toward the ATV and froze. Would his mother allow him back without the proper wife? It hadn't occurred to him until now. When Cole had wanted to turn part of Morning Creek into a horse rescue ranch, their mother had refused and when Cole threatened to leave, she let him.

Now he had another question to ask his older brother.

Starting up the ATV, he drove it out of the barn to find Logan leaving the house. He stopped and his cousin handed him a water.

"Grabbed one for you, too."

He looked at the clear bright sky. "I think we'll need a lot more than that before the day is over."

"I'll ride over on Black Jack."

He nodded and drove to his brother's brand new home on the ranch. The small barn nearby was all finished since he and Logan hung the doors.

Once arriving at Cole's house, he and Logan found the markings Cole had left. It looked like the new corral would be as large as the north one by the old house.

After two hours of digging holes, Dillon was absolutely sure the new corral was twice as big. "If I'm going to keep working in this heat, I need food and water, preferably the latter poured over my head."

Logan jammed the post hole digger into the ground. "We need an auger. This is taking too long. Let's head back. I'm going into town to see if the hardware store might have something. I can't believe Cole didn't rent us a machine."

Dillon laid his t-shirt on the back of the seat and got behind the wheel of the ATV. "Cole rent a machine when he has us as labor? Don't hold your breath."

Logan took his own shirt and wiped the sweat from his torso before untying Black Jack from the shady side of the barn. "You have another shirt I can use?"

He grinned. "Sure. If you don't mind the loose fit."

Logan lowered his brow. "Go hug a Saguaro."

He chuckled as he started the ATV. "See you at the house." Revving the machine, he sent it racing down the dirt road back to the main house. As he came to a full stop in front of the house, a cloud of dust covered him. Great, now he was sweaty and dusty.

Walking over to the hose, he threw it on full blast and let the water spill out onto his Gram's agave plants. Once all the hot water from the hose had emptied, he bent over and hosed himself down. The cool water was welcome until it turned real cold. Jerking the hose away, he stood up to find two trucks pulling in.

Returning the hose, he turned the water off and strode toward the newcomers. Dr. Jenna's truck he knew, but the other one he didn't. The driver side door of the truck opened and Hailey Pennington hopped out in a pair of very short white shorts, a peach tank top that bared her middle and brown cowboy boots.

Hell, the woman was hot. And here he'd thought he'd just cooled off.

Closing the door, she turned and noticed him. She stared at him for a moment, but he didn't know if that was good or bad because her sunglasses were too dark to see her eyes.

As if suddenly remembering she had them on, she took them off and gave him a smile. "Hi, Dillon. Did you go swimming and forget to take off your pants?"

He looked down to find the water from his torso had dripped down onto his jeans. Looking back at her, he shrugged. "A man's got to cool off somehow."

Dr. Jenna walked around her truck to join Hailey. "I'm more interested in the tall, dark and handsome man riding into the yard. Excuse me."

As the vet headed for Logan, Hailey approached. Shit, the last thing he wanted to notice was the lemony scent she always wore but turning away would be rude and he'd rather not have to apologize for that particular behavior again.

"I'm assuming you aren't wet for the fun of it. What are you working on?"

He hooked his thumb over his shoulder. "Cole wants another corral near his house. Logan and I were digging post holes, but he thinks we can get an auger in town." Stupid. She probably doesn't even know what an auger is.

"Ugh, I remember digging post holes."

"You?"

She nodded. "Oh yes. My father insisted we all know every part of the ranch from the cattle to the finances to the cooking. Some of us were better than others, depending on the task. Grey was always a whiz with the numbers and Cord had and still has the best handle on the livestock. Wes was all about the horses."

He couldn't resist asking. "And what was your specialty?"

He'd lay money down on cooking, decorating or possibly marketing.

"You'll laugh." She actually looked uncomfortable.

He'd never seen her appear anything but confident. He should shrug it off. His curiosity about this woman was bound to get him into trouble of one kind or another. "I promise I won't." So much for letting it go.

"I was good at carpentry."

"Carpentry?" He was too stunned to laugh.

She looked down at her dainty hands, which now that he focused on them, realized weren't as dainty as he thought. She wore no nail polish and there was a scar across the back of her right hand.

"What kind of carpentry?"

She looked up, obviously surprised by his interest. For some dumb reason that made him feel good. He really needed to get his act together.

"Pretty much everything. I've built tables, chairs, bookcases, but also sheds, chicken coops and I was one of the framers for Cord's house." She looked around as if to make sure no one had overheard. "Though I prefer to keep that a secret." She winked. "It would ruin my reputation."

He nodded, not knowing how to take that. He was still reeling from her confession. Carpentry?

"For your sake, I hope they do have an auger in town. That's a lot of post holes to dig if they don't. Then again, hard work builds character and muscle, or so my dad has always said." She grinned as her gaze moved to his arms.

He barely kept from flexing his muscles. What was wrong with him? What did he care if she found him attractive or not? She was off limits in his book. Irritated, he frowned. "From what I've found, hard work is just dirty and sweaty."

She laughed. "I totally agree."

"Hey, Hailey, ready to visit your horses?" Dr. Jenna strolled up to them.

"You bet!"

Hailey's pretty green eyes lit with excitement, causing his chest to tighten. Is that how she'd look if excited in a different way? "Holy shit."

"What?" Hailey turned from Jenna to look at him. "Something wrong?"

He waved her off. "No, just remembered something." He quickly spun toward the house. He needed to get his mind off the woman and onto something else, and he knew just the cure for that.

Ignoring the women chatting behind him, he strode into the house and started down the hall. Suddenly he halted and spun around, talking the stairs two at a time. First, he needed another shirt.

Grabbing another t-shirt, he slipped it over his head before heading back downstairs. He heard his Gram in the living room and stepped to the doorway. Little Charlotte threw a ball at Gram with one hand, the other hand occupied by her ever-present teddy. The little girl laughed as the ball bounced then landed in his grandmother's lap.

Gram rolled the ball back and Charlotte squatted down to pick it up. When she stood, she noticed him.

He smiled at her, his whole world seeming to right itself. His cousin was a very lucky man.

The ball hitting his shin was unexpected and he crouched down to pick it up. "Is this yours?"

Charlotte waved her teddy bear at him. "Mine."

He pressed the ball to his chest. "Mine."

"Oh, no. Don't you get her started now." Gram commanding voice left little impression on him.

A squeal issued from his little cousin. "Mine!"

He grinned and held the ball in front of him. "Then come get it."

Her eyebrows furrowed as she looked at the ball. Then her gaze lifted to his. He nodded.

Charlotte ran toward him, her hand outstretched, but her momentum carried her beyond his hand and as she grabbed the ball, she fell into him. He caught her soft little body in his hands. He always had a soft spot for kids and little Charlotte was his favorite.

Scooping her up, much to her delight, he strode from the room.

"Don't you be dropping that child, Dillon."

Gram's voice was no more than an annoying fly to him and he increased his pace. "Do you want to see Lucky?"

Charlotte looked over her shoulder and stretched her arm out, teddy firmly in her grasp. "My Lucky. Horsey mine."

He opened the door and strode out onto the porch. "And where is Lucky?"

Charlotte whipped her head around and pointed. "There."

He chuckled. "You are one smart little girl."

She spun her head back around and stared at him very seriously. "Yes. Smart." She nodded, and he swallowed the laughter that threatened.

He walked over to the south corral where Macy and Lucky were taking advantage of the shaded area that had been erected for a visiting youth group last summer before the colt was born.

"Lucky!" The yell from the little one in his arm came out of nowhere, causing him to hold her a little tighter.

"Let me get you closer." He stopped next to the rail closest to where the two horses stood. Lucky was busy drinking from his mother's teat.

He set Charlotte's feet on the top rail but wrapped one arm around her. It wasn't the first time he'd carried her around and after the first time when she made a sudden move and he almost dropped her, practically giving himself a heart attack, he knew better than to trust her. It had been a quick lesson in what it would be like to be a parent, something he actually looked forward to, though he'd never admit that to his family, especially not his mother.

An ear-splitting squeal suddenly issued from the mouth of the tiny child in his arms, making him rethink the whole parent thing in an instant.

"Lucky here!" Charlotte waved her teddy at the colt, who had looked up at her god-awful noise.

"Shh, you need to wait for him to finish his lunch."

Charlotte faced him. "Eating?"

He nodded. "Yes, that's how a baby eats."

She shook her head. "Me not a baby."

"No, you are growing big."

She smiled at him before turning back to look at Lucky, who was walking toward them as if he'd responded to her call.

Damn, the child was going to be spoiled by both the humans and the animals on the ranch.

When Lucky came close, he lowered his voice. "Be gentle. Soft."

Charlotte reached out her hand and pet the horse's nose. After four strokes, she grasped her hand to her chest and looked up at him in awe.

His heart melted all over again. "That was good."

The horse, obviously not satisfied with that amount of attention, butted his nose against Charlotte's legs, which immediately bent.

Thankful he had a good grasp on her, he stroked the horse on its neck with his free hand.

"Pet." Charlotte held out her empty hand, so he leaned her over and she stroked the horse again before letting out a squeal of excitement which sent the horse galloping away shaking its head.

She'd definitely needed to get control over her voice before they taught her how to ride. At the thought of teaching her to ride, his chest tightened. It was hard to believe he would have barely known her if he hadn't moved to Last Chance. Maybe things happened for good reason.

"Okay, we better get you back to Gram before she comes looking for us. Say goodbye."

Charlotte waved to Lucky by opening and closing her hand. "Bye, bye, bye, bye…"

She continued her litany as he strode for the house, feeling much calmer. But as he made the steps, the sound of another truck coming up the dirt road caught his attention. Turning back, Charlotte still saying bye to her horse, he watched as the fifth truck came to a stop, a horse trailer behind it.

The ranch looked like a truck stop and it didn't even include Cole's or Whisper's trucks. He waited to see who the newcomer was. Cole hadn't said anything about a new horse arriving and there was definitely a horse in the trailer.

The driver's door slammed shut and a woman appeared around the side of the trailer. Her slender form was almost boyish and her short, straight red hair was barely visible beneath her Stetson.

"Is this Last Chance ranch?" At her voice, Charlotte turned in his arms.

"Yes, it is. Can I help you?"

"I'm Riley O'Hare. Trace Williams said I could get room and board for some honest work."

Chapter Seven

Dillon gave Riley a welcoming smile. "That's right. You were the stable manager where Nizhoni and Phoenix came from. We thought you found another job when you didn't arrive."

One side of her lip curled up. "That was because of my creep of a boss. He said he'd sell me Domino while the police were there, then tried to go back on his word. Then he demanded cash. The guy's an—"

"Criminal. Yes, I know." He nodded toward Charlotte, well aware how quickly the little girl could pick up words. They'd finally taught her hello after Trace said hell one day in front of her.

Riley gave Charlotte a cursory glance. "Right. Sorry. Not used to being around children. Does she live here?"

"Three days a week. Gram is her babysitter." He moved his gaze toward the barn as Jenna and Hailey came out.

"I thought I heard a truck." Jenna stepped forward. "I'm Dr. Jenna, the local vet."

Riley shook her hand. "I'm Riley O'Hare. I'm the one who called the police on my employer. Are you the one that took care of Nizhoni's colt?"

"I am."

"Hi, I'm Hailey." As Hailey stepped up to meet the woman, he couldn't help but notice they were both the same height, had the same air of confidence, but where Hailey was curvy and feminine, Riley looked boyish and a little tough. "I want to thank you for stopping the abuse. That was a brave thing to do."

Riley shrugged. "I don't put up with anyone abusing any animal. It was the right thing to do. Sure, I'm out of a job, but I was told I could stay here, so once I got Domino I came."

"Stay here?" Hailey looked to him for confirmation.

He nodded. "Yes. Let me just hand Charlotte back to Gram."

"Oh, I can take her." Hailey strode toward him. "Charlotte, would it be okay with you if I took you inside?"

He looked at Jenna to see what she thought of that, but she was already heading toward the trailer with Riley.

Charlotte leaned away from him and held out her teddy. "Kissy teddy."

Hailey pretended to think about it. "If I kiss teddy, can I kiss you, too?"

Charlotte nodded and Hailey gave the teddy a resounding smack, much to Charlotte's delight. Charlotte scrunched up her face and Hailey gave the little girl an equally loud kiss. Charlotte laughed, absolutely thrilled.

"Now, unless you need a kiss, too, how about you hand her over and go show Riley where to stable her horse."

It took him a moment after she said the word "kiss" before he could move his gaze from her lips. They looked soft and the idea of pressing his own against them took root and wouldn't let go. Finally, he snapped his head toward Charlotte, who had no problem showing she wanted Hailey as she leaned her little body out over his arm.

"Whoa there." He finally looked Hailey in her eyes. "Keep a good hold on her. She's known for surprising you."

"No problem. She'll be safe with me." Hailey granted him a brief smile before focusing on Charlotte and holding her arms out.

With no real choice, he let Charlotte fall into Hailey's arms. As she adjusted the little girl, he swallowed a lump in his throat. Hailey was a natural. "She's heavier than she looks."

She frowned at him. "Go. I've got this."

He forced himself to look away and move toward the step. He was just concerned about Charlotte. He didn't know that much about Hailey. He glanced back once his feet hit the hardpacked dirt, but Hailey had already opened the door and was walking inside.

"Bye, bye, bye." Charlotte waved her teddy at him as she looked over Hailey's shoulder.

Now he was making a fool of himself and he didn't even know why. Resuming his course, he met the other two women as they led out a stunning black and white paint. He let out a low whistle. "That animal could make me switch from breeding American quarter horses."

Riley halted Domino and grinned, making her appear prettier than his first impression. "She *is* a beauty. Cost me a fortune because of that money grubbing—" She looked past him before continuing. "Asshole. But she's worth every penny. I was thinking if you have room, I'd like to put her near Nizhoni and her colt. Wait, you said the colt had a name now?"

"Yes, the woman you just met, Hailey, named him Phoenix and will eventually be taking them both home."

The redhead nodded. "It's a good name."

He agreed but didn't say so. What was wrong with him that

he couldn't give Hailey any credit, even in front of a stranger? "Domino is the perfect name for this mare."

"Not that the asshole had anything to do with it, which is a good thing." She scowled despite the fact she stroked the paint's neck. "He deserves life in prison for what he's done."

An image of Phoenix when he first saw him flashed through his mind and he fisted his hands. "Personally, I'd like to beat him to within an inch of his life, but my brother wouldn't tell me who your boss was. If you reveal his name I can promised retribution."

Riley's eyes widened before she let her gaze roam over his body as if checking to see if he could make good on his promise, yet her gaze did nothing to heat his body like Hailey's did. Maybe it was just that he preferred blondes.

Finally, Riley looked him in the eye. "I'm not sure that would be a good idea. If your brother is my new employer, I'd rather not betray him within minutes of arriving."

At the realization of what he'd asked of her, he backed down. "Good point. Come this way. I think we have a stall available opposite Nizhoni and Phoenix."

Jenna placed her hand on Riley's arm before she could take a step. "I'll need to give Domino a through going over. I hope you're okay with that."

Riley nodded. "More than okay. You just made me feel hundred percent better about my decision to come here. For me, the horses come first."

Jenna smiled. "Oh, you will fit right in here. Wait until you meet Whisper."

"Is that a horse?" Riley's eyes grew intense. She really was into horses.

"No." Jenna laughed. "She's Trace's girlfriend."

With a quick nod, Riley acknowledged that fact as perfectly ordinary and looked at him. "Lead the way."

Starting for the barn, he smiled to himself. It seemed Last Chance was not only home to rescue horses but also turning into a place for odd people as well. Even Hailey, who was only visiting on occasion, fit in better than he did. The longer he lived at Last Chance, the more he felt like the odd man out.

After reintroducing Domino to her former stablemates, Riley got her settled into her stall. Maybe he was just used to the horses at the ranch with strange behaviors, but this one appeared very well behaved. "Is your horse always so calm?"

Riley closed the stall door behind her. "She was only at my employer's for a couple months, but yes. She was very well trained."

He opened his arm to let her precede him out of the barn. "Do you know who did the training?" He would love to hire that person for Morning Creek. He swallowed hard. If he ever returned there.

"I don't, but I have it in her papers. Once I unpack my stuff, I can get it for you."

He strode next to her toward her truck. "No rush. Can I help you with your belongings?"

Riley opened the back door of the cab and pulled out a military issue duffle bag. "Sure." She held it up and tossed it to him. Its weight surprised him, and he almost dropped it. The woman was stronger than she looked.

When she closed the door, he frowned. "Anything else? Might as well make it one trip since I'm here to be your pack mule." He gave her a crooked smile.

She laughed. "That's all there is."

A woman with only one bag? He doubted Hailey could do that. Not happy his thoughts strayed to her again, he looped his arm into the strap and settled the bag on his back then started for the house. "Great. I'm getting off easy. You'll be staying upstairs in what I call the revolving room, since we never know who will be in it next. Unfortunately, there's only one bathroom, so you'll be sharing it with me."

They had reached the porch when Riley gave him another once-over with her eyes. "I've shared with worse."

Not sure if that was a compliment or an insult, he let it go. Opening the door, he motioned for her to go ahead. "Head right up these stairs."

Laughter from the kitchen distracted him. That had to be Hailey. What would she think about Riley staying at Last Chance? Would she care?

He shook his head as he headed up the stairs. For someone who wasn't interested in the woman, he certainly thought about her a lot. "Here you are, home sweet home. The bathroom is right there. Hope you don't mind a twin bed." He dropped the duffle onto one of the two beds in the room.

"I've slept on worse."

Not sure how to respond to that and not really wanting to know more about the woman, he ignored it. "I'll let you unpack, then."

She was already untying her duffle bag and nodded absently.

Leaving the room, he found himself anxious to find out what all the laughter was about. It wasn't that common on Morning Creek, but at Last Chance, there was so much family around that it seemed to occur all the time.

He stopped in the living room to look in on Charlotte. She was sleeping soundly in her playpen, her cowboy teddy clutched tightly in her small hand. His little cousin had no idea how lucky she was to have such great female role models in her life.

Stepping across the hall, he approached the kitchen doorway and stopped. Hailey had her head thrown back as she laughed, showing off her slender neck. She wiped her eyes and looked at Jenna. "Oh, that's nothing. You should have seen Grey's face when she took the gum from her mouth and offered to share."

Gram and Jenna joined Hailey in more laughter. He leaned against the doorframe, happy to be a silent observer, but Hailey spotted him.

"Hey, Dillon. Would you like to share some of your most embarrassing moments growing up?"

"I doubt I could compete with you ladies on that score, but I'm happy to listen."

A silent look passed between all the women before they broke out in laughter. He had the feeling the laughter was at his expense, but he was fine with that. It was just good to hear and seemed to fill a missing piece of him, one that used to be there back when he'd spend the weekend on Gram and Gramp's ranch playing rodeo round-up with his brother and cousins.

"You want to come with us, Dillon?" Jenna's question caught him off guard.

"What? Sorry, I didn't catch that."

She leaned into Hailey. "So much for listening." Hailey laughed again. It was the kind of sound that made a person feel warm inside.

She addressed him. "Jenna wanted to know if you'd like to go jet-skiing with us this Thursday before the crowds hit the lake."

Lake? "What lake? Lake Pleasant?"

She nodded. "Yes, that's where I've been staying while I learn how to fly hot air balloons and wait for Phoenix to come home with me."

She was staying that close by and had only shown up at the ranch three times in two weeks? His doubts that she was in league with his mother finally dissipated. A woman after him wouldn't have stayed away so long, at least none of the others his mother had thrown his way had. If that was true, he owed Hailey an apology, or at least a concession or two. "Jet skis aren't the safest sport, especially with big boats on the lake."

For the first time he noticed irritation cross Hailey's face before she spoke. "That's why we're going before the weekend crowds. I told you, I'm always safe in the activities I participate in."

Something about her irritation intrigued him and he actually wanted to see more of it. She appeared so perfect that to see her lose patience gave him a glimpse of what he considered the real Hailey. "That's what you've said, but if you had normal, less treacherous activities, you wouldn't have to be so careful. Is there anything you do that isn't a risk?"

She frowned before a slow smile crossed her face. "Sure. I like to plant flowers in my mother's garden and I like to go for hikes. In fact, I saw a sign for Pipeline Canyon Trailhead when I drove by on my way to explore the old Castle Hot Springs last year. Thought I'd try it. Have you done it?"

Hiking? It didn't seem like her, but then again, what seemed like Hailey in his mind was fast becoming completely false. "A long time ago. I had just graduated college, so years ago."

She slapped her hand on the table. "I can't believe it, we actually agree on something." She chuckled. "I was planning to hike it tomorrow. I'm assuming it's safe to do alone?"

Every protective instinct in his body woke up again. It was a long hike and though the last time he'd done it, he may not have been completely sober, the idea of her out in the middle of the desert by herself with the spotty cell coverage they had out there, had him tensing. "It's not a hard trail, if I remember correctly, but it's in the middle of nowhere and you can't depend on your phone if you get into trouble."

That she looked concerned appeased his sense of safety. "Jenna, you said you have to work tomorrow, right?"

Jenna nodded. "Yes, and if I'm going to use my day off doing something, I guarantee you I'll take jet skiing over hiking every time."

Hailey smiled, obviously not deterred. "I don't have a lot of friends up this way. I wonder if Whisper would go?"

"Go where?" Riley brushed by him in the doorway to join the crowd.

Gram, who hadn't said much yet, filled her in. "Hailey would like to do the Pipeline Canyon hike, but it's not safe to do alone and Jenna has to work. I can't do that long of a hike anymore."

His grandmother's admission shocked him. She never admitted to growing old. That concerned him.

She continued. "And I know that Whisper is going to Poker Flat with Lacey tomorrow because there is a new person coming in to work the stable over there and she wants Whisper to get a sense of how the horses feel about it."

Again, Riley took that information in stride. "Well, you can count me out. I've had enough hikes in the desert to last a lifetime."

Hailey's face fell, her disappointment obvious.

Before he could swallow his words, he spoke. "I can go with you."

Her eyes widened in surprise once again. "Really? Don't you have to work here?"

"I can take the day tomorrow." He gave Riley a commanding stare. "Now that we have more help."

The woman immediately nodded. "Right. That's why I'm here."

"That's fantastic." Hailey gave him the side-eye. "Are you sure this hike is tame enough for you."

He frowned at her. "Don't underestimate the rattlers or the

rocks. If I remember correctly, the last time you went for a walk in the desert you twisted your ankle."

She backed-off. "You're right, one reason why I won't do the hike alone. Thank you."

At her sincere thanks, he lost his scowl. It felt good that he could do something so simple for her. She seemed so easy to please that he wanted to be around her more. What was that about?

"Is there a chance I could get some grub?" Riley spoke to Gram. "I didn't have a chance to grab lunch today. I'm all unpacked and settled in upstairs and my stomach just reminded me."

"Of course." Gram immediately got up and moved to the fridge.

"Upstairs? You're staying upstairs?" Hailey glanced at him in question before returning her gaze to Riley.

"Yup. The room with the two beds. You're welcome to join me if you need a place to stay and if it's okay with Mrs. Benson."

"Please, call me Annette." Gram placed a plate into the microwave.

"Yes, ma'am."

Hailey coughed before finding her voice, but there was definitely no smile on her face. "No, that's fine. I have a place down the road. How long will you be here?"

Riley shrugged. "Don't know. Depends on how long these folks will have me."

Again, Hailey glanced at him.

Was she nervous? Jealous? Or just confused by how things worked at Last Chance. It couldn't be jealousy when she had that "friend" Austin. Still, she kept up with the glances as Riley devoured her lunch.

He'd give anything to know what was going through

Hailey's head, but the only way to get that was to ask her, and he wasn't about to do that in front of the women. However, tomorrow's hike would be the perfect opportunity.

A squeal from the living room had them all looking up and Gram rising from her seat. "Sounds like my cowgirl is awake from her nap."

He placed his hand on her shoulder. "You stay, Gram. I'll go get her. If I know my little cousin, she's going to want some cereal right about now."

Gram gave him a look of thanks and moved toward the cupboard. As he strode across the hall, he pondered her look. She never did that. Now he had something else he wanted to talk to his brother about.

Hailey pulled into the dirt parking lot, her headlights shining on the wooden sign designating this as the trailhead. No other cars were there, but it was before sunrise. She'd suggested an early start for two reasons. First, though it was October, it could still get hot and she'd rather be wearing a jacket than wishing she had no clothes on. Second, she knew how early cowboys were used to getting up, with the exception of her oldest brother, so she didn't want Dillon getting involved with something on the ranch.

Taking her sweaty palms from the steering wheel of her rented truck, she wiped them on her jeans. Now that she would have some alone time with the man she'd had a crush on for so long, her stomach was tighter than a swollen knot.

If she hadn't just learned that Riley was staying in the room she had stayed in and that the woman could very well run into Dillon in the near buff, she wouldn't have been half as nervous, but now she felt as if she had a time constraint. There was a good chance that Riley was exactly what he would want, since she loved horses and from their short conversation after Charlotte woke up, made it clear she had no family left to speak of.

That was everything Dillon's mother wouldn't want, which made Riley perfect in Dillon's mind. How was she supposed to compete with that? What if Dillon started to view her as a friend and asked her advice on Riley. That would hurt more than she cared to think about.

Already she was falling for him. When she'd come out of the barn yesterday to find him holding baby Charlotte, she thought her heart would turn to mush and leak out of her body. She offered to take the little girl because she would have made a fool of herself over him. A strong, good looking cowboy like him, gently holding that little girl made her think of having a family with him, which was getting way ahead of herself.

Still, she loved how natural he was with Charlotte. Had he thought about having children? Would he want to expose his children to his mother? There was so much she wanted to ask him but wouldn't. They weren't there yet…if they ever would be. She had a feeling he didn't see her as a pawn of his mother's anymore, but one false move on her part and he'd go back to that. It was frustrating because Beverly didn't have a clue she was even interested in Dillon.

Lights shone in her rearview mirror. It was time, whether she was ready or not. A lot was riding on this hike for both of them. It was her chance to get to know the real Dillon and for him to get to know her. Would he like what he saw?

Shaking off her doubts, she heard her mother's sage advice. *Just stop worrying and be yourself, sweetie. Trust me, if they're worth their salt, they'll love you. And if they don't, there's no reason for you to waste your time.* That particular advice had first been given when she had entered seventh grade, and the junior high school that was fed by a number of grammar schools. It came again with the first boy she was interested in and later in college and afterwards.

Taking a deep breath, she held the advice close to her heart and stepped out of the truck. It was even colder on this side of the lake, so she opened the back door and pulled out a fleece. Zipping it up over her purple sweater, she closed the door and turned to look for Dillon.

He was buttoning up a jean jacket that emphasized his broad shoulders. When he finished, he looked over the bed of his truck and waved. "Good morning."

She smiled. "Good morning. Do you think we'll have any view of the sunrise?"

He looked behind him at the lightening sky. "If we hurry, we might catch it on the first rise."

She looked up the trailhead. It seemed pretty far. "After you. You've been on this trail before."

He grimaced. "Yes, but I was half drunk."

"What? I didn't take you for a party animal." It just didn't fit with her image of him.

He shook his head. "I'm not. But last time I was on this trail at sunrise, I had just graduated college and partied all night to celebrate. After stopping at an all-night restaurant on Carefree Highway, me and my friends decided watching the sunrise from this trail would be a perfect ending to the night."

It was such a guy thing to do that she hid her grin and started for the trail. "Okay, so I'll lead for now."

"Good idea."

The trail was narrow at the start so he remained behind her which made it a lot easier to concentrate. "Did you actually make it to a hill in time to see the sunrise?"

"Actually, since it was still pitch black out, we made it to the third hill." He chuckled. "Just in time, too, because our flashlight was dimming."

She glanced at him over her shoulder. "I'm surprised you even thought to bring a flashlight in your inebriated state."

"We didn't. There just happen to be one in my grandpa's truck."

She nodded, being careful to watch her step. The last thing she wanted was to twist her ankle again.

"What did you do after *you* graduated?"

His question surprised her. She had to think for a minute. "I almost forgot. My girlfriends and I had gone to school with some guys who had a local band and they were playing in Tucson that night. So, we all piled into a couple cars and went to the bar. We danced and flirted with other patrons then when the bar closed we went with the band for pizza. I remember getting home just as the sun rose over the mesa on the east boundary of Ironwood."

"I didn't take you for a groupie. Was your boyfriend in the band?"

At Dillon's teasing tone, she looked over her shoulder and stuck out her tongue. "No, one of the band members wasn't my boyfriend." She said it in a sing-song voice so he'd know she thought the question silly. "My boyfriend was working that night, which is why I went out with my girlfriends."

"If I had a girlfriend when I graduated college, I would have made sure I had the night off to spend with her."

She stopped and turned around with her hands on her hips. "Seriously? At the age of twenty-two, you would have taken the night off, a chance to make some money, just to spend time with your current girlfriend." She let the full-on doubt fill her voice.

He stopped and a sheepish grin spread across his face. "When you put it that way, maybe I would have worked, too."

She nodded before turning back and continuing on the trail. "Besides, the next night he took me out to dinner. It was a wonderful evening." It had been. Very romantic and special. She hadn't thought of him in a long time. They had eventually gone their separate ways, each wanting something different from their lives. After that, she had only dated men who had a tie to the land, like her.

"In other words, you got lucky."

She rolled her eyes but didn't turn around. "That is none of your business."

"True, but you didn't say no, so that means you did. I can respect that."

She ignored him. How could he be such a good guy and then be such an ass…unless it was because he felt comfortable with her? She liked that idea.

They began to ascend the first hill and she glanced back at the Eastern sky. "Oh, I think we're going to miss it." She couldn't help the disappointment in her voice.

"No, we won't." Dillon stepped up next to her. "Give me your hand."

She took his hand but didn't have a chance to marvel at how small hers felt in it because the next thing she knew she was being pulled up the incline at a quick pace. Excited by the prospect of seeing the sunrise with him, she moved as fast as she could, slipping on the loose gravel sometimes, but he held her upright.

By time they reached the top, she was laughing over their scramble.

"Look." He pointed behind her.

Chapter Eight

Hailey turned around just in time to see the first rays break over the horizon in a bright beam of light. It bathed the desert in pale yellow, lighting up the tops of the Saguaro cacti and a tiny patch of water far in the distance. She sighed, enjoying the sight and the scent of the man standing behind her. She wanted more than anything to lean against him and have his arms envelope her, but that wouldn't happen. "That just never gets old."

"Do you watch many sunrises?" His voice so close to her ear sent shivers down her back.

She looked up and back at him. "I do. I love sitting on the porch at home and watching the sunrise." She looked back toward the horizon as more yellow light flowed over the desert landscape like water over a rock. "It's almost like the sun is cleansing the day, starting it off fresh."

"You must be a morning person."

She turned around but took a step back at how close they were. "I am. Of course, I don't forego the morning coffee though. That definitely is a must."

He chuckled as he gazed over her shoulder. "Yes, coffee is a requirement. Has been since before the west was settled. Though times change, some things remain the same."

He looked at her and she caught her breath. It was as if he was thinking that man and woman would always need each other. That had to be in her head. "Like coffee?"

He nodded before scanning the horizon again. "And sunrises."

She turned around again, but the sky had become very bright, so she shaded her eyes. She'd completely forgotten about her sunglasses which were back at the truck. Oh well. Facing him again, she smiled. "So, what else does this trail have to offer?"

He shrugged. "Like I said, it's been a while. Why don't we find out?"

"Good idea." He opened his arm for her to take the lead again and she did. They walked in comfortable silence except when she commented on a particular plant or bug. It always amazed her that such a barren environment as the Sonoran Desert could be home to so many living things.

They had just reached the top of the third hill when she stopped to face him. He'd been looking down, so he walked right into her.

Dillon grabbed her arms as he tried to catch his balance. Unfortunately, that just caused her to lose her own and they both went down. She laughed.

He was on top of her, but across her body. A wiseass remark about the lengths he would go to touch her came to mind but she silenced it. "Sorry about that."

He lifted himself off her. "It was my fault. I should have watched where I was going." He stood and held out his hand.

She took it and he helped her up. "Actually, that's exactly what you were doing. It was my sudden stop. I'll warn you next time."

He brushed off his jeans. "That would probably help."

She smiled and began brushing off her own jeans. Desert dust flew off since there hadn't been rain in months.

"Why did you stop?" His question came after he'd cleaned himself off completely.

Hmm, a neat cowboy. She liked that. "I wanted to ask if you remembered this hill. You said it was the third one you made it to when you saw the sun rise." She turned to look at the eastern horizon, shading her eyes with her hand. "I bet it was beautiful."

He chuckled. "A lot more beautiful than your back."

She looked over her shoulder. "What's wrong with my back?"

He stepped behind her and put his hands on her shoulders. "Just hold still."

Her heart raced as he proceeded to dust off her back and ass. Closing her eyes, she pretended he actually wanted to touch her.

"There you go, almost as clean as when we arrived."

She faced him, ignoring her rapid pulse. "Thanks. Guess I couldn't reach it all."

"Not a problem. Stopping here has actually triggered my memories. If I'm not mistaken, once we go down this next valley, the following hill will give us a view of the lake."

"Now that I'd like to see. I've only taken the boat out a couple times since arriving, but I'd like to see if I can recognize the area."

He frowned but started down the trail ahead of her.

Now what was bothering him? It didn't take long to find out.

They were only a few yards down the slope before he spoke. "Is this the boat of the man I saw you with at the Black Mustang?"

From his tone of voice, she'd agree with her friend that

Dillon was jealous, but for that to be true, it meant he liked her and she was still afraid to hope. "Yes."

"Will he be going jet skiing with you and Jenna?"

She grinned as her hope surged forward. "No. He doesn't live on his boat anymore, which is why I was able to stay on it. He has an apartment, now that he's a fulltime single dad."

Was it her imagination, or did Dillon's shoulders relax?

"Don't tell me someone besides Logan had a baby dropped on his doorstep."

She laughed. "Oh, no. Austin has been divorced for a few years now with only visitation rights, which he fought tooth and nail to get. Then one day he received this text saying he was granted full custody and to expect his kid within the hour. Then his ex disappeared."

Dillon looked over his shoulder. "That's got to be hard on the child. Are you helping him?"

She pointed beyond him where a small boulder blocked the trail. "No. We're just friends."

"Right."

She just couldn't let it go. She yanked on his arm.

Still it took a few seconds for him to stop. "What?"

"Austin and I have been friends since grammar school. I practically grew up with him. He's the twin I never had, but that's all he is. I think of him like a brother and to intimate that there is more to it is just well…" She couldn't think of a good enough word, so she went with the first one that came to mind. "Icky."

He raised both his eyebrows. "Icky?"

"Yes. Icky. The Wicked Witch of the West just never got it, but my brothers and friends do."

"Wicked Witch of the West?" He looked at her as if she'd completely lost it.

She huffed. "Austin's ex. She's the Wicked Witch of the West. She doesn't deserve to be called by her name."

He backed up a step and put his hands out. "Whoa, don't ever let me get on your bad side." His lips quirked up as he tried to stifle a laugh.

She swatted his arms to the side and stalked past him. Men.

Moving around the boulder, she continued up the path. At least she'd made her message clear. People who thought there was something between her and her best friend were idiots.

She heard Dillion trudging behind her as she climbed the hill. For the moment she was glad for the silence, so she could analyze their relationship. That he teased her had to be a good sign. That he was jealous of Austin had to be good too, as long as he could get over that. She wasn't about to give up her friends for anyone.

To be honest, she liked hiking with him. He was helpful and interesting to talk to but didn't have to talk all the time. She remembered a ranch owner she'd dated a couple years ago who never shut up. Unfortunately, only half of what he said was of any interest and that was when he didn't talk about himself. That had lasted a few weeks. She was a patient woman, but he took way too long to be comfortable around her.

Maybe Dillon—"Oh, wow." She halted on top of the ridge. Before her was Lake Pleasant, but not the wide-open area she was familiar with. It was the small inlets and waterways and then toward the open part all the many islands, making it look like brown bubble wrap with black liquid between.

Dillon stopped next to her. "No wonder I remembered this. It's impressive."

That was an understatement. She glanced at him to see he appreciated the view as much as she did. That's why she liked men connected to the land. They got it. "If this wasn't county land, I'd buy this hill and build a house on it, just so I could wake up to this every morning."

He looked at her then. "We don't have this, but we do have the river at Morning Creek. It's not as obvious from the downstairs, but when I wake up in the morning, I can see it rushing by. It doesn't sparkle because I'm downstairs and out the door before the sunrises."

She grinned. "Like today. I didn't realize you had a river on the property. Why is it called Morning Creek if you don't have a creek?"

He smirked. "You are only one of a handful of people to ask that question. Even my father didn't know why when he bought the ranch as a young man, but I was always curious about it and discovered the answer in some historical documents at the Bailler Museum in Tucson."

"Oh, you have to tell me. It's such an odd name. I'm shocked someone before you didn't try to find out."

He shrugged. "Guess it didn't matter to owners who were trying to eke out an existence. The ranch has been bought and sold too many times to count, nothing succeeding there."

"Until your dad bought it."

He grimaced. "So far so good, but I wouldn't call us a complete success yet. Our herd is still small and though we are starting to make a name, we'll be lucky to have a solid operation by time my children have children."

She swallowed hard at the thought of him thinking about children. None of the men she'd dated ever brought up the subject as if by mentioning it, she might suddenly want to have babies with them. Sometimes she wondered about men, but now she wondered about Dillon.

Pushing aside that thought to think about later, she went back to her original question. "So why is it called Morning

Creek. If I didn't know better, I'd say you are purposefully trying to lead me off track. Was it something nefarious like a gang of outlaws always met in the morning at the creek, even though it was a river, sort of a code?"

He laughed, one of those pleasant laughs that were full but not obnoxious.

"You have quite an imagination."

She cocked her head. "If you hung out with children as much as I do, you'd have a creative imagination, too." Even as she said the words, the image of him holding Charlotte in his arms came to mind and her heart warmed all over again. He'd make a great father.

"You hang out with children?"

"I do, but you're getting off track again. You *have* to tell me."

His lips quirked up just slightly, which proved he was stalling on purpose. He was far more fun than she'd expected. She grasped her hands together and fluttered her eyelashes at him. "Pleeeaaassseeee."

He jerked his head back and held his hand out in front of him. "Ugh, don't do that. You'll make me dizzy."

She stopped and stared pointedly at him. "Then tell me."

"Okay, just keep those fluttering eyelids under control."

She barely even blinked, not willing to say another word until he spilled the beans.

He dropped his hand and smirked. "It's not as exciting as your idea. Turns out when the land was first claimed there was a small creek running through it. That was over a hundred years ago. Nature changed as it does and it eventually turned into the river we have now, which is very advantageous to us."

Though he paused, she kept her mouth shut. She wanted the whole story and she already loved the first part.

He must have realized she wouldn't respond, so he continued. "The original owner at first had a small shack that he built next to the creek. As was not unusual for the time, he had headed west to find a place to homestead and planned to build a real home for his family before they followed. According to a letter he wrote to his wife before she came west and joined him, he would wake up every morning, open the door of his one room abode and say 'Morning, Creek' because he had no one else to talk to. My guess is his wife liked that he did that because that was what he called it."

It was a wonderful story and much more interesting than she'd expected and far more intriguing than her own family's ranch name. "That's a fantastic story. I'm going to tell that to the kids."

He crossed his arms over his chest, the denim sleeves of his coat stretching to their max. "So now you can tell me about these kids you keep referring to."

"Oh, it's just a literacy program I help out with when I can. It's for children who need extra help to keep up in school, but that all stems from not catching on to reading or not wanting to read because no one showed them how much fun it is."

He looked at her with the same look she got from others, like she was some kind of angel and she really didn't like that. Anyone who was viewed as an angel was bound to disappoint, so she quickly turned around and started down the trail toward the water. "Let's go see if this leads to the water's edge. Maybe they have a picnic table there."

Dillon didn't respond, but she heard his boots crunching on the loose gravel.

She couldn't help the bounce in her step. He was definitely the real deal and actually more than she'd hoped for. Since she'd had such a crush on him for so long, she'd been nervous she had made him out to be more than he was. But because of his resistance toward her, she'd seen his coarser side and his good side. He wasn't perfect, but neither was she.

She'd have to thank Austin next time she saw him. She probably would have given up on Dillon without her friend's insight into the male psyche. If only he could help her figure out how to get over the worst hurdle—Dillon's mother. Maybe some casual conversation would give her more insight.

She spoke over her shoulder. "You said Morning Creek is starting to gain a reputation, but you've moved in with your grandparents. Do you miss home?"

They continued down a few more steps before he answered. "I do."

"What parts about Morning Creek do you miss the most?" That should get him focused on the good things without involving his mother.

This time he answered more swiftly. "I enjoy choosing the mares and on occasion a stud. I also like caring for them and riding them and watching them grow from awkward foals to magnificent horses."

His excitement in his work was obvious. "Do you sell all but those you use to breed, or do you keep a few for yourself?"

"I don't keep any for myself unless it's for breeding. I know when they are born that they will be leaving. I'm proud when a buyer looks at what we have and his eyes widen in surprise."

"Is that why you bought Eclipse, so you wouldn't take one of the ones you bred?"

The silence told her she may have stepped into a sensitive area. If he chose not to answer that was his prerogative, but it was also her right to ask again. Turning around, she didn't get the chance. The loose gravel slipped out from under her feet, and she started to fall.

Dillon caught her before she did a face plant on the trail. He grabbed her under the arms, far too close to her breasts not to notice, then stepped closer to leverage her into a standing position.

"Are you okay?"

"Yes, thanks to you. I guess when they say curiosity killed the cat, they aren't kidding. I should probably keep my eyes on the trail." And if he'd just let go of her, she might even keep her heart from beating out of her chest. He must feel how attracted she was to him this close to each other.

He didn't let go though, instead, he looked at her as if he wanted to kiss her.

It took all her willpower not to lick her lips.

"I bought Eclipse because he is a magnificent animal, but I'd be lying if I said I didn't know it would piss off my mother. That was the added perk. The look on her face was something I haven't seen since I was eight and I painted the living room and her furniture with white paint left over from the corral fence because she wouldn't let me ride that day."

She cocked her head, a little disappointed. "So, when you bought Eclipse you were acting out?"

He shook his head and finally released her only to move one hand down the side of his face. "I was sending her a message. I'm a grown man, have been for sometime, and I can make my own decisions."

"Did it work?"

"No. She took it as a personal affront, which I guess it was." He looked away, obviously uncomfortable.

"At least you accomplished your goal of buying a wonderful horse. Do you think he'd be interested in Nizhoni?"

The change of subject was exactly what he needed. "He may be a great horse, but his taste in mares is questionable. He's been mooning over Macy since we arrived."

She turned around and headed down the trail again, this time watching her step. "I'm not sure that's questionable. Macy appears to be a great mother, much like Nizhoni. I'm thrilled that I came in time to meet Nizhoni and Phoenix. I hope Cole gives the okay for me to purchase them."

"He probably will. He's just careful not only with who the new owners of his horses will be, but also with the horses themselves. He'll want to be sure that Phoenix has no long-term effects from the abuse he suffered."

She nodded but kept her gaze on the trail as they were very close to the water now. "Whisper told me about Angel. I'm so glad that Lacey and Angel bonded."

"I think that was sheer luck, but then again, my brother doesn't do much without a lot of thought."

She slowed to stop as the trail brought them right to the water's edge. "What a great swimming place this would make." She turned to see what he thought.

He glanced beyond her and studied the lake. "I think I've been swimming here."

She unzipped her fleece now that it was warming up between the sun coming up and the exercise, but she didn't take it off. "I'll bet after graduation, you and your friends went skinny dipping here."

He looked shocked. "No. Why would we do that?"

"Really? A bunch of guys having had a few too many after celebrating a significant accomplishment in their lives didn't go skinny dipping in the early morning hours when no one was around?"

He honestly looked like the thought had never occurred to him.

She rolled her eyes. "You have a sister-in-law who works at a nudist resort and it never occurred to you? It certainly would have occurred to my brothers. Actually, they probably did, but they would never tell their only sister."

He looked at her curiously. "You're close to your brothers?"

"Yes, though not location wise. Growing up, they tried to treat me like a princess and when I was a teen they were *way* over protective, so I had to put a little distance between us. But we still have Sunday dinners at Ironwood when we can, especially now that Wes isn't riding bulls anymore. You and Cole seem close."

He nodded but was still looking at her as if he found her fascinating, which she didn't mind in the least.

"Did you two ever wish you had a sister?"

He took a step closer, shaking his head absently.

Obviously, he wasn't listening to her, but as his gaze moved lower to focus on her lips, she suddenly understood what he was thinking. The thrill started in the pit of her stomach like a lightning bolt, and it spread from her abdomen down to the juncture of her thighs and up throughout her chest.

As his head started to lower, her brain woke up. She didn't want to lose him and if she let him kiss her, her instinct told her he wasn't really ready. Quickly, she stepped back. "I always thought my mom should have given me a sister." She turned to face the water, not wanting to see his reaction. "I'm going to explore with Jenna tomorrow and try to find this spot on the jet skis. There's no picnic tables, but it still would be a great lunch place."

When he didn't say anything to that, she turned around to find him staring at the water. *Keep it light, Hailey. Make it look like you had no idea he wanted to kiss you. If he thinks you rejected him, you'll never see him again.* "Have you ever been on the lake?"

He looked at her. At first his brow was lowered, but his face relaxed at the question. "Yes. I used to go fishing with Gramps when we visited back in my high school days."

She turned away from the water and started down the trail again. "I haven't met your grandfather. Is he around?"

As he answered, she smiled inside. Things couldn't be going any better. Maybe, just maybe, he would want to see her again. She'd never had to work so hard in her life for something she wanted, but the more she learned, the more she wanted him. Now, if she could just make him see they would make a good team, she just might be in for the ride of a lifetime.

Dillon carried three posts over to where Cole waited. The auger Logan had rented had made the post holes a lot easier to dig and Cole and Logan had started setting the posts while he was hiking with Hailey but Logan had moved to other projects after lunch.

Now he finally had time to talk to his brother alone, but he wasn't sure what question to broach first. Setting the posts on the ground, he lifted one and set it in the hole. "What do you think of Hailey?" Shit, that was the last question he wanted to discuss.

Cole used the shovel to pack dirt around the post. "She's definitely sure of herself. I spent so much time avoiding her that until she came to buy a horse, I didn't know anything about her, except what mom told me about her family. Why? Is she bothering you? I can always tell her I won't sell Nizhoni and Phoenix to her."

"No." His response was too fast. "I mean, from what I've been able to tell, she already cares about those horses. You know women and animals, especially around here." Maybe couching it that way, Cole wouldn't think much of it.

"Good, because Lacey can't stop talking about her. You'd think they were BFFs or something."

He looked up at his brother. "BFFs. Really?"

Cole finished packing the dirt around the post and leaned on the shovel handle. "You should have seen Lacey on that trapeze." Cole looked off into the desert. "You'd think she'd been created to fly through the air. The instructor said she was a natural. I had to agree."

He rose to stare at his overly protective, overly safe brother. "And you didn't worry that she'd fall?"

"Shit, yeah. When we first arrived, I was fine as they showed us the safety harness and the net. They gave her a thirty-minute tutorial on the ground first and I was certain that was too short. I was thinking it would be a week of lessons before she ever got up there. But up she went."

"And you were okay with it?"

"Fuck, no. I was so blasted scared, it was all I could do not to climb up to that platform and grab her off it."

"I'm confused. If you were so worried, why didn't you just tell her not to do it?"

Cole stared at him as if he'd turned into a giant scorpion. "You're kidding, right?"

"No." He didn't get it at all. If Cole loved Lacey then why let her risk her life.

"Little brother, you have obviously never been in love. Because I love Lacey, I couldn't deny her. She'd dreamed of being in a circus since she was a little girl. She always felt that she missed out on her calling, but as a responsible adult, she understood that would have never been a happy life for her. That's why when she asked me, I couldn't say no. It was a small thing that would make her happy."

"And when she's happy, you're happy."

"Yes, there's that. But it's more. I had to let her try this, despite my own hang-ups." He held out his hand to stop any comments. "Yes, I'm well aware I go too far with safety precaution, but that's because of my profession and the amount of times I see the results of a lack of safety. This trapeze place took all the precautions they could. Lacey even missed the grab the first time."

"Hell, what'd you do?"

"I started forward as if to catch her, but not only was the net in my way, which had a much better chance of saving her than me, but she had a harness on and they lowered her into the net gently. They told her they did it on purpose so she would get rid of any fears of falling."

"Did you breathe?"

Cole chuckled. "Not for a full two minutes. But when she flipped over the net to land on the ground, she came right up to me, more excited than ever, and told me it was the second-best thing she'd ever done and she was going back up."

It was hard for him to wrap his mind around the fact that Cole had allowed Lacey to risk her neck to make her happy. "I guess I've never felt that strongly for a woman."

Cole motioned for him to grab another pole. "I hope you do. There is nothing in the world like the love from the right woman."

Even as he set the pole in the next hole, he wished to find exactly that. Maybe he could have found her already if his mother hadn't kept pushing the high society women at him. That reminded him of another question he wanted to ask Cole. "Do you think if I found someone like Lacey and married her, mom would let us move onto Morning Creek. I don't mean in the main house, but I could probably have something small built."

"I doubt it."

Cole's quick answer was not what he'd hoped for.

"Why? Because I didn't marry one of the women she approved of?"

Cole packed the dirt around the pole as he spoke. "Yes. With me, as the oldest, she was determined to see me marry 'well' as she put it. She even sabotaged my relationship with Lacey when I was in high school. I didn't realize it then because she didn't start to push the "respectable" women on me until after I graduated college and had 'sown my wild oats' as she put it."

"But you did marry Lacey after all." He stepped away now that the dirt was in.

Cole stamped on the ground around the pole. "That was sheer luck that I ran into her and that was only after mom and I had our falling out."

"What did she do to you?"

Cole tugged on the pole to make sure it was solid. "It was more the deal she tried to make with me. I told her about my idea for bringing horse rescues to Morning Creek. I had recently been volunteering for an animal rescue place and had seen that they couldn't keep the large animals more than a week. Many of them were sold at auction."

In other words, sold for meat or worse.

"She told me that if I married one of her approved women, she would let me have the rescues at Morning Creek."

"What? You never told me that." Dillon's anger with his mother grew.

Cole shrugged. "It was a side of Mom I was still trying to grapple with. I refused and came to Gram and Gramps with my idea. If they refused I would have found a cheap piece of land and started from scratch."

He hefted the last pole and put it in place. "Why? Why is Mom so bent on us marrying into what she deems as prestige? You'd think she'd be happy if we fell in love and married period."

"I have no idea. Even Gram is stumped. Aunt Bonnie is the complete opposite of Mom. I do envy Logan and Trace for that. Unfortunately for you, because I escaped Mom's clutches, she was even more determined to marry you off to the right woman."

"Yes, I know."

"You never told me why you came barreling up to Grams and Gramps' house that night, crashing into Jenna's car."

And he wasn't ready to, either. "I had no choice. I would have hit her dog, even if I did think it was a desert tortoise. I couldn't have lived with hitting an animal, never mind my cousin's, girlfriend's dog. I think smashing up her car worked out for everyone in the end."

Cole agreed and continued to work on the pole.

Dillon moved to the pile of poles and pulled three more. So where did that leave him with his mother and his interest in Hailey? Even now she was jet skiing all over the lake and he itched to head over there and make sure she was okay. The only thing that stopped him was he had no idea where she and Jenna would be. How the hell did Logan deal with that?

Chapter Nine

Dillon pulled into the parking lot of the marina. He had no idea why he was there except he had an urgent need to know Hailey was okay. Though she'd invited him to join her and Jenna, he'd turned her down, not willing to watch her risk her neck for fun, like Cole had with Lacey. He hadn't expected that being so far away would bother him just as much.

Walking through the carded gate as a couple walked out got him past the first hurdle. She'd told him if he changed his mind he could find her on dock A, slip 11. Signs clearly marked the docks, but slips were another matter. The boats ranged from small twenty-footers to what had to be eighty-foot, two-decker houseboats. One houseboat was three decks with the name "Sexsea" on the side, but he couldn't imagine Hailey, or even himself, steering that thing into the docks.

At the sound of female laughter a few slips up, he picked up his pace. He'd swear that was Hailey, which meant she was fine. He could turn around and walk away right now, but his need to see she was physically okay was too strong.

Walking by one of the big houseboats, he found her and Jenna, sitting in deck chairs in the open back of a two-deck small yacht, maybe forty feet long. The name of the boat was emblazoned on the back—The Adventurer. How fitting.

Hailey smiled, as usual, and sipped on a bottle of iced tea.

"I better get going. Logan can make dinner, but Charlotte will put up a fuss if I'm not there to tuck her in." Jenna stood and gave a now standing Hailey a hug. "Thank you for a wonderful day."

"My pleasure. I'll be here a couple more weeks, if you want to go again."

Before either of the women noticed him, he ducked down the finger dock between two houseboats and waited for Jenna to leave. He'd rather no one on the ranch knew he was here. In fact, he could leave now. Hailey was obviously fine.

He waited, debating which way to go. Leave or reveal himself. Hell, he didn't shower and change into shorts and flip flops just to take a drive. Stepping back out onto the main dock, he walked by the houseboat and stopped at the yacht. Hailey wasn't there but the slider into the lower level was open and the inside curtains blew inward, giving glimpses of the white interior with blue accents.

Hailey, in a sexy string-bikini top and a short white skirt, emerged with a fresh ice tea bottle and noticed him. "Dillon, what a great surprise! If you were looking for Jenna, you just missed her."

"No. I finished my work and thought I'd take you up on your offer to see the lake again. It's been while."

"Perfect. I was just going to go sit out on the bow and watch the sunset. I don't like to take the boat out alone. But if you don't mind untying, we can motor out and enjoy it on the water."

He didn't want to point out that they were on the water right here. It had been a long time since he'd been on the lake. Living south at Morning Creek had him so busy that he hadn't visited his grandparents as much as he should have. "I can do that."

"Great. I'll grab the key and get the engine started, if you want to untie the front ropes."

She ducked back into the interior, and he moved down the finger dock. Loosening the first rope, he untied it and threw it up over the railing. The front of the boat boasted a large cushion that a few people could sit on and lean their backs against a row of upper windows. That would be the perfect place to watch the sunset. He'd check it out when he knotted the ropes over the railing once he had the boat untied.

Walking to the other side, he did the same as Hailey started the engines. He waited on the main dock at the back of the boat until she was ready to leave. He watched the upper deck, waiting for her signal.

She finally came into view and shouted over the engines. "We're good to go!"

Quickly, he untied the ropes on the port and starboard sides of the stern and hopped in. Kicking off his flip flops, he pulled the loose stern ropes inside then made his way to the bow just as Hailey eased the boat forward and out of the slip. He tied the port rope to the railing then made his way over the bow to the starboard side.

"Dillon!"

Hailey's shout had him looking up. She pointed. Two jet skiers were racing between the boat and the tires that marked the edge of the marina.

He grabbed the railing and sat quickly just as their wakes hit the boat, rocking it hard. Once the jet skiers were gone and the water calmed, Hailey steered the boat slowly toward the marina exit, expertly maneuvering around the floating tires that marked the boundary. He tied the other rope then moved along the side where there was an entrance to the helm.

"That's a no wake zone." Hailey spoke before he even

made it up to her. "It's one reason I don't go out on the lake on the weekend. People who don't know the rules of the water do stupid-ass stuff. Those yo-yos must have just arrived."

He agreed but didn't say anything. Instead he enjoyed watching her steer the boat around the tires to the wide opening before increasing the speed and heading out to the open water. Seeing her at the helm did weird things to his gut. She looked confident, strong and very sexy in her bikini top and short skirt.

But there was something very relaxing about being on a boat, floating and rocking with the waves. Calm, happy memories assailed him of heading out with his Gramps before the sun came up to get a special fishing spot. He found himself smiling.

"The best view will be in the middle of the open lake, though my favorite section is the Aqua Fria."

The Aqua Fria was the river that fed the lake. It was closed for many months early in the year if the Bald Eagles had eggs, which was pretty much every year. It had been so long since he'd been down there, he found himself anxious to see it. "Then let's cruise down there after the sun sets. I'm assuming this thing has lights because that means it will get dark before we return."

She chuckled. "Oh, this thing has all the bells and whistles."

He stood slightly behind the captain's chair, which was anchored to the boat, but Hailey stood in front of it, her hands on the wheel, her golden blonde hair whipping out of the clip that was supposed to hold it up on her head. The urge to touch the strands straying so close to him was hard to resist.

He was about to give in to temptation when they hit a cross wave and he grabbed onto the back of the chair instead to stay upright.

Hailey laughed before slowing the boat. "We should be good here. I'll turn off the engine. We'll drift, but we're far from everything, so that shouldn't be a problem."

He turned a full three-sixty to scan the water only to discover she was correct. The few boats in view were heading into the marina and far behind them now. Land was a good distance away on every side.

"Can I get you something to drink?"

He glanced at the sky which had started to striate into bright orange and pale yellow. "Sure. Iced tea is good."

"One iced tea coming up. I'll meet you out on the bow." She nimbly descended down to the back deck and disappeared.

He took steps down and walked along the port side before taking a seat on the cushioned area he'd noticed earlier. He crossed his legs out in front of him and leaned back against the windows. It was the perfect angle for watching the sunset.

Hailey came around the starboard side. "Here you are."

She handed him the bottle and he took it, his fingers touching hers for a moment. Their softness made him wish he had an excuse to hold her hand...but he didn't.

She sat down next to him, crossing her legs beneath her. "Thanks for coming. It's so much nicer to watch the sunset from here. The docks on Friday nights can get a little loud with everyone coming in for the weekend."

He took a sip of the cold tea, happy to have a reason to look at her. "How long have you been here?"

She grinned. "A couple days before I almost crash-landed on Last Chance."

"How are those hot air balloon lessons coming?"

"Great. I only have a few left. I'm not an expert or anything, but I know how to control it, steer it, and lift off and land. It's a lot easier than a plane, but like a plane, wind makes everything a bit more complicated."

"You know how to fly a plane?" He didn't hide the surprise in his voice, though if he thought about it, he shouldn't be surprised.

"Not a big plane or even a jet like my older brother. I fly a small sport plane. It's a RANS Coyote with a 503 motor."

Since he didn't know anything about planes, he didn't reveal his ignorance by asking any more questions.

She leaned back next to him and straightened her legs. "Ah, now it's getting pretty."

He finally looked at the sky. She was right. The oranges had become more brilliant and striped the sky with both bright and pale pink shadows in between. He often watched the sunset from the ranch, but it seemed much more striking tonight. Maybe it was being on the water, floating along peacefully that made it so spectacular.

Or maybe it was the person he was sharing the view with. He took a quick glance at Hailey. A small smile remained on her lips as she stared at the sky with awe.

He moved his gaze back to the sunset, but he didn't see it. Instead, he saw her lips and yearned to kiss them. He wanted to see them lift in a smile after he kissed her, too.

Holy shit! Somewhere between designating her off limits and now, he'd connected with her. The fact was, he really liked her and wanted to know everything about her. When the hell had that happened? For all he knew, she had little interest in him. She did have a friend who was a guy. Would she put him in the same category?

He didn't want to be a friend. He wanted more. It wasn't because she was beautiful, which she was. It was all about who she was—honest, kind, forthright, confident, and as she mentioned herself, an angel and crazy. He hadn't wanted to admit it, but he loved all parts of her and wanted to delve into them more—understand why she was who she was.

"Oh, wow." Hailey's breathless exclamation had him refocusing on the sky.

It was now every color common to Arizona sunsets. This moment was always fleeting, when the orange, pink, purple and pale blue graced the sky. "It never gets old." His own emotion had the words coming out just above a whisper.

He felt her look at him and turned his head to meet her gaze. Her green eyes were muted by the sky, but her stare was intense, her smile gone. "That's what I think, too."

It was as if, in that moment, they were on the same page, as if they had connected on a significant level, beyond words. It felt right.

She was the first to look up again. "Oh, look." She pointed at a plane high in the sky, the bright orange colors reflecting off it and its white tail leaving an orange streak against the darkening background.

If he'd been one of those poetic cowboys, he'd probably have compared her to the sunset, but he was pathetically weak in that area, so he kept his thoughts to himself. As much as he liked looking at the sunset, he liked looking at her more.

When the bright pinks had paled and the purples moved to lavender beneath the darkening sky, she sat up. "That was pretty amazing. Much better than a movie. We can stay for the end, but if we do, you won't be able to see the Aqua Fria well enough to appreciate it."

He sat up as well, ready now to see what was ahead for them in more ways than one. "Then let's head out, Captain."

She chuckled. "I'm not a licensed captain, but I do have my boating card. As I've said before, I'm always safe."

She hopped up onto her feet and moved around the port side. He followed, enjoying her ass in what he'd thought was a white skirt, but from when she jumped up, he knew to be shorts of some kind.

They had drifted with the wind and were now closer to the north side of the lake, so once she started the engines, it took no time to enter the river. The lake was down about a hundred feet, about halfway to its low winter mark, so the cliff walls of the river loomed large on either side. Sometimes one side would gentle into no more than a hill like the ones on the trail they'd hiked and one spot was almost a field, where three wild burros warned them not to come any closer as they grazed between the prickly pear cacti and mesquite trees.

Of course, the burros' warning caused Hailey to laugh. She was always filled with joy, which reminded him of himself when he was younger. He liked that version of himself. She made him want to be like that again. The more he was with her, the more he wanted to be around her. Had he become addicted? Is that why he had to come to the marina?

"This spot will be the first place where we can see the stars if you want. I can anchor us and grab some snacks while we wait." She'd slowed the boat to under idle speed between two large cliff sides. It was already darker than any other spot they'd gone by.

He should offer to anchor, but his boating skills were rusty. "Why don't you anchor and I'll find the food."

"Sounds good." She left the engine running and hit the switch on the anchor.

He made himself go below though he preferred to watch her. She knew what she was doing. She always did, except when she was learning. Her words the day she almost crashed came back to him. *I have to do it myself. I have to make my own mistakes and learn from them.* It was similar to what his father used to tell him, which was that he would learn more from his failures than his successes. His dad would like Hailey.

But his mother liked her too much. How could he forget that? No matter how much he liked her, he couldn't have a relationship with her. It would be a dream come true for his mother and as wrong as it was, she was the last person he wanted to make happy. Not after all she'd done.

He opened the sliding door to below and the curtains blew into his face at the movement. A citrusy scent engulfed him and he stilled. But what if Hailey made *him* happy? He could feel a tug of war starting in his gut and quickly focused on his task.

Swiping the curtains aside, he stepped down the two steps into the main cabin. It was definitely plush and the bits of blue he'd seen earlier turned out to be blue rope lighting, expertly placed beneath soffits against the ceiling and around what would be dark corners. The mariner motif was everywhere from pillows with blue anchors printed on them on the very large couch, to the bronze tall ship at the center of the table.

Except for the hint of lemon in the cabin, it didn't feel like Hailey. He moved to the cabinets, which all had a small latch on the inside that he had to push in to open them, something he was familiar with since they used the same latches in the kitchen at Last Chance to keep Charlotte from emptying the pots and pans onto the floor. Something he'd been told she'd done more than once before they were installed.

The first cabinet he opened contained dishes. The next one boasted vitamins, aspirin, seasickness prevention tablets and— What? He moved his gaze back to the vitamins. One jar was for active men. Did Hailey have someone in her life? She'd said the Austin guy was just a friend. Despite his brain telling him that's all it was, jealousy reared its ugly head.

About to close the cabinet, his eye caught something else. Picking up the bottle, he shook his head at his stupidity. Varied colored gummy vitamins crammed half the jar. Hailey had said Austin was a fulltime father, like Logan before he met Jenna. Austin may just be a friend, but would he want Hailey to help with his kid?

Anxious to spend more time with her, he closed the cabinet and opened two more. Finding a tray in one of them, he loaded it with chips and crackers and then raided the refrigerator where he found more iced tea, cheese, salami, and a box of chocolate mint cookies.

When he exited the cabin, he found Hailey leaning over the starboard side. "Everything okay?"

She straightened. "Yes. I was just making sure the anchor caught. On the river, it can be hard to catch something. Oh, that looks good. Let's go back on the bow."

He let her lead the way and when they sat, he made sure to sit next to her with the tray in front of them. He cut up the cheese into cubes and placed it on a cracker before handing it to her.

"Thank you. I've been living on the boat by myself for so long, I'd forgotten how nice it is to share a meal."

He raised his brow. "Don't you go to the restaurant here on the marina?"

She shook her head. "No. I ordered a couple times and had it delivered. I prefer to keep to myself so word doesn't get out that I'm up here. I'm having such an awesome time. I can really be myself if there are no cameras around."

"Is that a problem for you?" It had never occurred to him that she might be followed by paparazzi.

She shook her head. "Hard to believe, isn't it? But when there is a slow news day in Tucson, they come looking for my family. You'd think with the dozen or so stars living around Phoenix they would follow them." She shrugged. "I think it's an Arizona thing."

He put another cube on a cracker and handed it to her.

"Today has been one of the best days I've had so far here."

Surprised by her statement, he had to ask. "Why?"

"Well, first I had a lot of fun jet skiing with Jenna. She loves the water and we got to explore the side of the lake where you and I hiked. I couldn't find a water access to the exact spot, but that could be because the lake is down. Maybe I can get Hector to let me pilot the balloon tomorrow in that direction so I can see the area from the air. If not, I'll take my plane up and check it out. I usually follow this river when I'm up here because the scenery is so unique." She bit into her cracker and licked the crumbs from her lip with her tongue.

A spike of desire hit his gut and traveled to his groin. Ignoring the sensation, he tried to keep the conversation going. "Is that all you did with Jenna?"

She swallowed. "Oh, no. We went swimming, had a picnic, stopped at the other marina to listen to the live band they had, then headed back in. She loved it so much, I gave her Austin's phone number. I think he'd love to take Jenna, Logan and Charlotte out on the water."

The idea of his little cousin on the boat had him tensing. Hell, he was going to be an overprotective parent for sure.

"And then you came by and we watched the sunset and now I'm having a lovely snack with a handsome cowboy as I wait to stargaze. I mean, how could it get any better?"

A few answers flew through his head, like kissing her and making love inside the cabin all night, but he discarded them all until he found one that was acceptable. "How about some chocolate mint cookies?"

She laughed. "Absolutely. Those will definitely make it better."

He opened the package and held one in front of her mouth. "Open up. I'm sure you are better at this than Charlotte."

She gave him a smirk before opening her lips.

He swallowed hard as her teeth came down on the cookie he held, and she bit it in half. He waited while she chewed then found his voice again. "You have to eat all of it."

She obediently opened her mouth again and this time her lips brushed over his fingers as he placed the cookie on her tongue. She wasn't smiling anymore. In fact, she was looking at him very seriously.

He moved his gaze to her lips where chocolate crumbs remained. He couldn't resist using his finger to gently brush the crumbs away.

"Dillon?"

He looked into her green eyes, still easy to see in the fading light. Curiosity shone in them and something else. Expectancy?

"I like you, Hailey." The words came out before he could stop himself and his gut tightened, stealing himself for her reaction.

She sucked in her breath and slowly let it out. "I like you, too. Actually, I like you a lot."

In the back of his mind, he recognized their conversation as one a couple high schoolers might have, but he didn't care. He was waiting for her to say "but."

Instead, she looped her hand around his neck. "Kiss me."

He needed no further encouragement. Pulling her to him, he tasted her lips for the first time. They were soft and yielding as his nostrils filled with lemon scent. He barely kept a moan from becoming vocal, and instead brushed her lips with his tongue.

She opened for him, inviting him in. He accepted and

swept his tongue inside to taste mint, chocolate and all that was Hailey. It was intoxicating and far more potent than any liquor.

Her hand played with his hair as her tongue met his. They tangled and explored together, two equals coming together.

He wanted more, to feel her against him, so he pulled her closer which sent the tray skittering off the cushion and onto the fiberglass bow.

She broke their kiss and looked at it, then gazed into his eyes. "It was in the way anyway." Her hand moved down his shirt and started to work the buttons. "This is, too."

His gut twisted with desire so intense he didn't move until she pushed his shirt over his shoulders, kneeling to make that happen.

Her cleavage was directly in front of his face and he didn't even try to resist. Sticking out his tongue, he stroked it from bottom to top.

Hailey stilled. "Do that again."

Happy to oblige, he licked again, but this time he went farther, moving up one side of one breast and down the other.

She dropped his shirt and put her hands on his shoulders.

Shaking off his discarded clothing, he held her waist and took one side of her string bikini top in his teeth and pulled it to the side. The whole panel moved along the bottom string, leaving her full breast bare.

His conscience was telling him to move them downstairs because someone might see, but he ignored it, the hard nipple before him begging him to lick it. And that's what he did. Flicking the hard nub a few times with his tongue, he watched it grow harder, the skin of the areola puckering.

Keeping her steady with his hands, he leaned forward and sucked her nipple into his mouth. Her loud moan tightened his groin as his cock responded. He played with the hard nub, exploring the texture and small nuances. Then he sucked harder, gauging her body language until he understood what she liked.

Loosening his suction, he maneuvered her nipple between his teeth and rolled it. Hailey's hands dug into his shoulders as she arched, pushing her breast into his face. He took the opportunity to move his hand to her back and pull the tie that held her top in place.

Immediately, she pulled her breast from his mouth, catching her breath as his teeth scraped along her nipple.

Concerned, he looked up at her, but she grasped her top and pulled it over her head to bare herself to him.

The stars must have aligned just right for this to be happening. In the growing darkness with only the pale golden boat lights bathing her torso, she looked like some goddess come down to Earth to gift him with the ultimate pleasure. The shadows enhanced her attributes, giving more depth to her breasts, her waist, the hollow at her neck, and he wanted to taste it all.

Her hands grasped his head, tilting upward as she lowered her lips to his and kissed him, showing him with her mouth exactly how much she wanted him.

He grasped her ass, kneading it through her clothing, wanting to feel her bare skin.

She lifted her mouth from his and pushed away again to unbutton her skirt. As she moved to push it down, he stopped her.

"Not yet." He didn't give her time to respond. He cupped both breasts in his hands and rubbed his thumb across the hard points even as he dipped his head to kiss her belly. The lemon scent was strong, but it was mixed with her desire and his erection strained against his shorts.

Removing his hands from her breasts, he wrapped them

around her body and held her to him, his face pressed into her soft skin as he tried to find his control. His attraction to her was so strong, but he refused to let it rush him.

Her hands rifled through his hair before brushing over his shoulders to finally push him back. "I want to feel you against me. Please, don't hesitate. I couldn't bear it."

It was as if she read his mind. He nodded, but couldn't speak, his desires and emotions too twisted together. Breaking their contact, he unbuttoned his shorts and pushed them down his legs. She wanted him as much as he wanted her and despite her words, he would savor every moment, every touch. She was worth that. He knelt to face her and stilled.

Chapter Ten

Hailey pushed her skort off faster than an eagle snatched a jumping fish. She was beyond excited Dillon wanted her and she wasn't about to delay that for even a second. Shimmying out of her bikini bottoms, she threw them to the side. If they fell off the boat, she couldn't care less.

Dillon wanted her. She had to repeat that fact to herself because after hoping for over a year, to actually have him was almost beyond comprehension. She glanced around to check for any night time boaters in the area, but all was calm…except her.

She knelt on the cushion and watched as Dillon removed his shorts. His body was sigh-worthy and the need to feel him inside her became almost unbearable. Finally, he faced her.

She couldn't resist touching him. Grasping his shoulder with one hand, she ran her other over his lightly furred chest, loving the soft feel of the hair there as she glided over ripples of muscles. She wanted to press her breasts against him.

"I don't have protection."

At his words, she stopped, her hand on his hard stomach. "I'm on the pill and haven't slept with anyone since I was tested." She quirked her lips up. "I'm as clean as a whistle. What about you?"

His shoulders relaxed. "The same."

She moved her hand lower. "Good. I'm glad we are both safe when it comes to that." She rifled through the dark pubic hair until she found the hard cock she wanted. Grasping it in her hand, but not too tight, she moved over it, feeling every ridge and vein. With her thumb, she brushed off a drop of liquid that revealed his excitement. That alone had her sheath filling.

Dillon was a very considerate lover. He seemed to be taking his cues from her. He put his hand on her shoulder as he ran his other one between her breasts, over her stomach, to the small patch of short hair on her mons.

She grasped his cock harder, not moving a muscle, anticipating his next move. She wasn't disappointed as his fingers moved between her thighs to find the moistness that covered her entrance. She forced her knees to spread apart, hoping he'd explore more.

His fingers continued, but not what she was expecting. She'd hoped to feel them inside her, but instead he encircled her clit, moving her own silkiness over it in circles, causing her excitement to grow. Her tension built, and she forced her hand to release him, afraid she'd hurt him. Instead, she grasped his other shoulder, to stay upright.

A slow smile spread over his face at her movement and at first, she wasn't sure why. But when he traced his other hand down to her breast it became clear. With her holding him to stay upright, he was free to play with both hands.

Her heartbeat raced as his hand reached her breast and squeezed it gently. When his fingers found her nipple, hot need raced from there to the juncture of her thighs. She closed her eyes, the sensation he conjured filling her with warmth and excitement. He continued to roll and pinch her nipple while his other teased her clit, building her orgasm slowly as if he had all the time in the world.

Just as she imagined what his cock would feel like, he moved his fingers over her nub and into her sheath. Her orgasm hit her hard and she rocked on his fingers, yelling to the stars her pleasure. As she was swept away into the universe, she grasped him hard, keeping him as her anchor, until finally her spasms lessened. He held her against him, kissing her hair as he grasped her butt.

She turned her face to his and found his lips, thanking him for the amazing experience. When he broke the kiss she became acutely aware of his erection pressing against her. Moving her legs out from under her, she sat back, her legs spread on either side of him as he leaned with her lowered position. "I'm needy. I want you inside me."

He released her to look around them. "Do you want to go inside?"

She laughed. She couldn't help it. She felt so good, so happy. "No. I don't care if anyone sees us. I just want you now."

His nostrils flared and her heart skipped a beat as his gaze on her body grew intense, but he still didn't move.

She grew anxious. To come so close and have him refrain because they were on top of the boat was too much. Her heart was living too close to the surface and she blurted out what she thought she would never say. "Unless you don't want me."

Pressing her lips together at baring her soul, she held her breath. Would he decide to turn away? She was positive he'd either pounce on her or rise and dress, but he did neither.

He reached his hand down and cupped the side of her face. "I want you more than you know, more than I should." His brow furrowed, but then a small smile graced his lips. "You are an amazing woman. I don't doubt why I want you."

Her heart lightened, and she raised her arms. "Then find joy with me."

He gave the smallest of nods before moving his hand from

her face and leaning over her, his torso propped up by his strong arms, his cock nestled between her legs. "You're a beautiful woman, from the inside out."

At his declaration, her eyes misted. "And you're more than the man I expected."

He raised his brows at that, and she grinned. "Now make love to me."

At her words, his smile fled and warmth filled his eyes. He didn't say anything, but he didn't have to. He leaned in and gave her a heart-stopping kiss as he adjusted himself over her.

She opened her legs to him as she opened her heart, more than hopeful that they could make it work. As his tip touched her entrance, all thoughts moved to his hard body. Instinctually, she waited for him to make the first move, but she hinted with her tongue as she thrust it into his mouth.

A low, almost growl came from deep in his throat, sending her body into hyper alert. He broke the kiss as his cock slowly and steadily pushed into her. As every inch of him entered her, she felt more and more fulfilled until he stopped, completely sheathed, pinning her to the cushion beneath.

She opened her eyes to find his closed, his breathing labored as if stopping went against everything he wanted. Her own breaths were short because she had no control with him. He lit up every corner of her being.

Lifting her legs, she wrapped them around his butt, and he slid another fraction deeper into her. This is what she wanted.

Dillon opened his eyes and looked into her own. No words passed his lips, but he didn't move his gaze as he lifted his hips then slid back into her.

Her whole body shivered with desire before he pulled back again and slowly pushed inside. She was ready for him the minute he'd entered her, so his movement heightened her excitement.

His rhythm slowly increased, teasing her every time he pumped into her, but still he held her gaze, making the experience truly shared and even more intimate. Soon he was pushing into her at a regular pace, her body wound tight as his demanded more of her.

Just when she thought she couldn't wait any longer, he broke her gaze and yelled, filling her and sending her spiraling out of control. She held on tight as he pumped into her with his joy, spiking her own.

As soon as she could think beyond the pleasure coursing through her, she opened her eyes to find him looking at her once again, his own body still racked with their shared ecstasy. It filled her heart to be so connected to him. It was as if they were one, one body, one heart, one soul.

Eventually, they both came down from such an incredible high, their breathing becoming more regular, their gazes still locked. She'd never felt so a part of another person in her life. He had her heart. He was the one.

"Wow." It was the only word she could think of to explain their lovemaking. She expected smugness from him, but that's not what she got.

"Yes." He looked a bit baffled.

Would he pull away from their intimacy? He actually initiated it. But her connection to him, though real, was new and she feared it breaking. She reached her hand into his hair and pulled him down for a kiss.

At first, he hesitated, but she persisted and he returned it with a sweet, 'I care for you,' kiss. When they broke apart, she smiled warmly. *I love you.* She clamped her mouth shut to avoid saying the words aloud, her instinct telling her it was too soon for him.

She was so enjoying the feel of him inside her and his

intense gaze that it took her a moment to realize there were blue flashes hitting the cliff wall near them. "Oh, no. We have company."

Dillon looked up and must have seen the flashes on the other wall. Quickly, he pulled out of her, his groan echoing her own.

She scrambled for her bathing suit as he slipped on his shorts. Men were so lucky that they only needed one piece of clothing to appear decent.

Her skort was on, but she had no top and the lights coming up behind them were a lot closer. In the dim light, she scanned the bow for her bathing suit top, but it was nowhere in sight. Maybe she could duck inside without them seeing her.

She looked around the side to see the Sherriff's boat was almost even with her stern. She spun around to find Dillon handing her his shirt. As soon as she grasped it, he moved to the port side and waved, drawing the boat to the opposite side while she quickly thrust her arms in what was short sleeves for him. Buttoning the most important buttons, she quickly joined him.

The Sheriffs cut the flashing lights and pulled up alongside, but their boat was much shorter than Austin's. Dillon untied one of the bow ropes and dropped it down to them. "Can we help you, sir?" His voice sounded completely normal.

Did someone see them and call the sheriffs? The media would love that. She could see it now—Hailey Pennington arrested for indecent exposure on friend's yacht.

"We're looking for a lost hiker. Have you seen anyone?"

Hell, she'd only had eyes for Dillon. She stepped around the corner to stand next to him.

"No, we haven't." Dillon put his arm around her waist and pulled her against him. "How long have they been missing?"

The sheriffs looked at her then back to Dillon. "Since

yesterday afternoon, but we just got the call this evening. Are you staying overnight out here?"

Dillon responded. "Yes, we are."

They were? That was exciting in itself.

"We'd appreciate it if you kept an eye out for anyone moving around out here by themselves. People who camp out this way don't usually do it alone, so if you see anything or hear anyone calling for help, call us on Channel 16. You do have a radio, right?"

She jumped in. "Yes, officer. We do. Could you tell us if it's a man or a woman?"

"It's a sixty-two-year-old female regular hiker, which is why her family wasn't concerned at first. They said she's in good shape and knows how to take care of herself in the wild. We have the Game and Fish Department starting a search at first light."

Dillon's hold on her grew a little tighter. "Was she headed out this way, or are you just checking all over the lake?"

"Her family says she's been hiking around the lake for a couple decades, but that just makes it harder with all of the tributaries." The sheriff lifted his ballcap and scratched his head before readjusting it. "I just hope we find her in time. You folks have a good night and let us know if you see or hear anything."

She was quick to answer. "We will." The idea of a woman past her mother's age alone in the desert concerned her. Rattlesnakes were a threat, but so were scorpions, mountain lions, javelinas, coyotes, and even burros could be nasty. The treacherous desert ground with all its loose rock could cause the woman to twist her ankle and not be able to make it back.

"Good luck." Dillon caught the rope the sheriff threw him and waved as they left.

The river narrowed significantly up ahead, but the sheriff's small boat could go places The Adventurer could not because of its size and engine draft.

Dillon pulled her around to him and held her tight. "See why I worry about you being safe."

Her heart skipped a beat at his admission. He was worried about *her* safety. She hugged him back. "Thank you. That's why I wouldn't have gone on that hike without you. I'm so glad you came with me, not just for safety's sake or the views." She looked up at him. "Having you there made it a memory I will always cherish."

He lowered his head and gave her a gentle kiss. It wasn't exactly what she'd hoped for, but she wouldn't push. He had to come to terms with his feelings for her despite his mother.

Dillon released her lips, then let go of her altogether to tie the rope to the railing. When he finished, he looked behind her and smirked. "I think we still have some unfinished business here."

She turned around to find the food they had started to eat was at one end of the bow, the tray at the other and still no bathing suit. "I couldn't find my top."

He moved to the end of the bow and carefully gathered up the food. Luckily, the cookies were in a package but the cheese and crackers he brushed off into the water. She imagined the fish below happy dancing.

Coming back, he shook his head. "I think your top might have gone overboard, but you look good in my shirt."

She smiled. "It's comfy because it's so big." And it had his juniper scent to it, which she loved.

"Then if you're that comfy, how about we watch those stars we came out to see."

"I'd like that."

He took her hand and led her back to the cushion. They sat next to each other, the tray of food on his other side.

She leaned back against the bank of windows. Did he really mean for them to stay the night? Would they sleep together? She hoped so, but their relationship was new, and she'd go at whatever pace he wanted.

"There's one." He pointed with his free hand toward the west.

She sat up. "One what?"

He looked at her as if she were clueless, which she was. "A shooting star. This area is known for shooting stars and meteors."

"Really?" She let her doubt be clear. "I didn't think there was a particular place on Earth that had a better view of those things than another."

He shrugged. "I don't either, but ever since I was a boy, Gramps told me this lake was the best place to see those things."

"Oh, then that's good enough for me." She grinned at him before laying back next to him. They stared at the night sky in silence. She was happier than she ever remembered being. To be here with Dillon, who admitted he—" There's one! Oh wow, your Gramps is right."

"Told you."

Yes, he did. He'd told her a lot of things tonight, and she was going to hold on to every one of them.

Dillon whistled as he saddled Black Jack. This last week he'd actually felt happy, almost content. There was something about Hailey that caused that to happen, far beyond his growing feelings for her. She seemed to have that effect on everyone.

Today, there was an added peace to his life. He didn't have to worry about her crashing a hot air balloon. He'd dropped her off at the school yesterday and followed her solo flight in his truck. She'd maneuvered the large balloon like a pro and set it down gently on the landing spot. Watching her work it from below reminded him of her confidence with the boat.

Not only was he happy to have her back on the ground again, but he had a growing confidence in her abilities. The fact that he was worried at all was proof of how strongly he felt. He should have noticed that earlier.

With Black Jack ready to go, he walked him outside where Eclipse waited. His family hadn't remarked on how much time he was spending with Hailey, but he was sure that was coming. He just hoped no one decided to enlighten his mother. At least not yet.

He was torn on that account. It seemed that if he continued his relationship with Hailey, which at the moment he couldn't see ending, he would be happy and his mother would be happy. As wrong as it was, after what his mom put him and Cole through, the last thing he wanted to do was reward her by doing exactly what she had hoped for.

Yet, if he denied his mother her dream, then where did that leave him? And where did that leave Hailey? He wasn't sure, but she seemed very into him. He didn't want to break her heart because of his mother. It was a quandary he needed to solve sooner rather than later. Every day that went by, there was a chance someone from his family or the public would say something, and his mother would hear. That would force him to make the decision earlier than he might be prepared to do.

At the sound of a truck on the dirt road to the ranch, he turned from the horses and strode toward the other side of the front yard, such as it was.

Hailey came to a stop and jumped out, wearing jeans, a pale pink sweater and her brown cowboy boots, with her hair pulled back in a simple pony tail. "Hi there, cowboy."

He grinned as he strode toward her.

She ran to him and hopped up onto him, wrapping her arms around his neck and her legs around his waist. "Did you miss me?"

"More than you know." He leaned his head forward and caught her lips with his own. The kiss quickly turned passionate, and he had to remind himself where they were before he could end it. "Are you ready for our ride?"

"I've already started."

He turned around with her in his arms to check the ranch house. Seeing no one at the front door or windows, he walked with her to the horses. "Yes, you have."

He was halfway across the yard when he stopped. "What the heck? Look at that."

Hailey dropped her legs and let go of his neck to turn toward the horses. "I told you."

Macy, who hadn't even looked at Eclipse, was suddenly at the corral fence where he and Black Jack were tied. Eclipse was so excited he lifted his head and nickered before stamping his feet. Black Jack looked at him as if he were the strangest horse he'd ever encountered.

Hailey laughed. "I guess I win the bet."

"No, we never made that bet. You refused, remember?"

"Good thing I did, too." She wiggled her eyebrows. "I'm looking forward to riding with you. I wish I could take you up in my plane later, too, but it's a one-seater."

His stomach tightened all over again as he helped her to mount Black Jack. "You're flying home?" She only lived a couple hours south, but it still bothered him…a lot.

She shook her head. "Not yet. I never got to fly the balloon over the Pipeline Canyon Trail, so I want to explore that from the sky plus do my favorite run, which is along the Aqua Fria. That river holds a very special place in my heart now."

At her wink, his stomach loosened a little, but he still worried about her flying. He tried to tell himself he just needed to see her doing it, like with the balloon, but it didn't help much.

He untied Eclipse and mounted. As he led the way around the ranch house, he couldn't help but admire how well she sat her horse. Macy followed them as far as the corral allowed until all she could do is watch them ride into the desert. That horse had kept Eclipse hanging for so long, Dillon didn't feel a lot of empathy for her.

He led them to the dirt road to Cole's house when Hailey shouted. "Race you to the end!"

She took off before he could respond, and he kicked Eclipse into a gallop. That woman was going to break her neck. Eclipse was a powerful horse, but Black Jack was fast and he seemed determined to test his speed.

He kept his eye on Hailey, his heart pounding with worry. Halfway down the road, he pulled abreast of her at the same time admitting she was an excellent rider. Focusing on her ability, he forced himself to concentrate on the race instead of on her seat.

Lowering his body over Eclipse, he urged his horse on. He was in the lead by a length until near the end when Black Jack must have decided he'd had enough of Eclipse's dust and pulled ahead. As they approached the very end of the dirt road, Dillon gave Eclipse the go ahead and the animal pulled even with his competitor, leaving them at a tie.

Smartly, Hailey slowed Black Jack as he ran onto the untouched desert ground. "That was great!" She laughed, even as she pulled out her elastic tie and gathered her golden hair together to pull it back again.

His heart lurched at her beauty even as his mind reminded him she wouldn't be around much longer. He would miss seeing her every day. How did that happen?

"So where is this trail you talked about. You know I'm always up for a new adventure and new sights."

That was very true and one of the things he both loved and feared about her.

He stilled. *Loved?*

"Dillon? Something wrong?" She moved her horse closer. "You look like you just saw a ghost." She glanced behind her as if to make sure there was no such thing.

He sidled away from his realization. He could imagine she'd love to discover a ghost in the hills, or worse, in one of the abandoned copper mines that littered the state like the one he was about to show her. If he hadn't already promised her, he'd take her somewhere else. "No, just remembered something. This way." He pulled Eclipse's reins to the right and walked the horse in the direction of the mine.

Hailey sighed as she turned her horse to walk with him. "I hope one of these days you'll be comfortable enough with me to tell me what's really on your mind."

He snapped his head around to look at her. Shit, she could read him that well already? Fine, then he'd tell her what was on his mind. "When it comes to you, there's a lot on my mind. Right now, I'm wondering when you'll be going home?"

She studied him, probably trying to decide if he wanted her to go.

He couldn't blame her as his stupid bet came to mind. He quickly added to his question. "I'm hoping it's not soon."

She smiled brightly at that. "In a few days. I have to go

back for Monday because my family has to be at an event to benefit a museum we support. It was actually my grandmother's pet project, so we always all show up." She looked him over as if trying to determine what size clothes he wore. "You could be my date. I'd love to see you in a tux again." She frowned. "Then again, I'd probably have to fight off all the other ladies. Maybe that's not such a good idea. Of course, you in a t-shirt and jeans could cause a stampede." She wiggled her brows again.

He didn't smile. He felt like he'd been kicked in the gut. She'd return to her society life in just a few days. Where would that leave him?

"Dillon, what's wrong? Obviously, something is bothering you. Is it me?"

"No." He snapped the word out. "I want…" He let his voice trail off. It was hard to explain, especially to her.

They rode in silence for a while. He kept trying to figure out how he could tell her he couldn't decide what to do about their relationship.

"Does it have to do with your mother?" Her question, said so softly, was too close to the target to ignore.

"Yes." What else could he say? That he wished he had a mother like Trace and Logan's? That he didn't want his own mother to be happy? Even he struggled with that reality.

Hailey slowed Black Jack and walked him around so they faced each other. "Why did you leave Morning Creek and come to Last Chance?"

The woman's insight was scary, but he couldn't hide it from her. She deserved to know. "My mother went too far."

"How? Tell me."

He rubbed his hand down one side of his face. There was no way to avoid it. It made his mother look bad and it made him look bad. "After Cole married Lacey, mom's efforts to marry me off tripled. At first, out of respect for her, I attended everything, but it started to get in the way of the ranch, so I cut it back. She wasn't happy and began trying to make me feel guilty. Even if I went where she wanted me to, a country club tea or a theatre production, she still complained that I was disrespectful every time I turned something down."

He paused, the hurt he'd felt closing his throat for a moment. He'd been raised to respect his parents, but the day he realized his mother had brought him up that way to manipulate him had been the worst day of all.

"Finally, I told her no more. She was furious, trying to make me feel guilty, but I stood my ground for a complete month. It was irritating her and started to affect my parents' relationship. Desperate, she told me about a charity event for orphans being held in Tucson. She said I just needed to dress as a glitzy singer for the kids. She'd even buy me the clothes to wear. I caved. Then when I arrived at the event, I discovered it was a bachelor auction for the charity. My mother had planned to auction me to the highest bidder in her never-ending quest to marry me off to a prestigious family."

He looked at Hailey. "What the fuck is wrong with *our* family?" He moved his gaze away from the sympathy in her eyes. She was too easy to talk to. He shouldn't have told her and he new better than to swear in front of a lady. She was definitely that, but he couldn't seem to move his lips to apologize with his throat so tight.

"I thought so."

At her bald statement, he swung his gaze back to her. "What?"

She nodded. "I was at that auction. I wasn't going to go, but when I saw you were one of the bachelors, I knew it had to be your mother's doing. She's well known among my friends, some of who tolerate her, some who, to be frank, bad-mouth her."

He stared in shock. "You were going to buy me?"

"Of course. Not that I planned to hold you to the date. I figured you deserved to get let off the hook your mom had dangled you from. It would have been different if you had volunteered, but I knew you hadn't."

He had underestimated Hailey, lumped her in with the women who willing accepted his mother's invitations. She was far smarter than any of them. "And if I'd volunteered?"

She grinned. "I would have bid, but only to raise it for the charity. I don't need to buy a man to get a date."

No, she wouldn't. She was everything a man could want. Smart, beautiful, and good at too many things to count. His mother would love her background. His father would love her horse sense. His brother already loved her for telling Lacey about a safe place to realize an old dream. And he loved her. He did. The warmth in his chest grew, until the idea of telling his family chilled him to the bone.

"Dillon, can we stop playing twenty questions and you just tell me why it's a problem that you go to the charity event with me on Monday?"

His lip quirked up. "Yes, we can, but let's keep walking."

"That works for me." She turned her horse around to walk it beside him and they continued. "Okay, spill it."

He took a deep breath, not use to talking so frankly to a woman, but Hailey was special and important to him. "As you guessed, it's my mother. Being with you would make her the happiest woman in the world."

"And?"

He gripped the reins a little tighter. "And I don't want her to be."

"Ah, I see. You want her to suffer like she made you and Cole suffer."

He glanced at her. "Yes. I know it's wrong, but that's how I feel."

She chuckled. "That doesn't make you a bad person or even a bad son. What that makes you is human."

Her simple statement loosened a knot he'd been carrying around in his chest for months. "I am human. Very human. I make *a lot* of mistakes."

"So do I. As I told your brother, I'm not an angel and I'm not crazy. I'm somewhere in between."

He nodded. "I can see that. I can also see why he thought you were both crazy and an angel as I've had the same thought as well."

"Dillon, tell me you didn't."

He shrugged. "I may make mistakes, but I'll never lie to you. I have thought that, especially when you crash-landed here." He held up his hand to keep her from speaking. "*Almost* crash-landed. And I'm proud of you for learning how to pilot a hot air balloon."

"Thank you." She smiled at that. "I can take you up some time."

"No. No, that's okay. I do trust your skills, but I don't trust the equipment. Too much can go wrong that is out of a person's hands."

"You don't know that."

She was right, but he believed that. "I guess we'll never know."

"In other words, agree to disagree?"

He grinned. "Yes." Though he did hope to keep her feet on the ground more often than not. He led them around a small butte.

Hailey slowed to examine the skinny projection as they walked around it. When they came to a stop on the other side, she moved her gaze to him. "I think I understand now. You don't want to be seen with me and make your mother happy, so going to the museum fundraiser would be out. I'm fine with that, but I think you have a bigger decision to make."

From what he'd been thinking, he had more than one to make, and they all involved her. "And what is that?"

"How long do you plan for us to hide our relationship from your mother, and what will you do when she finds out."

By her serious face, it was clear she expected him to break it off with her. Just the thought of that had his gut in a knot. "Whatever it is, we'll decide together."

That seemed to ease her concern a bit. And just the fact that he made her feel better had him pleased with himself. Shit, he had it bad.

Chapter Eleven

Hailey strode into the hanger of the small-plane airport not far from both the lake and All Hot Air. She was anxious to get back into the sky to enjoy the sights, relax, and think. Her conversation with Dillon earlier kept swirling around in her head. On one hand, she had the feeling he was as anxious to continue their relationship as she was, but on the other, his resentment of his mother was so strong, he might break it off with her for that reason alone.

She would be a lot angrier if she'd never met his mother, but the problem was, she didn't want to give the woman the satisfaction either. So where did that leave them?

After walking into the airport office and letting them know she was flying out, she headed back outside toward the parked planes when she spotted movement around the side of the hangar. Curious, she investigated.

Surprised, she yelled as the was person about to light up. "Austin! Give me that!" She strode forward with her hand held out, palm-side up.

"I didn't know you were flying today."

"I didn't know you were either. Now stop stalling and hand it over."

Reluctantly, he placed the lighter in her hand.

Dropping it into the front pocket of her jeans, she gave him a scowl. "I thought you quit smoking. What happened?"

"Fatherhood."

She reached her hand out again. "That's even more reason to quit. Give me your cigarettes, too."

"You weren't supposed to be here. I thought you were hanging out at the Hatcher ranch. How's that going?"

She just stared at him until he finally gave her the pack. "Really? You can spend two hours at a bar drinking beer without a cigarette, but you go flying and you need one?"

He shook his head. "No. I was doing well, but then—never mind. It's complicated. And you're right. I need to find another way."

She gave him a sympathetic smile. "I know it's hard and I can't begin to understand, but I promised to look out for you."

He nodded. "You're right. And I promised to look out for you. Thanks."

She wrapped her arm around his waist and nudged him back toward the tarmac. "I'm going to investigate a trail I hiked. I want to see if it connects to the lake. With the water low, it may not."

Austin stopped walking, forcing her to halt as well. "I am curious. How are things going with the Hatcher guy?"

She smirked. "His name is Dillon, and it's complicated."

He grinned, accepting her right to hold off talking about it for a while, just like he was keeping things tight to the vest with his new parenting role. "I just got back. I did a final fly-by the Aqua Fria and spotted Bald Eagles. Might want to check it out. I'm thinking they may end up closing it down to boat traffic soon."

"Oh, I hope their eggs hatch. They are such majestic birds." They had a few on Ironwood and they were fascinating to watch when they were hunting.

Austin looked at his watch. "I better get home. Good babysitters make a mint these days." He chuckled uncomfortably.

"Of course. I'm just going up for a short run. I'm having dinner with Dillon, his brother and Cole's wife, Lacey. We have a lot to talk about."

"Did the office tell you to keep and eye out for the missing hiker?"

She nodded. "Yes. Or rather they suggested I keep my eye out for vultures. I can't imagine doing something you've done for years and then suddenly everything goes wrong and you die." She shivered. "It's that she died alone that curls my stomach."

"Well, if you don't want to die alone, you better nail down this Hatcher guy."

She gave him an exasperated sigh. When she opened her mouth to respond, he held up his hand.

"I know. His name is Dillon. Just giving you a hard time." He stepped closer and gave her hug. "See you on Monday. Be safe up there."

She smiled as she stepped out of his embrace. "Always am." Then she turned and headed for her plane.

Hers was the only blue plane parked at the airport, though to be fair, it had a black underbelly and it stood out because of its clear cockpit. The wing, which was mounted above cockpit was one piece and a bright white. She took very good care of her plane, making sure it was in top condition and keeping up with the regular maintenance schedule of both the manufacturer and the FAA. She loved her Coyote.

After doing her pre-flight, she strapped herself in and radioed the tower. They were expecting her and gave her clearance on the runway. The little airport had maybe two or three dozen fliers a day except on the weekends, but they took safety as seriously as she and Austin did.

Getting up to speed, she was soon airborne. As she soared high above the desert floor, a rush of happiness filled her. It was a great feeling, being so light and to view the world from the sky like a bird. She wanted to share this with Dillon. Maybe purchasing a two-seater should be on her to-do list.

She headed the plane toward the west finger of the lake. At least that's what she called it. From the air, the lake looked like a hand without a thumb. It was fun to explore by water and air, and now she'd discovered it could be fun to enjoy by land as well.

The fact was, she wanted to enjoy it with Dillon. She wanted to enjoy everything with Dillon. The last couple weeks had shown her that everything she'd thought about him was true, and yet had learned other things she hadn't expected. He was a bit old-fashioned, but it was charming, especially when she pointed it out.

She chuckled. Even at the mine that afternoon, she'd forced him to let her determine if it was safe. He grumbled but let her investigate, keeping a vigilant watch over her. It was hard to keep from laughing when she told him it wasn't safe. His relief was more than palpable. It was physically visible. He'd even promised to take her to an old copper mine that *was* safe to explore.

She had grown to love how protective he was. It had to mean he felt strongly about her, though he hadn't said the words. He wasn't just protective of her, but of his brother's and cousins' women, too. He was protective of Gram and little Charlotte and even of the horses at the ranch. Everyone he loved had him going on high alert, so if he was protective of her, that had to mean he felt strongly about her.

Banking the plane as she reached the lake, she stayed west and headed north toward where the Pipeline Canyon Trail was located. Having Dillon with her on that hike made that trail her favorite to date. She may have had a crush on him for awhile and had become totally infatuated with him after seeing him almost naked that morning at the ranch, but it was that hike that started her falling for him fast.

She wouldn't say anything yet, but she was totally in love with the man. That she had to go back to Ironwood at the end of the week for the charity event was upsetting. It wouldn't bother her at all if she could take Dillon as her date. They didn't live *that* far away from each other and with her plane she could fly up at a moment's notice. She'd even studied the dirt road into the ranch to see where holes needed to be filled in and how much straight away there was after a wash, just in case she wanted to start landing there.

The fact was, she wanted to spend every day with Dillon. If he were to tell her he loved her tomorrow and asked her to marry him, she would. Just thinking that had her heart near to bursting with happiness. She'd found the man she could see herself with for the rest of her life. That was huge!

The warmth of her love had her smiling to herself even as she flew along the lake's finger, studying the shoreline and waterways. After two passes, she concluded the lake was too low to reach the inlets near the trail, but she had a feeling in the spring when it rose to its full depth, there would definitely be boat access.

She and Dillon would have to spend the day exploring in the warmer weather. They could even go swimming. They'd already had the last warm surge of heat for the year. This week had been cold. People from out of state didn't realize exactly how cold it could get. When she'd woken this morning on the boat, the temperature had just reached forty and the winds on the lake were frigid.

As she finished her last pass by the west finger she headed northeast. The sky was already showing its brilliant colors and she'd need to return soon. She'd head for the end of the Aqua Fria, fly south over it then east until she came back to the airport.

Though she was enjoying her flight, she kept wishing Dillon was with her. She was sure he would enjoy the sights, even if he was cautious about flying. She'd noticed a distinct change in him when he'd come with her for her solo flight in the hot air balloon. Though he hadn't gone up with her, he had followed her and met her when she touched down, a big proud smile on his face. That's what she wanted in a relationship. Someone to share everything with, successes and failures—sweet moments and craziness.

And there were only two things standing in her way. The first was Dillon. Did he love her? Her gut said yes, but she wanted to hear it, have him admit it out loud. Her concern was he may not until he'd figured out what to do about his mother, and that was the real crux of the issue. For them to become a true couple would fulfill all his mother's dreams, and he didn't want to do that after all she put him through.

She didn't want to give the woman that satisfaction either, but she wouldn't give up her own happiness to spite Mrs. Hatcher. Would Dillon?

Even in her worried state, she kept her focus on the scenery below. The tiny little tributaries that fed the river were below her. The flat area would give way to the ravine the river carved out and eventually to the place she and Dillon made love.

She didn't see any eagles yet, but she wasn't close enough to the top of the cliff. She could fly a little—

The engine shut off.

"Fuck." After a few seconds of her stomach moving into her throat, she took a deep breath. She'd trained for this.

Adjusting the flaps, she kept the glide down shallow and hit the switch for ignition.

Absolutely nothing changed. She checked her fuel. She still had plenty. What the hell was the problem?

She tried the ignition again. Nothing. She stared at the propeller on the nose of the plane. "Okay, listen. If you don't turn, we're both in trouble. So, let's get our act together, okay?"

She hit the switch, but the propeller remained inactive and the plane kept descending. Panic sped up her chest and the faeries in her stomach fought to get out and escape. She wished she could too.

"Okay. Okay. Think. You're going down. Oh, crap I'm going to crash! I'm going to die. I'll never see my family again. I'll never see Dillon." Her heart, already pounding, felt like it was about to explode.

Looking out the clear cockpit, she was heading for the plateau on the east side of the Aqua Fria. The ground looked so unforgiving. If she hit nose first, she'd be dead in an instant. Even if she managed to land, she'd be sure to flip over and be crushed or worse, burned to death as the gas exploded.

Instinctually, she used the updrafts of the last heat of the day to bank the plane gently to the right, controlling the rudder with the pedals as she lined it up on the river as best she could. At least there'd be some give…if she didn't sink immediately and get trapped inside. The river was deep, even when the lake was low. Over a hundred feet deep in some areas, and she'd be sinking into that.

Panic rose again, closing off her throat and airways. She couldn't breathe. Desperate, she pinched herself hard. Air whooshed into her lungs, feeding her brain. Panic wasn't going to let her see Dillon again. Panic was the enemy.

The plane continued to glide down. If it slowed too quickly

she'd drop like a stone, but if she hit the water too fast, she'd break apart like she would on land. She checked her speed and adjusted until she was where she needed to be.

Okay, she had this. Stay focused, stay upright, nose a little higher. Don't want to dive straight to the bottom. Her air cut off again and she forced more in. "I'm not going to die. "I'm not going to die."

"Oh shit!" A curve in the river caught her by surprise and the plane glided over the hard plateau by mere yards before the river straightened again.

Frantically, she reviewed her memory of the Aqua Fria as the plane dipped below the cliffs. If there was one more curve, she'd smash into a wall.

The plane glided lower, the darkness of the shadows keeping out the sunset, making it dark before it really was. Shadow and water started to blend.

Nose up. Nose up.

Smack!

Chapter Twelve

Hailey closed her eyes as the plane smashed into the water, the sudden stop, almost pulling her arms from her shoulders as she gripped the steering column.

Get out! Her brain kicked in, and she popped her eyes open. She'd landed. She was alive!

She had to get out. Unbelting the straps that held her in, she opened the cock pit door.

The light plane rocked with her movements. Though it was dark in the ravine, the purple sky gave a little illumination, and she could see the water lapping at the side of the plane just beneath her feet. Carefully, she stepped on the exhaust pipe that ran along the side to the nose and climbed on top.

The plane began to sink. What could she do?

Climbing up the windshield, she crawled onto the fixed wing, the top most piece of the plane. She pulled out her phone, pretty sure there was no signal, but she'd try anything. She pushed it and the words "no service" showed up in the corner. That's what'd she thought. Powering it down, she stuck it back in her back pocket. The dark water surrounding plane continued to come closer as it slowly sank.

Shit! It was November and the water would be frigid. In the limited light, she looked at both sides of the ravine walls.

One side went straight up from the water, the other had a small beach because the water was down, but it was not that long and it was farther away.

Oh, God. The water was now beneath the wing. She had to do something. She had to swim for it. Scrambling, she pushed off her boots and shucked off her jeans. Pulling her sweater over her head, she rolled up the jeans and wrapped them inside the sweater. The air was already cold and the thought of jumping into the water had her shaking.

Desperately, she double knotted her bundle of clothes with the sleeves of her sweater then slipped off her bra. She had no idea if her plan would work, but she had to try. As she fed her bra through the knot of clothes, tears ran down her face. She wiped at them as she tried to see what she was doing in the fading light.

The water continued to lap at the wing.

She stopped. She wasn't sinking anymore? She might be able to stay right where she was? Undecided now on what to do, she waited. She kept her eyes on the spot where the water licked at the wing to her left. It wasn't changing. Was it? Was she floating?

Water touched her fingers, and she whipped her head around. The other end of the wing was starting to disappear beneath the water. Scooting backwards, she quickly stuck her bundle on top of her head and tied it tight with her bra beneath her chin.

Shaking from cold and fear, she finally let herself slide off the wing and into the cold black water.

It was mind-numbing. She'd freeze in a second and sink to the bottom.

Self-preservation kicked in at that thought, and she struck out for the far shore. She wasn't into her swim four strokes before her feet started to go numb. She kicked furiously, hoping she was making a direct line, but it was dark in the river now and the shore blended with the water.

When something jarred against her leg, she pulled it in to her chest, almost going under and swallowing a mouth full of water. Whatever it was, was big and her mind started imaging things that couldn't be. It was a shark, no a whale, no an alligator. Fear fueled her muscles and she sped forward only to find her legs getting stuck. No, not stuck. It was sand.

She'd made it!

Crawling out of the water, she took her first deep breaths, the air feeling so much warmer against her ice-cold skin. She tried to stand, but her legs gave out from under her, and the clothes on top of her head slid to the side, sitting on her shoulder. With numb hands, she crawled away from the water's edge and whatever terrors it held, all the way to the cliff wall.

Turning around, she sat with her back against it and stared into the darkness. There was no sign of her plane. It was gone.

She wrapped her arms around her and started to cry. How could this have happened? Why her? She was always safe? There was nothing wrong with her plane. Nothing! It was a perfectly good plane. She'd never had a problem with it. There was no reason for the engine to just stop working!

As her anger grew, so did her awareness of her surroundings and the fact that she was shivering. The air temperature no longer felt warm, and she was still wet. Her hands were starting to tingle as feeling came back to them. They hurt.

Desperate to get warm, she fumbled at the ties under her chin, but the water had swollen the material. It was too much. She lowered her head and with stinging hands wrenched the bundle off, giving herself a rope burn in the process.

She tried to untie her sweater but her hands hurt too much. She focused on deep breaths and counting until the tingling became bearable. As quick as she could manage, she pulled apart her sweater and yanked it over her head.

Immediately, her body started to warm and her shaking slowed, but now her feet began to burn. "Arrrrrr!" She let her pain out, knowing exactly what would come next.

Dillon paced across the porch. Where was Hailey? They were supposed to be at Cole's house thirty minutes ago. She was never late. He'd noticed she was more likely to be early. Taking out his phone for the eighth time, he called her. It went straight to voice mail.

Something was wrong. He looked at the western sky as the last shades of purple turned dark gray. What if she had crashed?

Even at the thought, his chest tightened so much he couldn't breathe. He refused to believe that. She probably just landed late and was in the shower on the boat. That's all it was. Or maybe she never did fly this afternoon. Maybe she got caught up in something else.

Walking a hole in his grandparents' porch wouldn't give him the answers he needed. First, he had to find out if she'd flown. The problem was, he had no idea what airport her airplane was at. There were three small airports in the area, one west of them and two east.

His hand fisted over his phone as helplessness crawled up his back. He would just call all three airports. One of them was sure to know—Austin. Austin would know which airport.

He didn't have Austin's phone number, but he knew someone who did. He quickly dialed Logan's number. When his cousin answered, he didn't even let him finish saying hello. "I need Austin Leighthall's number from Jenna."

"Austin who?"

"Just ask her."

He waited as Logan called for his girlfriend. Then he came back to the phone. "She's coming. What's wrong."

He didn't even care if he was over-reacting or being overprotective. "Hailey was supposed to fly today and meet me here half an hour ago. She's not here and she's not answering her phone."

He half-hoped his cousin would suggest a viable reason, but he didn't. "Shit. We're on our way. Here she is."

At his cousin's reaction, his fear escalated, making it hard to memorize the number. Jenna finally texted it to him.

As soon as it popped up, he hit it. "Austin?"

"Yes, who's calling?"

"This is Dillon Hatcher. Which airport does Hailey have her plane at?"

"It's at Deer Valley, why?"

She claimed Austin was a good friend. "She was supposed to be here half an hour ago and her phone is going to voice mail."

"Fuck. I watched her take off earlier. We need to get over there and see if her truck is still there. She's never late."

That's what he was afraid of. "I'm on my way." He hung up and ran down the steps to his truck. He was about to open the driver door when Cole's truck came speeding up the road from his house. Cole jumped out. "What did you find out?"

He swallowed the lump in his throat, obviously Logan and called his brother. "Hailey flew out of Deer Valley late this afternoon. I'm headed to the airport to see if her truck is there."

"We're going too."

He nodded, happy to have Cole with him though he was still holding onto the idea that she was just in a very long shower. Twice on the way to the airport, he had his truck dial her number, but both times it went to voice mail.

As he pulled into the lighted parking lot, his heart sank. Hailey's truck was the only vehicle there. There had to be someone else on the premises. If she flew out, didn't someone have to be there when she returned?

He drove his truck around the hanger and found an office building. Two vehicles were parked there. Maybe she was inside talking to the staff. He looked at the planes parked on the tarmac, but he had no idea what hers looked like. If she'd been the type of society woman he originally expected, she wouldn't even fly a plane, but he knew by now the plane wouldn't be pink.

Opening the door, he strode inside. "I'm looking for Hailey Pennington."

The man and woman chatting behind a small counter stopped at his pronouncement.

The man moved toward the counter. "Is she a pilot?"

"Yes. She flew out of here this afternoon and her truck is still in the parking lot." He tried to keep the panic from his voice. He needed their help, so he kept his fisted hands beneath the counter so they wouldn't see his level of frustration.

"Do you know her plane number?"

He barely kept from rolling his eyes. How many planes would actually fly out in one afternoon. "No, I don't, but I know she flew out sometime after two this afternoon." She hadn't left the ranch until then.

The woman rose from her chair and moved to another before a computer terminal. "That should help."

He opened and closed his hands as he waited for her to find the information. Behind him, the door opened and Cole walked in along with Logan. "Now all we need is Trace."

Cole stepped up to the counter next to him. "He's on the way as is Detective Anderson."

"Why did you call him?" Anderson was friends with Cole, but his experience with the Williams-Hatcher family had not exactly been good…for him.

"I'm just covering all bases."

In other words, if Hailey was a missing person, they needed to involve law enforcement and Anderson was known and trusted.

The woman looked up from the computer. "She flew out just after three." She looked at him. Sunset was at 5:21 p.m."

Cole glanced at his watch. "It's almost seven now."

He didn't like where this was headed. Did she run out of gas and set down somewhere? "Would she have enough fuel for that long?"

The woman tapped her keyboard and the man blocked his view by standing behind her.

Maybe she set down somewhere without service and was even now trying to walk back to civilization.

"Yes." The man had turned around. "Her Coyote has plenty of fuel, and she gassed up before she left."

His stomach loosened a bit at that. "She was supposed to be back at six. Could she have landed at another airport?"

The man nodded. "There's quite a few small airports within that range."

The woman smiled at him encouragingly. "Would you like me to contact them. It may take some time. I can start with the closest?"

That's what he wanted. Someone to tell him that Hailey

was okay and safe and he just needed to drive somewhere and pick her up.

"Yes, please do that." The strange voice behind him had him turning around.

"Detective Anderson."

"Dillon." Anderson turned to Cole and his expression relaxed a bit. "Cole."

"Thank you for coming. My brother's girlfriend was supposed to be back at the ranch at six but she didn't show up. We traced her here where she flew out in her plane a little after three but has not returned."

"And you think she may have gone to one of the other airports if she had trouble. Good start. We'll wait to see what these people can tell us."

Dillion watched the woman typing on her keyboard. Screens went by on her computer that he couldn't read. What if Hailey had to set down in the desert and was bit by a rattlesnake. Even now she could be lying somewhere in the dark dying.

Unable to stand there and cool his heels, he strode outside without a word. His step faltered as he found Jenna, Lacey, Whisper and Riley talking in hushed tones. Lacey looked like she was shivering. He addressed her. "It's warm inside. You can go in."

They looked up at him in surprise. Whisper nodded toward the building. "Did they find her?"

He shook his head. "Not yet. They're checking other airports in the area to see if she put down there."

"She has to be alright." Lacey's worry cut into his gut.

Everyone of them liked Hailey. He didn't blame them. She was…perfect.

A truck sped into the parking lot and screeched to a halt. When the door opened, Austin jumped out. "I had to wait for the babysitter. If Hailey's truck is here it means she's out there somewhere."

Dillon's jaw tightened and his cheek started to twitch just beneath his right eye. "They're checking the other airports to see if she went to one of them."

"She didn't." Austin's absolute confidence in that, had Dillon suddenly feeling nauseous. "She went to the south finger and then was coming back the Aqua Fria. If she didn't return, it means she went down along that route."

The blood pounded in his ears, making it impossible to hear anyone. Jenna ran into the office and Whisper appeared to be yelling, but he couldn't hear anything as panic set in. "We have to find her."

The office door burst open and Cole, Logan and Trace poured out.

Cole clasped him on the shoulder. "Jenna says Hailey went down along the lake. If that's true, we'll find her."

He wanted to ask the question they were all wondering. Was she alive? But he couldn't get his mouth to form the words. He *had* to find her. "Someone needs to cover the south finger. She planned to see if the lake connected to the water we saw while we hiked the Pipeline Canyon Trail. I'm taking the boat and heading up the Aqua Fria. I need someone to hit both areas by land."

"I'm going with you." Austin interjected. "After all, it is my boat."

"Fine. Cole can you take the land side of the Aqua Fria? I think it's accessible from Poker Flat."

"Of course, I'll take Lacey and Riley. The more eyes on the land the better."

Logan stepped forward. "I'll talk to the marina and see if they can take me and Jenna to the south finger by boat."

He nodded, antsy to get going. "Trace, you and Whisper can take the trail since you have the ATV on your truck."

"Will do."

"Wait." Lacey stopped on the way to Cole's truck. How will we let each other know if we find her? The phone coverage is non-existent out there."

Fuck. He didn't care, just as long as they found her. "Send up freakin' fireworks. Whatever it takes."

Cole grabbed his arm. "Hold on." He yelled to stop everyone from getting in their vehicles. "Everyone hold on!"

They froze, but Dillon whipped his arm away from Cole. Every second counted now.

Cole glared at him before addressing everyone. "I have flares in my truck. Come over and grab one and if you find her, send it up. Also, if you don't have a blanket or water, I have that in my truck as well."

That was Cole the Fire Captain. Always prepared. Dillon looked at Austin who simply nodded. They were good to go. He jumped in his truck and tore out of the parking lot. He drove with his high beams as the night was dark and there was no moon. The last thing he wanted was to hit a burro and get derailed.

Austin was right behind him and they both hit the pavement running when they got to the marina. Once on the boat, he pulled the ropes and Austin set the course. When they were out on the open lake, he gunned it.

Dillon went downstairs and pulled out blankets and brought them above deck. One of them came from the bed and had Hailey's distinctive scent. He brought it to his nose and inhaled. As his eyes started to tear, he swore and dropped the blankets on the seat before heading out to the bow.

When they entered the river, Austin slowed the boat. He put on his search light and had it scan back and forth.

Dillon stood at the bow, his eyes examining every nook and cranny along the shore. He had to believe she was alive somewhere. The thought of her buried a hundred feet below the inky darkness was more than he could stomach.

~~*~~

Once the pins and needles subsided in her feet, Hailey stood, bracing herself against the cliff wall to brush herself off. Removing her soaked panties, she pulled on her jeans, thankful for the temporary warmth. Taking her phone from her back pocket she turned it on for a light. The beach wasn't that long ahead of her.

Turning to scan the beach the other way, she froze. The light landed on the torso and face of a dead woman washed up on the beach. Her stomach decided it had enough and she bent over and vomited.

When she finished, she felt drained, hungry and hopeless. She didn't want to end up like the female hiker. She should pull the body ashore so the authorities could give closure to the family, but the idea that she might end up the same way had her recoiling from the thought.

Oh, God, please Dillon, come look for me.

Unable to face that end of the beach, she walked the other way and found a small indent in the cliff wall to huddle out of the wind. They always said Lake Pleasant had its own weather and the river acted like a wind tunnel. She was cold enough as it was without the stupid wind.

It made her feel even more lonely because all the night sounds were wiped away by the wind's howl. On calm nights on the lake, she could hear the burros talking, but not here. It was just her, the cold, the wind...and the dead body. She shivered as much from the gruesome aspect as the cold. It was so hard without someone to share her worries with.

The words of Josiah from the bar floated through her mind. *It's when you're alone that you have to worry. That's when you come face to face with yourself and find out exactly how brave you are…or aren't.* She was beginning to understand. Did he also feel like her that he didn't care if he was brave or afraid as long as he got out of the situation?

Turning her phone off, she tried to put it in her front pocket, but there was something in there. Sticking her hand in, she found Austin's lighter. At the reminder of her friend, she started to cry all over again. The last thing she'd done was berate him for smoking. He'd always remember her doing that.

A lot of good it did for her to look out for him when she was down here. Would he come looking for her. He'd promised to look out for—she stared at the lighter and started to laugh hysterically.

It took a while to get herself back on track, but she finally calmed, wiping the tears from her eyes. Austin's lighter could help her after all. Getting up, she stuck the lighter back in her front pocket, turned on her phone light and searched the area for anything that would burn.

The wind picked up, but she gathered everything she could from the one end of the beach. It was a sad pile and wouldn't last long. She'd seen a larger piece of driftwood at the other end but she didn't want to go there.

Come on, Hailey. It's about survival. What happened to the little girl who slayed dragons and pierced the bad guys in the eye with her arrows? "She grew up. Get off my back." Her voice in the hollow sounded eerie, so she clamped her mouth shut.

She stared at the small pile of wood. There was no help for it. She didn't want to survive a plane crash only to die of hypothermia. Steeling herself, she rose and turned on the light on her phone. Keeping the beam away from the water's edge, she found the large piece of wood and dragged it back to her hollow.

Her teeth were chattering now, but she went back to the other end and gathered every scrap of wood she could. It still wouldn't last the night and she doubted they would search in the dark. Didn't a person have to be missing twenty-four hours for the sheriffs to get involved?

Maybe she could start just a small fire and keep it going for as long as possible. She was no survivalist, but it seemed like a good idea. Anything to keep her teeth from chattering. At least she'd been camping with her brothers, so she knew how to build a fire. Luckily, it hadn't rained in over a month, so the wood was dry. It caught quickly, despite her shaking hand...it burned up quickly, too.

Putting the precious lighter back in her pocket, she held her hands over the warmth. Once they heated, she pressed them against her face. It was addictive, and she soon found herself leaning her face over the fire directly.

The wood burned fast, but the heat felt so good. Finally, she let it burn down to just coals. She still had her big log and a small amount to get the fire started again. Leaning back against the cliff wall, she dozed.

"Hailey!" Dillon ground his teeth. They had to go slow but every minute could mean the difference between finding Hailey alive or...he wouldn't even think it. To have found her then to lose her so quickly was not worth contemplating.

He kept his eyes on the shoreline on both sides. They'd

been looking for over an hour now. She had to be out here somewhere.

The radio crackled which meant Logan was checking in. Thanks to Channel 16, they could keep in contact with him though the signal was sometimes blocked by the cliffs.

Austin's voice interrupted his periodic calls. "Logan says nothing yet. No flares."

It was the same as it was for the last six check-ins.

"This is the last section of deep water and then it gets too shallow for this boat. You should think about what you want to do then."

If it was too shallow for the boat, he'd get out and walk it. He wasn't stopping until they found Hailey. He kept glancing up, expecting to see the sky lit with red by Cole. There had to be more room to land a plane on the desert than on the water. He didn't care who found her, as long as she was found alive and well.

As they entered an area with two high cliffs on each side, he recognized the place. It was where he and Hailey had made love. That was when he'd finally let her into his heart. He called out again. "Hailey!"

He listened as they floated forward. The night wind making it hard to hear. For all he knew his voice was being carried back to Austin, but he wouldn't stop calling. It was a piercing wind, too and the sweatshirt Austin had lent him did little to keep out the chill.

Was Hailey in this, too. All she had on was the sweater she wore as they rode to the copper mine earlier in the day. It had been a beautiful day in the seventies. Now it had to be about fifty with the wind chill making it colder and the temperatures dropping.

Scanning right and left, he took a double take. "Cut the light!"

Austin cut the search beam.

He pointed. "There." He was afraid to hope. It looked like a campfire behind an outcropping in the cliff wall. It could be campers, but it was damn cold for camping. As the boat drew closer, he could see a figure huddle next to the small fire. "Hailey!"

"Dillon?"

Chapter Thirteen

At the whisper of Hailey's voice, his spirits sored. "We found her!" He turned to yell at Austin. "Portside! We found her!"

"Holy shit!"

He ran up to the helm and grabbed a blanket before returning to the bow, ready to walk across the water for her.

"That's as close as I can get and still get us out of here. Can you make it?"

He didn't answer. He held the blanket above his head and jumped off the bow. The water came up to just over his knees, which was far shallower than he expected. Slogging toward the shore, he moved as fast as he could.

Hailey stood, shivering, her arms crossed over her body, her feet bare, her hair a tangled mess as the wind whipped it about her, but to him she was the most beautiful woman he'd ever seen.

"Dillon. You came." The wonder in her voice almost started the tears he'd been fighting all night.

"Of course, I came." He held the blanket out and wrapped her in it in his arms and kissed her. Her lips were cold and he tried to give her his heat.

When he broke the kiss, she leaned her head against his shoulder. "Thank you for coming."

He didn't hesitate but scooped her up in his arms and walked to the waiting boat. Austin waited on the bow and he lifted her up to him. There was no ladder there, so he had to wade deeper to the side ladder. He was up to his chest by time he climbed out and when the wind hit him, the chill seeped into his skin. Fuck! The thought of Hailey feeling that bite, had his heart constricting.

Once on board, he took Hailey from Austin and walked into the boat. All he cared about was warming Hailey up. Quickly, he wrapped her in more blankets and put her in bed.

He stripped off his clothes and sat next to her. "I almost lost you."

She smiled sleepily. "I hoped you would come. Can I have some water?"

He was such an idiot. "Yes." Getting up, he walked to the refrigerator and grabbed a bottled water. When he returned, he found her staring at him. He opened the bottle and lifted her so she could drink. "That wasn't much. Do you want more?"

"No." She closed her eyes and smiled. "I just wanted to watch your naked backside."

He forced a smile in case she opened her eyes, but when she didn't and her breathing evened out, he rose.

Wrapping a blanket around him he went topside to talk to Austin.

The man was all smiles. "We did it."

"Yes, we did. But she's not well. Radio for an ambulance. Did you send off the flare yet?"

Austin shook his head as he started the boat out the way they had come but at a slightly faster speed, the tight quarters making anything speedier impossible.

Dillon bent over and grabbed one of the emergency flares. Moving down to the back deck which was wide open, he set it off.

Austin called down. "Ambulance will be waiting for us at east the ramp."

That was all he needed to know. Opening the slider, he went inside to watch over his heart.

Hailey opened her eyes to find herself in a hospital bed with her mom, dressed in a pretty aqua tunic, sitting next to her. "So, it really happened?"

"Ah, you're finally awake. You gave us such a scare." Her mother leaned over and gave her a hug.

She held on, happy to be safe in her mother's arms.

When her mother pulled away, there were tears in her eyes.

"Oh, mom. Don't cry. I'm fine."

Her mother nodded. "I know. But I can't imagine what you went through. Crashing into the river, swimming ashore and…I'm sorry." Her mother wiped at new tears.

"How do you know what happened? Haven't I been asleep? Last I remember, Dillon was bringing me to the boat."

Her mother's eyes widened. "That's all you remember?"

She nodded.

"You don't remember sleeping for a short while then waking up and telling Dillon everything that happened?"

She shook her head. "Everything?"

"I think so. He said you even told him you vomited and cried and that you thought the lake would connect with the water by the hiking trail when the water level was higher. I think he was glad that you told him. He even told the authorities about that poor hiker you found."

She told him everything. What did he think? Last she remembered he was kissing her on the beach then he swept her up and brought her to the boat without her having to get wet again. She tried to remember what happened afterwards, but it wasn't there.

"You were suffering from mild hypothermia. You've had a traumatic experience. You'll probably remember when you can process it all. The good news is that you can come home today."

But she didn't want to go home. She still had three, no two days left with Dillon. Did he tell her mom about their relationship?

There was a knock on her door and Austin peaked his head in. "Hey, you're awake. Can I can come in?"

She nodded. "Absolutely. I heard you were one of my heroes."

He came over and gave her a warm hug. "I just drove the boat." He sat down next to her. "Dillon wouldn't stop. He was determined to find you."

That thrilled and terrified her. He didn't like that she took risks, at least in his eyes. How would he deal with her crashing her plane in the river? The fact that he'd come after her had to be a good sign of how he felt about her. "I'm grateful."

"I can't believe you crash landed your plane on the river and walked away from that. You are more talented than me."

"No. You would have done the same things. It was all what we learned in our flight school. The hardest part was keeping my panic at bay."

He winked. "But you had so much to live for, right?"

She glanced at her mother, not sure how much she would like hearing about Dillon Hatcher, son of *that* Hatcher woman. "Actually, it was your lighter that kept me alive. I had stuffed it in my jeans pocket when I caught you with it and forgot about it."

Austin's eyes got misty. "I'm glad I was able to help in some small way."

"Is Dillon here?"

Austin sat back. "He went home to change. I'm sure he'll be back. I dropped him off at the ramp and he rode in the ambulance with you. They wanted to admit him too because his clothes were all wet, but he refused. He waited until they were absolutely sure you would be one hundred percent back to normal, then he left."

Her mother patted her hand. "The poor man didn't get any sleep all night. He was here when I arrived this morning. He's nothing like his mother."

She shook her head absently. "No, he's not at all."

"Austin called me and I told your brothers, but when I discovered you were going to be okay, I told them not to come since you'd be home soon. Grey might stop by though, since he's in the area."

She moaned. "Great, just what I need. A lecture from my oldest brother."

Her mother grinned. "I do hope so. It saves me so much time."

Hailey rolled her eyes as Austin laughed. "It's not funny. For a man who professes not to want children, Grey is an expert at making you feel guilty. Be careful or I'll have him lecture you."

Austin put his hands up. "Okay, okay."

With no warning, the hospital door opened and Dillon, complete with black cowboy hat, stood at the end of her bed scowling at her. "What were you thinking?"

Her heart sank as her belly tensed. "I wasn't thinking, I was pilo-"

"No, you weren't thinking. But I've been thinking…a lot.

What's wrong with you? Why do you need to live on the edge? Do you have a death wish?"

"Of course not. I just enjoy trying new things, but I told you, I'm always safe."

"Safe? You call crashing into a river safe? You could be at the bottom of that river right now."

She interrupted, trying to calm him down. "But I'm not because I was trained to handle all kinds of situations."

He gave a harsh laugh, revealing exactly how angry he was. "Well, I'm not. I haven't had the Hailey Pennington training and I resent you making me join you on this ride. You force yourself into my life, make me fall for you, then do this." He waved his hand at the hospital bed.

Her heart started to crack. "I'm sorry. I didn't mean for this to happen. The engine just stopped. I had all the s…" She stopped talking at the fury in his eyes.

"Don't you care about those around you? Do you even think about the people who love you who have to stand on the sidelines or by the phone and just hope that you'll come home safe?"

"I—"

"You don't. All you care about is the new experience, the better view, the excitement of accomplishment. I'm here to tell you, those aren't worth a damn compared to the joy in a little girl's eyes when she sees her own horse or the grin of satisfaction on a grandmother's face when she watches her family devour her special meal. It doesn't even come close to the feeling a man has for a woman he loves as he takes her in his arms and kisses her with all he has in his heart. That's what's worth something."

"I do value that."

"Not enough, Hailey. I'm done. I did my shift, now it's

someone else's turn to watch you. I don't want anything to do with you. I don't need this." He threw his arm to the side then turned on his heel and stormed out.

"That bastard." Austin rose.

Her heart was in her throat, so all she could do was grab her friend's arm and shake her head as her tears started to fall.

Austin looked down at her. "Oh, no. This time I'm looking out for you for real." He pulled his arm from her hand and walked out.

She turned to her mother. "How could he? It wasn't my fault the plane stopped working. He acts like I planned it. I don't understand." Combined with the hurt was anger that he could blame her after all she had done to be safe.

"I do."

Her mother's calm words shocked her and she stared. "You do? Then could you explain it to me?"

"Hailey, that man's in love with you. You mean everything to him, but you just showed him what it would be like if he lost you. He doesn't want to go through that again."

She frowned. "I would never put him through that on purpose."

Her mother shook her head. "So you will never fly a plane or a hot air balloon, or swing on a trapeze, or climb a cliff, or jump a wash again?"

"I will, but I'm always safe about it."

"Honey, I know your 'always safe about it'." Her mother took her hand. "But every day since you were seven years old, I've dreaded the day something went wrong and yesterday it did. It doesn't matter how safe you are when you're dependent upon equipment that can break."

"You dreaded?" That was a strong word for her mother, who was a strong woman herself.

"Yes. Every time you came home excited by a new adventure, I died a little inside."

Now her heart was breaking for a whole different reason. "Oh, mom. Why didn't you tell me I couldn't?"

"We tried that the first time when you wanted to learn to ride, but you were a determined little girl, and did it anyway without proper supervision. That's when your father started to stress the safety issue." Her mother looked away. "We should have been stricter, but you were my little girl. I didn't realize how hard it might be for the man who fell in love with you. I didn't think that he would have to go through what I have."

"It's not your fault mom. I'm a big girl now and I've made my own decisions."

"And what decision will you make about Mr. Hatcher."

She sighed, her heart hurting too much to think clearly on that subject. "I'm not sure I have a decision left to make."

Dillon strode out of the elevator and headed for the lobby doors. He'd thought about it overnight while waiting to hear Hailey's prognosis and he'd made up his mind. He would leave her alive and well.

Now he could get on with his life knowing she was fine the last time he saw her. He wouldn't be the man that waited nervously for his wife to come home, knowing that there was a good chance she wouldn't because some accident was bound to befall her.

It was one thing to enjoy a dangerous sport. It was another to do multiple ones, constantly taking up new ones and for what? He couldn't even call her an adrenaline junkie because she wasn't. She was a level-headed woman who needed something he couldn't give her.

And he'd be damned if he'd lose her again. It was better to let her go than keep her and—

A hand grabbed his shoulder and he twisted away, only to find Austin standing there. "What?"

"You have no right to talk to her that way."

"I don't plan to talk to her in any way again. But you do, don't you? You encourage her to risk her life. You could care less if she dies."

"You have no idea what I do. You have no clue who Hailey really is. She was an idiot to ever set her sights on you."

The anger boiling below the surface was threatening to erupt. He held himself rigid, his hands fisted at his sides. "She set out to do this to me on purpose?"

"Shit man, it's not about you. She just freakin' almost lost her life. Do you have any idea what that's like? Did you just pretend to like her so you could get her in bed?"

It was too much. His fist was swinging before he could even think about the consequences. The man went down on the sidewalk outside the hospital front doors. "Stay away from me and mine."

Turning away, he strode for his car, his anger helping him to bury the pain of losing Hailey forever.

Hailey took a sip of wine as she watched the sunset from her parents' house. The concrete block, adobe porch was comfortably warm, retaining the heat from the sun despite the quickly cooling temperatures. She propped both feet up on the railing and relaxed.

After days of alternately crying and getting pissed, she'd finally found her usual mental balance. The problem was, she was no closer to moving on with her life than she was when Dillon stormed out of the hospital.

Oh, she was pissed at him for decking Austin, but her instinct told her his anger toward her was far stronger. She would have passed off everything he'd said at the hospital as more of his stick-in-the-mud, over protective attitude, but her conversation with her mother hurt and made her re-evaluate.

They hadn't talked about it since. Her mother tiptoed around the subject and her father just scowled, but her brothers were much more vocal. Austin obviously held a grudge because he'd taken her defense to a whole new level, forcing her to forbid him to find Dillon and fight him. He grudgingly agreed, then promptly went next door to her brother's house.

Her brother Cordell had come storming into her bedroom. He lived in his own home on the ranch and just her luck, he arrived during one of her crying bouts. He was the most level-headed of them all and to see him riled up had made her thankful she had him to lean on. He sat on her bed as she explained the whole story.

Unfortunately, he was ready to search out Dillon and teach him a lesson by the time she was finished, so she'd had to extract a promise that he not go near Dillon as well.

Then when Greyson, her oldest brother, came down from Phoenix for Sunday dinner, she'd been careful with her words. Grey was hard to read, keeping his emotions tightly under control. It was partly why he was such a great businessman. He handled all the finances for Ironwood. Still, despite his calm acceptance of her shortened version of the story, she'd still extracted a promise from him not to go near Dillon, just in case. There had been something in his eyes that had her instinct kicking in.

She lifted her wine glass and took another sip, thankful for the shawl she'd grabbed before heading out to watch the sunset as the temperatures were dropping. Growing up in the busy household, she'd often treasured her time alone, but now she wished she had someone to talk to. The problem was that the someone she wanted to talk to was the source of her heartache.

She actually had her youngest brother, the most volatile of the group, to thank for that realization. The family had kept him in the dark about everything on purpose, especially when he couldn't make Sunday dinner. Then when she didn't show up at the Monday charity event at the museum, he'd wanted to know why.

Sure enough, he left the event and bee-lined-it straight for the ranch. Luckily, she wasn't crying at the time. Still, he demanded the whole story which she didn't give him, but it was enough for him to find fault with Dillon and to promise retribution. The more he slandered Dillon, the angrier she became on his behalf. Her arguments defending Dillon surprised her and made Wesley even angrier. He downright refused to promise her anything, and that worried her.

In fact, it worried her so much that she'd thought of driving up to Last Chance to warn him, but that would be a betrayal of her brother. The whole thing was a mess. She did try to call Dillon, but he didn't answer. Her mother waved off Wesley's threats, saying Dillon could handle himself. She was probably right.

She sighed and took another sip of wine. The sunset was spreading its bright pinks across the sky, but there were dark clouds interrupting the scene. It looked like a storm, though that was just for show. Half the time any rain that did fall never made it to the ground, drying up in the desert heat on its way. However, the clouds did make for an interesting sunset.

The backdoor opened behind her and she looked over her shoulder as her mother, wrapped in a warm fleece shawl, came out. "Mind if I join you?"

She smiled. "I'd love it. The sunset is different tonight. Beauty with angry clouds."

"A lot like your heart right now." Her mother pulled the wooden rocking chair over.

She thought about that for a moment. "I think my clouds have become nothing more than empty threats as well."

Her mother started to rock. "Then you've made a decision?"

She shook her head. "No. I don't see that there is a decision to be made. He hates me for scaring him. It doesn't matter how scared I was. In his eyes, I did it all on purpose and he doesn't want to have anything to do with me. You heard him."

Her mother squinched up her nose. "It would have been hard not to."

He *had* been pretty loud, especially for a hospital.

"You will have to show your face in public eventually and when you do, you'll need to know what you'll say." Her mother's voice sounded way too innocent. "Have you talked to your girlfriends?"

She gave her mom the side-eye. "Okay, spill it. What is the press saying?"

"That you were so depressed you tried to kill yourself."

She rolled her eyes. "Good. Then maybe they'll leave me alone. They act like no one ever had a plane accident before."

"Have they found the plane to determine why it stopped working? That would probably help dispel the latest rumor."

She shook her head. "Detective Anderson said the dive team went as deep as they could, but they couldn't find it. I wonder if it got swept farther down stream toward the lake in an undercurrent. It was a very light plane."

Her mother frowned at the news. "I'm concerned if this rumor grows, you'll never have a chance at love again."

She chuckled. "Mom, you are an optimist. I don't want to find another man. I'm still in love with Dillon."

"Oh, but you'll get over that. You have to since he doesn't want to have anything to do with you."

Her heart sank. "Do you really think there's no way for me to get him to forgive me?"

Her mother's eyes widened if fake surprise. "Forgive you? But you didn't do anything wrong."

"I think I did. I owe him an apology at the least." She gave her mom a sheepish smile. "I think I owe you an apology, too. All those years I was having fun, enjoying new adventures, I never thought how worried you would be. Dillon was right. I was selfish."

"Oh, honey. You weren't selfish. All your life you've given to others."

"But to the people that mattered most, I was selfish. I've been thinking a lot about what you said in the hospital, and you're right. For me, it wasn't the excitement so much as conquering something difficult. I should have tried to master calculus like Greyson or cattle breeding like Cord, but I wanted something of my own. It was stupid."

Her mom leaned over and clasped her hand. "You are not stupid. You simply didn't have all the information on which to base a smart decision. Part of this is my fault. Instead of giving in to your desires, I could have nudged you toward other pursuits like embroidery."

She pulled her head back. "Embroidery? Really mom?"

"Don't brush it off so quickly, young lady. You try getting every tiny stitch to look perfect without a mess in the back. Trust me, it's impossible."

She laughed. "Maybe I should."

They sat in companionable silence as the sun's rays

completely disappeared and the sky darkened. She'd been afraid that her accident would ruin sunsets for her, but they didn't. She had too many happy memories of them, the last one of being with Dillon. What was he doing right now?

"You know, honey. Getting Dillon back would be a challenge to conquer."

She looked at her mom. "A challenge? That's putting it mildly. That would be a mountain higher than Everest. That would be like tightrope walking while juggling four flaming batons. That's not a challenge, that's an impossibility."

Her mother's lips quirked up. "That's never stopped you before." Rising, her mother pulled the rocking chair back to its spot against the house then patted her shoulder. "Think about it. That man loves you like I want to see you be loved."

She looked up at her mother. "You think so?"

"I know so."

Dillon chalked his cue and focused on the ball, ignoring the sound of the televisions and conversations among the bar patrons. Bringing his stick back, he gently hit the ball. The solid nine ball teetered on the edge of the side pocket then fell in.

"You're on fire tonight, Dillon. I'm going for a beer."

He set his pool stick against the wall and pulled out the balls. Setting them in the rack, he lifted it off and hung it back on the wall. He looked at his watch. The call Cole got must have been more than a false alarm. That meant he might not show at all.

Dillon picked up his beer and took a swig. He wouldn't be surprised if one of his cousins showed up instead. He should resent the constant company all three of them had decided he needed, but he was too happy to have anything and anyone take his mind off of Hailey.

Even his mother's call asking him to come home had been welcome, if just to have someone keep him focused for a while. He'd actually dragged out the conversation, asking about Salud, who as it turned out had foaled. They'd have a new mare for breeding if she turned out like her mother.

It had been especially nice to inform his mother that he wouldn't be home because he hadn't found a wife yet. The silence on the other end had been deafening until she started to suggest one of her favorite picks. That was when he suddenly had to go because he had to help Trace bring in the horses.

Seeing that the man he'd been playing pool with was still waiting for his drink, he grabbed his stick and took a few practice shots. The bar wasn't exceptionally busy on a Wednesday night, but the game was on and Cutter, the bartender, had a tendency to get distracted.

He'd just made a pretty good corner shot when he noticed he had company on the other side of the pool table. Looking up, he found Austin, his eye an ugly yellow and green color, with three other men. He had to be kidding.

He stood, his pool stick still in his hand, one end resting on the floor. "You don't look so good, Austin."

"That's okay because I'm feeling very good."

He raised his brows but didn't say anything. Let the man come up with his own repartee.

"I thought you'd like to meet some good friends of mine. "This is Greyson," he pointed to a man in an expensive suit, "Cordell," who was a cowboy, his jeans showing some dust, "and Wesley." That man had a championship belt buckle, but his cowboy hat was some designer type thing.

He was about to tip his hat in fake cordiality when the

names sent off warning bells in his head. He scowled instead. "Hailey's brothers."

The one named Wesley scowled right back at him. "You didn't think you could break our sister's heart and get away with it, did you?"

He snorted. The man had it upside down and backwards. "That woman doesn't give a shit about anyone." *Except maybe the homeless, animals, children, the elderly*—He shoved the thought aside.

"Whoa, Wes." The one named Cordell held the other one back. "We know that's not true." Cordell pierced him with his gaze. "And so do you."

The brother in the suit spoke. "Which is why we're here."

If they thought he'd go and apologize, they'd be waiting until the day the sun didn't rise. "And why *are* you here?"

Cordell spoke. "We want your word that you will stay away from Hailey."

That was easy to give, but he didn't plan to be bullied into anything.

"And that you don't say anything about your relationship with her to the press." At Greyson's explanation, it became clear. Hailey had sent them up to save her reputation. If the public knew she'd been seeing Beverly Hatcher's son, she'd probably be embarrassed.

"And you can't tell Hailey we came here." The one named Wesley appeared to add the comment for good measure.

Austin looked at the glitzy cowboy. "I think if we have his word he'll stay away from Hailey, that will cover it."

Wesley shook his head. "Ever heard of phones?"

All four looked at him expectantly. There were two ways he could play this. Agree and get on with his lackluster evening. Or refuse and have the chance to let out his anger and frustration on them before being beaten to a pulp. He let a slow smile form on his lips. "I refuse."

Greyson and Austin appeared surprised. Cordell was obviously concerned, but Wesley grinned. "I was hoping you'd say that." The man put a knee on the table, ready to come at him, but Greyson held his collar.

The bar patrons were oblivious to what was happening, which meant no help there, but at this point he didn't give a damn. Then the door to the bar opened and he re-thought his options.

Greyson shook his head. "I think you should reconsider. Do you have a sister at home?"

He shook his head. "Nope."

Austin grinned. "No, but he has sisters-in-law, all who like Hailey, by the way."

His gut wrenched at the reminder. That was probably why none of the women had spent more than three minutes in his presence, except Riley, but she hadn't been involved with Hailey at all. Were the women mad at him or did they not want to rub salt in his wound. He shrugged. "They're my cousins and brother's problems."

"Dillon, is this a private party or can anyone join?" At Cole's voice, the four men turned.

He grinned for the first time all night. "Speaking of my brother, this is Cole."

Behind Cole were four other men dressed in the fire department t-shirts. It was an impressive sight.

Cole nodded. "And these are my men." His tone of voice was authoritative. The four men with large biceps stretching their shirt sleeves gave one nod in unison. Hell, it looked like a damned Special Forces unit.

He dropped his smile and spoke to his brother. "I was just playing pool. I could use some good competition."

Hailey's brothers looked at him, their mission a complete failure and they knew it. Greyson spoke for them. "We were just leaving." He pierced Dillon with an intense gaze he didn't expect. "I hope you'll think about what we said." There was a promise and a threat in that look that he wasn't oblivious to and his hackles rose.

But before he could respond, the four walked through his brothers' men and exited the bar.

"Grab us some beers guys." Cole waved toward the bar then faced him. "What the fuck was that about?"

He took a deep breath as his adrenaline rush dissipated, leaving him with a feeling of emptiness. He shrugged. "Just Hailey's brothers and Austin threatening me. They wanted me to promise to stay away from her."

Cole's eyes widened. "And you didn't?"

"Hell, no. I'm not going to be bullied into doing anything."

"Is that the only reason?"

Cole's stare was penetrating, so he turned away and grabbed the chalk. "I thought we were here to play pool."

The last thing he wanted to think about was Hailey and the real reason he wouldn't promise to stay away from her. He had to forget her. She was alive and whoever she found to love her would take care of her. He had to believe that and move on.

But the idea of another man in her life gnawed at his insides and wouldn't let go.

Chapter Fourteen

Hailey took the dirt road to Last Chance slowly to spare her little Beetle as much pain as possible, but she itched to get there. Damn, her stupid brothers. They were so going to regret confronting Dillon. Now he'd be even more resistant to her.

What the hell had they been thinking to make Dillon promise not to see her? That Wes had bragged to her about it just infuriated her. She would come up with a fitting punishment for every single one of them, including Austin. He was the last person she'd expected to come up with such a dumb idea. Fatherhood had seriously played with his brain.

As she pulled into the yard, she sucked in her breath. Dillon's truck was parked there, which meant he was around somewhere. Luckily, Dr. Jenna's truck was there, too. When she'd called Jenna, she'd asked if she could visit her horses, though they weren't hers yet. That was another hurdle she had to get over, convincing Cole she wanted them.

As she exited her vehicle, she could see a couple trucks at Cole's house. His cousins were probably working over there, but in reality, they could all be anywhere on the ranch. Wiping her sweaty palms on her jeans, she headed for the barn, her warm blue sweater suddenly a bit too warm.

Walking inside, she inhaled the scent of hay as she reminded herself that Jenna had been happy she called and hadn't sounded angry at all.

When she stopped at Phoenix and Nizhoni's stall she caught her breath. Dillon was holding Phoenix's head as Jenna examined the healing wound on the side of his face. Nizhoni wasn't just watching, but crowding Jenna.

Dillon didn't notice her because he had his back to her, but Jenna did. "Oh good, you're here. Can you grab a halter and slip it on mama here? She's really getting in the way."

Dillon looked over his shoulder and stared. "What are you doing here?"

She wanted to tell him, like she had when she first arrived, that she was here about the horses, but as much as she wanted to see them, she wanted to see him more. "I came to see you."

He let go of Phoenix and Jenna huffed. "I can see I'm not going to get this done now." Grabbing her bag, she brushed past Dillon and exited the stall, giving Hailey a wink as she passed.

"I don't want to see you. I thought I made that clear."

She nodded. "You did, but I had to see you to apologize."

That caught his attention. "For what? Sending your brothers? Don't bother."

"Send my brothers? I didn't send them. The idiots took it upon themselves to come up here and I promise you, they're going to pay for that stunt."

"Whatever. Like I said. It doesn't matter." He walked to the stall door, opened it, and stepped out into the main aisle of the barn. "If that's all." He motioned toward the exit with his hand.

"No, it isn't. I still need to apologize for scaring you. I'm sorry."

"Why?"

She cocked her head. "Why? You mean why am I apologizing for scaring you?"

He crossed his arms over his chest. "Yes."

At least he hadn't walked out yet. "Because I understand now what you went through."

"No, you don't. I thought you were dying, lying in the desert somewhere with rattlesnake bite poison slowly creeping through your body. I thought you had crashed your plane in the middle of nowhere and were slowly bleeding to death. I thought you were at the bottom of the lake, caught inside your plane as it filled up with water."

She swallowed at the images he painted. He was right, she hadn't realized truly what he'd gone through. She forced herself to speak past her dry throat. "I was afraid of all those things, though the snakebite hadn't occurred to me. As I panicked after the engine shut off, there was one thought that brought my brain back online." She paused to see if he would ask what it was, but he didn't.

"I thought I'd never see you again if I didn't calm down and get control of the situation as best I could. Then once I was ashore, I was so scared and cold I just kept hoping you would find me. You, more than anything else, kept me going. You were my reason for staying alive."

He didn't say anything, just looked at her as if trying to decide if she was telling the truth.

"Since that night, I've had a long time to think. For the first time I looked at why I feel the need to fly planes and hot air balloons and hang-glide."

"You hang-glide?" He looked at her in utter disbelief.

She could hide it, but she needed to put everything on the table. "That and many other activities that you would not be happy with."

He went back to scowling at her.

"I didn't realize what it was like for others who loved me to know I was doing these things. My mom confessed that it scared her to death. Her actual phrase is that she 'died a little inside every time'. I was clueless. She'd never told me. But I'm not laying blame at her feet. I'm a big girl and I should have thought about that. I never had anyone I loved attempt the activities I did, so it never occurred to me."

He raised his brows. "Did?"

She licked her lips. "Yes, past tense. I don't want to hurt those who love me anymore. I may take all the safety precautions, but those activities include equipment, and it can fail as I have learned." She looked away. "When I saw the face of that hiker, swollen with lake water, her eyes lifeless, I saw myself. It scared the hell out of me."

Dillon dropped his arms. "But that is part of who you are."

She shook her head. "No, it's not. Like I said. I reflected on why I love to do everything most people consider dangerous and I don't feel a rush when I'm piloting the hot air balloon. I feel the rush after I've landed it perfectly. I have a need to master difficult things."

Dillon studied her now. "And you think you can be happy mastering difficult things that aren't life threatening?"

She grinned. "I know I can. My mother jokingly mentioned embroidery. She was right. It *is* hard but look." She pointed to the embroidered duck on her blue sweater. "I did this!"

His eyebrows rose in disbelief. "Embroidery?"

She nodded, even now feeling happy to show off her accomplishment. "Yes. I never thought to look at a skill like that as a challenge, but now that I have, there's a whole world of possibilities. I want to learn pottery, glass blowing, chess, and darts."

He looked askance at her. "And you would be happy with non-life-threatening activities?"

"Yes, but if I run out of ideas and feel a need to do something a little risky like survival training, I thought that we could do it together, or you could be involved, like you were with my first solo balloon flight. I was excited when I landed because I'd mastered it, but having you there to witness it and share my joy made it twice as exhilarating."

He stood there staring at her like she was either an angel or crazy. Maybe she was. She didn't care anymore as long as she could have him in her life. "Of course, none of this matters if you don't love me as much as I love you." There, she'd finally said it.

At her declaration, he finally moved. Taking the two steps between them, he cupped her face in his hands. "I do love you. I can't stand the thought of losing you again."

She smiled. "You'll never have to worry about that, I promise."

His lips came down on hers and she melted into him, loving his taste, his hard body, his heart.

As their tongues tangled she looped her arms around his neck and moaned.

Dillon broke the kiss when they were both almost breathless. "We need to find a room."

She laughed. "I agree. There's another thing I want to master. That's being a mother."

He froze.

Oh, shit. Did she overstep again?

"How soon did you want to work on that?"

Surprised, she gave him a shy smile. "We can practice now, but I think in a couple months we could give it a try."

The smile that spread across his face was breathtaking. "Hailey Pennington, will you marry me?"

Joy exploded in her heart for one brief moment before reality set in. "What about your mother?"

Dillon truly growled this time. "To hell with my mother. This is about us. Will you marry *me*?"

Happiness filled her soul at his declaration. "Yes. Definitely, yes."

He hugged her to him and spun her around before setting her on her feet and kissing her breathless once again. When they finally broke apart. She grinned. "Now about that room…"

He laughed. "I know where there is one nearby." Taking her hand, he walked her out of the barn.

They were half way across the suspiciously empty yard when her curiosity got the best of her. "How do you want to tell your mother?"

He shrugged. "I don't know. First, I need to get you a ring so we can make it official. I know my mother will—" A slow triumphant smile spread across his face.

"What Dillon? What?"

The screen door opened and Trace strolled out. "Hey, are you guys going to get hitched or what?"

Dillon nodded. "Yup."

Trace stared in shock for a moment then ran back into the house. They could hear the cheer that went up inside the kitchen from where they stood.

He pulled her in his arms and gazed at her with love in his eyes.

She felt tears of joy welling up and she laid her hand on his cheek. "I told you I learn from my mistakes."

He turned his face into her palm and kissed it. "And I promise to always be your safety net."

She pulled his head down for a loving kiss just seconds before the screen door slammed against the outside of the house and the family poured out. She laughed and turned toward her soon-to-be new family but kept her hand in Dillon's. She was never letting him go.

Epilogue

Dillon held Hailey's hand as he turned down the paved road that led to his parents' ranch. He felt the hard stone of her engagement ring against his fingers. His whole family and Hailey had agreed with his plan for his mother, which was important. There would be some minor sacrifices on his and Hailey's part, but they all deemed them worth it.

"Wow, you have a paved parking lot, too?"

He slowed the truck as they entered under the sign declaring it Morning Creek Ranch. "Yes, mother insisted. She said we needed to look like a first-class breeder. I've been to many first-class breeders and only a handful have paved parking lots, but that's my mother. She's all about impressions and appearances.

"Is it wrong that I'm excited by this?" Hailey squeezed his hand.

He parked the truck then looked at her. Her smile was wide and happy and she looked fantastic in her brown leather coat, green turtleneck that matched her eyes, jeans and cowboy boots. The only thing missing was a stylish cowboy hat. "No. This has been a long time in coming and don't forget, she's still getting her dream come true, so it's not wrong."

She nodded, still smiling as she pulled the engagement ring

off and tucked it into the front pocket of her jeans. "Okay, let's do this."

He jumped out of the truck and opened her door. "I hope you're a good actress."

She frowned. "How's this for acting. Do I look thrilled to be here?"

He chuckled. "No." He reached for her hand but she hid it behind her back.

"Uh-uh. Remember, we aren't madly passionately in love."

"Right. That's the hardest part to remember." He opened his arm for her to proceed him and followed her to the front door. He hadn't believed himself homesick, but at the scent of his mother's garden along the front porch and the views of the horses in the corrals, his stomach clenched with yearning.

Hailey stopped at the front door. "I do hope you show me around afterwards."

"Of course. Ready?"

She nodded and he opened the door for her.

When they stepped inside he could smell the juniper and sage scent his mother loved to fill the house with. "Mother, I'm home!"

Footsteps sounded on the center stairs of the open concept great room. "Dillon? Is that you?"

He rolled his eyes. "Yes, it's me and I brought a—"

"Oh, my God! It's Hailey Pennington. Please, come in. Come in. I think Susan made some peanut butter chip brownies this morning. Can I get you a cup of tea, coffee, a glass of wine maybe? It's so good to see you. You know I was just talking to the Mayor's daughter the other day and commenting on how I hadn't seen you and here you are."

They followed his mother through the large kitchen to the

area with the oak table that sat twenty, while she kept up a steady stream of discourse.

As they walked by the kitchen counter, he grabbed up his mother's phone and stuffed it into his rear pocket.

His mother pulled out a chair for Hailey. "Please sit. Tell me what I can get you."

Hailey smiled politely through the entire monologue, but he wasn't that good an actor. His mother irritated him so much that just her breathing was enough to have his cheek twitching, which made him feel guilty as hell.

"Nothing for me. Please sit. We need to talk to you about an important matter."

His mother gave him the 'Oh really' look. "We?"

"Yes, mother. Please sit."

She finally did, though she didn't stop talking.

Hailey grabbed his mother's arm. "Please Mrs. Hatcher, this is serious matter and we need your undivided attention."

"Oh." She closed her mouth, obviously insulted and not taking it seriously at all.

He counted to ten to keep his anger under control. "Because you have been relentless about marrying me off to some high society woman, I've finally decided to acquiesce."

His mother's eyes lit with delight and she opened her mouth, but he held up his hand. "However, I have an important stipulation, which if not adhered to by you, will cancel all contracts."

"Contracts?" His mother looked from him to Hailey.

"Yes, Mrs. Hatcher, contracts. As you know I am a very rich woman and to protect the family money, myself and my brothers must fulfill certain obligations before we marry if we want to continue to receive funds from our trusts."

His mother looked confused. "Marry? I mean, of course

you do. Marry? Do you mean to marry my son?" His mother's shock was fascinating.

"Yes, mother. That is why we're here." Sometimes she just didn't concentrate. "As I said, I am bending to your wishes and Miss Pennington has agreed to an arrangement."

An ear-splitting scream filled the house and he cringed, his cheek starting to twitch.

"Oh, my God! You've made me the happiest woman on Earth!" His mother got up and grabbed Hailey and hugged her. "I have to tell Cynthia and Rebecca and— where did I put my phone?"

"Mother, please. We're trying to talk to you."

She waved him off. "Oh, I know sweetie, but this is important."

He followed her into the kitchen and took her by the shoulders. "You have a very important guest sitting over there, and I don't think you want her to call the whole thing off, do you?"

His mother's eyes grew round.

He raised his brows at her to indicate that that could happen.

"Oh, you are so right." She laid a hand on his arm before turning back to the table. "I'm sorry Hailey. Please continue."

As his mother took her seat, he rejoined them.

"As I was saying Mrs. Hatcher, I—"

"Oh, please. Call me Mom."

Dillon grasped the back of Hailey's chair to keep from yelling.

"As I was saying, Mrs. Hatcher. I have an obligation to fulfill before I can marry or I lose my money. Therefore, we cannot let anyone know about the engagement. If word gets out before I'm married, I'll lose my funding. I can't allow that to happen."

He could tell his mother really wasn't listening. She was thinking about what she'd tell her friends.

Hailey continued on. "If word gets out prior to the wedding I will simply call the whole thing off and go on my way. I will not lose that money for anything or anyone."

She was so convincing, he almost believed her, but not only did he know she never thought about money, but he was also privy to the fact that there were no stipulations. They'd actually come up with the idea together while watching a Christmas movie, though why they were on before Thanksgiving, he didn't know.

"Do you understand, Mrs. Hatcher?"

His mother nodded absently.

Hailey looked at him in concern and she had a right to be. His mother wasn't paying attention. She tended to ignore things she didn't want to hear.

"Mother. Mother!"

"What? You don't have to yell at me dear. I'm right here."

He sighed. "Did you hear what Hailey said? You can't tell anyone about the engagement."

"What? Why?" She looked to Hailey for an explanation.

When Hailey's explanation was heard, his mother looked to him and gave him a sly smile. "Oh, I'm sure you two wouldn't call off the wedding just because someone heard about the engagement."

"In a heartbeat." Hailey looked sternly at his mother and he suddenly could see her as a mother herself. His chest warmed knowing she had that side to her.

His mother looked to him. "Really? You'd let that happen?"

He shrugged. "Of course. I'm only marrying her to get you off my back and come back to Morning Creek and help dad with the breeding."

She appeared to think about it all for a moment. Then a sly smile curved her lips. Shit, what had they not thought of.

His mother reached over and patted Hailey's hand. "You know, we have plenty of money. You can tell the world about your engagement. You don't need your money."

He felt his cheek start to twitch and rubbed his hand over his face.

Hailey responded immediately. "But I *do* need my family. They are everything to me. I think I failed to mention that along with losing my trust, I would also be disowned."

"Disowned?" His mother's high voice as she digested that piece of information had him fighting a smile. Damn, Hailey was good.

His mother took a deep breath. "No one can know? As in anyone?"

Hailey nodded. "Correct."

"Can I tell my husband?"

He jumped in. "No."

His mother had tears in her eyes. "But I can't keep a secret from him."

Hailey looked up at him and nodded.

"Very well." At his mother's elated look, he qualified it. "I'll tell dad. You can talk to him about it, but if anyone overhears, a stable hand, a mower, the gardener, the wedding is off."

Immediately her face fell. What had she been planning.

Hailey gave his mother a soft smile. "I know this is hard Mrs. Hatcher, but my family is everything to me. If word gets out in any way, I'll have to call it all off and move on. I hope I can trust you to keep the secret."

His mother's face grew determined, her chin coming up as she looked at Hailey. "I promise. How long do you need this kept?"

He jumped in. "One year."

His mother's shoulders slumped. "A year?" The words came out in a whine.

Hailey stood. "Yes. Can you do that? If you can then I will be your daughter-in-law."

His mother stood, her resolve back in place. "I would love to welcome you to our family. If a year of secrecy is necessary, then that's what I'll do."

"Good." Hailey gave his mother a real smile.

He took his mother's phone out of his pocket and placed it on the table. Then looked at his mother. "My future is in your hands."

He turned to Hailey. "Shall we tell my father?"

"Of course."

They strode out of the kitchen and he led Hailey to the back door. Once outside, he glanced in the dining room window. His mother was stroking her phone. He sincerely hoped she kept silent. He and Hailey were willing to live in sin if necessary to teach his mother a lesson, but he would prefer to give his children his name. He'd have to talk to her about a secret marriage if it came to that.

After telling his father who was very happy for him and actually pleased with the secret arrangement, they headed back to his truck. They were silent until he pulled out of the parking area and they had turned the first curve in the road.

"That was fantastic!" Hailey broke into a smile and grabbed his hand. "I didn't realize how truly desperate your mother was. I even felt sorry for her when it looked like she was going to cry."

He shook his head. "Don't. She does that whenever she wants to get her way because my father could never deal with tears."

"Oh, wow. Do you think she'll keep her mouth closed?"

"I have no idea. It all depends on which is more important to her, having you for a daughter-in-law or bragging to her friends. If she thinks about it, she'll realize she'll look like an idiot if she brags and then the wedding is off, but she doesn't always think clearly about things like that."

Hailey squeezed his hand. "Only time will tell. Now on to the next punishment."

He grinned, feeling no guilt at all about Hailey's plans for her brothers and Austin. "Is Austin coming?"

She grinned. "He sure is. I made sure of that by making arrangements for his babysitter to be available first. Let's just say she's getting a little bonus."

He laughed. "You are a devious woman."

"Only when those I love cross me."

"That won't happen with me, but you never know what our children will do."

Her face took on a soft look. "Well, there are exceptions to every rule."

That was true. She was the exception to his own rule about not marrying anyone his mother chose. He was grateful that he'd made that exception.

"I've been thinking."

He grinned, always interested in her next idea. "Yes."

"About Nizhoni and Phoenix. I don't think I should bring them down to Ironwood, only to have to move them to Morning Creek a few months later. I think we should let them stay at Last Chance until we're married. What do you think?"

What he thought was that he already felt happily married, making a decision together. He was such a sap. "I think that's a good idea. It will give Phoenix time to grow and Nizhoni time to trust people again."

She looked over at him. "I don't think Cole would have let me buy them if I hadn't agreed to marry you."

He shook his head. "No, my brother isn't like that. He's very objective about what's right and wrong. Drove me crazy when we were younger and he wouldn't side with me sometimes because he knew I was in the wrong. With the rescue horses, he will always put their welfare first. If he felt you would take care of them after inspecting your stables and talking to your staff, he'd let you buy them. The only difference was he didn't come down to do an inspection because he could count on me to do it."

She chuckled. "That's good to know. But now that we are going to bring them to Morning Creek, he'll probably feel even more comfortable." She didn't say anymore for a few miles, so when she did speak again, he was all ears. "Maybe we can give Phoenix to our first child."

His chest tightened at the idea and he glanced her way. "I think that would be perfect." It wasn't the first time she'd brought up children in the last few days.

That she wanted to be a mother to his children had opened a whole part of himself he was still learning. He found himself asking Logan more questions about raising Charlotte and even thinking about which room at Morning Creek would make a good child's room. He'd always figured he'd be a dad one day, but having Hailey as his fiancée made it more real.

It wasn't far to Ironwood from Morning Creek and they arrived long before it was time for the family dinner. It was at first a little awkward finally meeting Hailey's dad, but her mom was genuine in her welcome, and he soon relaxed.

As each brother arrived, his mood became lighter. They'd all been told about the engagement and to keep it under wraps for the time being, so they were the ones feeling awkward around him, and he didn't mind a bit. Austin's eye had healed, but he still stayed on the other side of the room.

Once everyone had arrived, Hailey stood in the middle of the large living room. "May I have your attention before we eat?"

"Are you going to make a speech, sis?" Wesley laughed.

"No, I'm handing out a punishment."

That had all four men sobering. He should stop smiling, but he couldn't help it. His soon-to-be wife had landed on the perfect plan.

Greyson finally spoke. "What's the offense?"

She scowled at him. "As if you don't know. I told each and every one of you not to contact Dillon, but what did you do? You immediately when up north and did just that. And then to make it worse, you told him to stay away from me. How dare you determine what is best for me?"

"We were just looking out for you, Hellion." Cord held out his hands. "You can't blame us for that."

Her gaze swiveled to him. "Oh, yes I can. It would have been one thing if you took it upon yourselves without talking to me. But every one of you spoke to me first and promised not to approach Dillon."

"I didn't." Wes brought her attention to him. "I would never disrespect you by breaking a promise."

"Right, you'd disrespect me by refusing to do as I requested and butting into my love life."

Dillon smirked. He was really enjoying this. Hailey was magnificent when riled. He'd just make sure he stayed in her good graces.

"She's right." Austin spoke up. "We did interfere when she didn't want us to and I doubt any of us would want her to do the same to us."

Cord and Grey nodded, but Wes disagreed. "I'd be happy to have her interfere in my love life. Maybe then I'd have one."

"Wesley." The stern tone came from Mrs. Pennington and Wes lost his smile.

"Okay, Hellion. Give it to use straight. We can take it." Cord looked down the line of men before returning his gaze to her. "What's our punishment?"

Somewhat appeased, Hailey's stance relaxed and she took a sip of her wine as she looked at each man. "Since my wedding to Dillon will be a circus of reporters and photographers, I can't see getting married here in Arizona. I need a place where no one knows the Pennington name, so I've decided on an island wedding."

"Oh, that sounds lovely." Mrs. Pennington looked at her husband, who nodded in agreement.

She looked back. "Thank you, mom." She faced the men again. "So, I'm sending each of you to a different island to check out a venue I've picked out as a possible place to get married."

"What? I don't know anything about weddings." Wes's exclamation was agreed upon by all the men if the head nodding was any indication.

"Then you better learn. This is an important decision for me, so I need you to give it your full attention." She turned her focus on Cord. "Since you were the first to promise me you wouldn't interfere, you will go as soon as Mom and Dad get back from Spain."

The other men looked at Cord with sympathy in their eyes. To his credit, he took it like a man. "Where are you sending me?"

Hailey smiled. "To Momi, a Hawaiian island! There's this boutique hotel there that looks perfect for our two families, but I know pictures and websites don't tell the whole story. So I need you to check it out. I want a full report on everything from cleanliness to table settings to other things to do besides getting married."

She looked back at him, her excitement transferring to him. He rose and joined her, standing behind her as he looked at each man in turn. "This is important to her. She's depending on you, so don't let her down."

"She's our sister, we never let her down." Wes's attitude was grating.

He couldn't resist replying. "If that were true, we wouldn't be standing here right now, would we?"

The man grabbed up his beer and took a swig.

Hailey looked up at him. "I think we're done here. Shall we go out on the porch until dinner is ready?"

"I would be happy to." Offering her his arm, he walked her outside, the warmth of the day already waning. He knew his fiancée, and she was anxious to let out her excitement.

No sooner had the door closed then she turned around and faced him. "I loved that. Did you see their faces?"

He smiled. "I did. It was perfect revenge."

She moved up to him and pointed her finger into his chest. "Now, it's not revenge, it's punishment to help them learn from their mistakes."

He grasped her finger and held it in his hand. "It's punishment from you, but revenge from me. If my brother hadn't walked into the Black Mustang, I can guarantee you I'd still be in the hospital right now."

She sobered. "I'm thankful to Cole because I'm not sure I could ever forgive my brothers and Austin if they had done that to you."

He kissed her finger then dropped it to loop his arms around her. "Then I'm doubly glad because I don't think your brothers and Austin are actually bad people, and I'd hate to cause a rift between you and your family.

She sighed as she laid her cheek against his chest, turning her face to the final rays of the sunset. "I'm so glad I took a chance at Last Chance."

He grinned. "Me too."

They stood in silence, watching the changing sky. He was one lucky man that she had been so persistent about getting to know him. He would be grateful every day of the rest of his life that he had dared to love her.

And the rest of their lives started right now.

The End

Read on for an excerpt of *Aloha Cowboy*.

Chapter One

Leah Pennington picked up her pace at the sound of a guest's raised voice in the open-air lobby of the Puanani Resort.

Who was at the front desk today? Oh no, it was Ulu. He was probably making his interest in the male guest far too clear. Stepping around the corner she sucked in her breath.

Aloha cowboy. Emotions swirled within her, from excitement at seeing the back of a broad-shouldered cowboy who reminded her of home, to fear he might be someone she knew.

She continued toward the front desk, her professional persona in place, and glanced at the man next to the cowboy, his black hair tied back in a short ponytail. Two such muscular men visiting Momi would be news and all over this side of the island by tomorrow morning. Giving Ulu a quick reprimand with her gaze, she stepped behind the counter to face the men with a confident smile.

She held her smile by force of habit, barely stopping her eyes from widening in surprise. The two men, around her age, couldn't look more opposite. The cowboy's deep green eyes were crinkled at the corners as if he found something amusing. His nose was straight, his lips a pale mauve and his chin hard. As he doffed his hat at her appearance, he revealed very short brown hair, which though shaved close above his ears was thick about his head. In his white shirt with western pockets and new blue jeans, his appearance sent a pang of homesickness tugging at her heart.

The other man, just as tall and broad, had bright blue eyes

shadowed by his dark lowered brows. His nose was slender, though also straight, his lips fuller and his cheek bones were far more prominent. The darkness of his hair was accented by his tight black t-shirt and blue jeans. He was the first to address her.

"There's been a mistake. I sincerely hope you can rectify it." The irritated tone was no surprise since he'd been dealing with Ulu, who continued to gaze at the men as if they were his own personal eye-candy.

What was a surprise was the guest's accent, which she couldn't place. "I'm sure we can take care of everything." She moved her gaze to Ulu and raised her brow. "Let me see what we have."

Ulu pouted before reluctantly turning away and disappearing into the small office behind the counter. She had no doubt he would be glued to the two-way window at one end to further ogle their guests.

She stood in front of the reservation screen and quickly read it through. Pennington? Her heart leapt again. Everyone in Arizona knew that name, the very same as her own. She wanted to ask if he was one of *the* Penningtons, but since she hated people asking her that, she kept her question to herself. She looked directly at the cowboy. "Mr. Pennington, I see you have the honeymoon suite."

He grinned sheepishly. "Yes, my sister, Hailey booked the room. She sent me to scout your resort as a possible place for her to hold her wedding."

She smiled more warmly at that exciting news. "Oh, she would love it here. I'll be happy to show you what we can do for her." A wedding at the Puanani would be good for their precipitous bottom line. Auntie would be thrilled if they could make it happen.

"Let me see what the problem might be." She looked over the reservation, but there was only one name. Understanding dawned. Ulu thought the two men were gay, which was right up his alley. She hoped he hadn't ruined their chance to impress the men. He was too forward since his last break up. She'd have to talk to Auntie about his behavior…again.

Just to make sure, she looked at the dark-haired gentleman. "I'm guessing you two are not together?"

"Yes."

"No." The cowboy raised an eyebrow at his friend.

She cocked her head. "I think I'm confused."

Mr. Pennington smiled at her, showing perfect white teeth. She wasn't sure if the yearning in her belly was for home or him. She blinked quickly to clear her head.

The cowboy looked at her name tag before speaking. "Leah, we are together in that we're friends and traveling together, but we expected there to be two rooms."

"Oh, then perhaps there are." She bent her head and prepared to type. "What's the other name?"

"Phillipe du Bourbon," the other man replied. As his deep voice with the accent hit her, she bit her lip to keep from chuckling.

Bourbon? Really? She keyed in the name and came up with no reservation. Shoot, not good. She quickly moved through a few more screens, finally finding what she needed—an open room, sort of.

She lifted her head and smiled at Mr. Pennington before moving her gaze to Mr. du Bourbon. "The reservation was only for one room, but there's no problem. I have another I can give you. How long are you staying?" Her gaze drifted back toward the cowboy, probably because he kept his sense of humor, and it was easier looking at a smile than a frown.

He replied for them. "I'm here for a couple weeks, but Phil will be staying longer, right?"

Phil nodded. "At least a month. Is your free room available that long?"

She nodded. "It is, but I'm afraid it's in another building. However, we are a very small resort, only twenty rooms, so it won't be hard to find each other."

"Is there a chance you have a normal room for me in that building? Maybe something less expensive?" The cowboy, who was quite tall, looked toward the computer as if he could see what was listed there. "I don't know what my sister was thinking."

She shook her head. She didn't want him to know that the room she'd found for his friend had been on tentative hold for a personal friend of hers and was the only one left. "Not at the moment, but I might in a few days if you want to move."

"Yes. I don't mind moving."

She moved her fingers over the keyboard, making adjustments. She wasn't surprised he wanted a less expensive room. Some of her old friends back home were cowboys and they didn't exactly make a ton of money. Then again, neither did she. It also meant he'd answered her question. He was definitely not one of the original families who settled in Arizona. *Those* Penningtons were ridiculously rich.

When the computer gave her the confirmation screen, she smiled. "All set. Let me get you your keys and a map of the property. We're small, but we have a lot to offer."

She looked down to pull a couple maps from the shelf below when a hand touched her shoulder. She ducked beneath it and turned to face whoever was behind her. "Oh, Auntie Loke." She turned toward their new guests. "Gentlemen, this is Auntie Loke, one of the owners of The Puanani."

The older woman grinned widely, her gaze quickly taking in the eye-candy in front of her. "It's a pleasure to have you."

Leah handed each man a map. "Auntie, Mr. Pennington's sister has sent him to investigate the Puanani as a possible place for her wedding."

Auntie's gaze turned calculating. She was a shrewd business woman and hadn't kept the boutique hotel going by missing opportunities. "Pennington? Are you from Arizona?"

The cowboy nodded. "Yes, Ma'am."

"Then you must know Leah."

Oh shoot. Leah sucked in her breath.

"I'm sorry ma'am. The state has millions of people in it. I'm afraid I just met Leah."

Auntie shook her head. "I thought with the same last names that maybe you were related. Oh well, you know each other now."

The cowboy's gaze snapped to hers. "You're a Pennington as well?"

"Yes. And no, I'm not one of *the* Penningtons."

He laughed. "I see you get that question a lot, too. People seem to think there's only one Pennington family in the whole state."

She nodded before she pulled out two room cards and swiped them through the machine to activate each for the appropriate room.

Auntie scanned the area. "Where's Ulu? He has the front desk today."

Before she could say anything, the man bopped out of the office.

"I'm right here, and I'll be happy to show you the way to your room." He gave Phil a wink.

Leah groaned silently as their guest stiffened.

"Nonsense, you man the desk. That's your job." Auntie swiped up the small folder with the room number and key inside and sauntered out from behind the check-in desk. "I will show…" She glanced back.

Leah supplied the name. "Mr. du Bourbon."

Auntie raised her brows before she gave the man a warm smile. "Is that French?"

The man loosened up for the first time since Leah had seen him. He nodded politely and held his arm out for Auntie. "It is. I am Phillipe, but my friends call me Phil."

As her boss escorted Phil away, she finished inserting the honeymoon suite key into the folder. "Here you go, Mr. Pennington." She held out the folder.

"Please, call me Cord. Let's leave the whole Pennington business behind us." He winked.

Her heart fluttered in her chest just like it had when she was in high school. How dumb was that? She was a grown woman who'd grown up among cowboys. It had to be the reminder of home that caused her breath to catch.

Ulu started to walk past her. "I'd be happy to show you where your room is, Cord."

She stepped back, cutting off his escape from behind the desk. "You heard Auntie."

Ulu pouted as his shoulders fell. "You take all the fun out of my job."

Cord laughed.

She gave him a relieved smile, thrilled he didn't mind Ulu's forwardness. "The suite is at the other end of the property. Would you like me to call a staff member to bring your bag for you?"

He shook his head. "No, just you to lead the way."

She gave him a quick nod before moving out from behind the counter. "It's this way." She opened her arm toward the archway that led to the pool courtyard at the center of the property.

Cord threw his duffle bag over his shoulder, the muscles in his forearm moving in stark relief as he settled it on his back before he donned his hat and gave her a nod.

She turned to focus on their direction, her belly tightening at how attractive he was with his hat on. No wonder Ulu was practically salivating. She didn't have to wonder if Cord followed because the sound of his cowboy boots on the tile was loud enough for the guests by the pool to look.

As she led him around the flower-shaped pool toward the Hibiscus building, a woman in a polka-dot designer bikini, white sun hat and dark glasses rose from her lounge chair and blatantly watched them walk by.

Leah wanted to smack her. It figured that Deidre Snyder would be staying here. At least she was in a building on the near side of the grounds. The woman preferred the Executive suite because it had an adjoining room that allowed her to spread out, as she put it, and it was on the second floor, which gave the best view, according to her.

Finally, they reached the shaded walkway between buildings at the other end of the pool, and Leah halted to explain where they were headed. Cord must not have expected her to stop because when she turned, he grabbed her arm as he walked into her.

At the contact she flinched, and quickly stepped away, breaking his hold.

"I'm sorry." He scanned her as if looking for a wound or something. "Are you okay?"

"I'm fine." She brushed it off without explanation. "Your suite is at the farthest point from the lobby. Are you sure you don't want me to get a staff member for your bag?"

His brows lowered, clearly affronted. "Leah, a saddle weighs more than my clothes."

"Of course. I apologize. We don't get many stateside cowboys here." She turned and headed down a set of flat stones placed strategically to form a pathway over the sandy ground. "In fact, you're the first since I've been here."

He didn't respond until they reached an area of heavy bushes where the path split. "I was hoping to visit a ranch while I'm here. Are there any nearby that wouldn't mind a visit from a 'stateside cowboy'?"

She turned to the left and led him along the path before stopping in front of the honeymoon cottage. *Remain professional. Don't let him see that he rattles you in more ways than one.* "The Pono Ranch isn't too far. I'd be happy to make arrangements for you." She held out her hand for the folder she'd given him. "Once you see this room, you may not want to switch."

He looked over her head at the small building. "If it's that nice, then Hailey will probably love it, which means I won't. My sister and I have opposite tastes." He held out the folder, and she pulled it from him, taking the key out to open the door.

Usually, the bellmen did this. She'd shown guests to a room before, just never the honeymoon suite. As she stepped inside, it suddenly occurred to her how it would look to a cowboy who was not on his honeymoon. The whole suite screamed "love nest" and she became acutely aware of the man behind her.

Cord stepped in as Leah moved aside. Well shit. Wasn't this just the perfect place for a couple of newlyweds. It was one large room with a kitchenette, table for two, loveseat, and huge four-poster bed with gauzy white draping over the top.

Even worse was the hot tub he could see outside on the patio with the ocean view. Trying to ignore the obvious purpose of the room, he looked to the painting on the wall closest to him, but that didn't help. It wasn't erotic by any means, but the suggestion of sex was blatant in the woman's face as her lover kissed her bare shoulder from behind, his hands clasping the silk wrap against her, revealing the hard nubs of her nipples pushing out the material.

"There is a closet over here with a safe, and through the door over there is the toilet." Leah pointed across from the bed where a glass enclosed shower was located in full view of most of the room. Next to it was a sink set against the wall, the only "private" area being the commode.

He moved his gaze to Leah to get his mind off the room, but as she walked toward the sliding glass door, he couldn't help staring at her ass as her hips swayed in her white sleeveless dress with the large purple flower print.

It was the very reason he'd almost knocked her down when she'd stopped, and now, imaging her wearing a thong beneath her form fitting knee-length skirt didn't help his concentration at all. In fact, his jeans began to feel tight.

She opened the sliding door to reveal a huge, secluded patio surround by a half-wall of concrete. Flowering bushes surrounding the patio gave privacy on both sides almost all the way out to the beach where the water lapped at the yellow sand, while floral scents filled the area with a sweetness that wasn't overpowering, but definitely there.

The secluded patio was mostly in shade except at the farthest-most end where Leah stood. The sun there made her strait, shoulder-length brown hair shine with deep red slivers of color that were hidden in normal light. The purple flower behind her right ear paled in comparison.

She turned around and leaned against a gate nestled between the bushes. "As you can see, it has everything a newly-married couple would want, plus it comes with a private butler that can be called upon to arrange any service from massages to a midnight snack to a private sunset cruise."

"I'm more likely to request a pizza for breakfast and a ride to the ranch."

She laughed, the sound as enticing as her voice. "We can make those arrangements, and don't worry, I'll be sure not to assign Ulu to the duty."

Her confidence was attractive, as was her dark brown eyes. So much so that it took him a second to process what she said. "Are you the manager here?"

Her head came up a little higher, her pride in her position obvious. "I am. Graduated from Arizona University, top honors in the hospitality program."

He gave a soft whistle. "That program has a great reputation. No wonder you landed a sweet position here in the Hawaiian Islands."

Her smile faltered as pain flashed in her eyes before she turned and opened the gate. "This walkway will lead you down to the ocean. If you're an early riser, you can catch spectacular sunrises here."

What was that?

Aloha Cowboy

Read on for an excerpt of Riley's Rescue (Last Chance Series: Book 6)

Chapter One

Riley O'Hare stepped out onto the porch of the two-story ranch house of Last Chance Ranch and halted, the screen door still in her hand. "Well, shit."

Letting the door slam behind her, she jogged down the three steps to the hard-packed Arizona dirt and ran for the south corral. Cyclone, their resident Clydesdale, and technically Dr. Jenna's horse, ran circles around the enclosure.

Looking over her shoulder, she scanned the area in front of the house. Only her pick-up truck sat there of the more than four that usually graced the yard. In her peripheral vision, she noticed dust on the dirt road to the ranch, but didn't have time to focus.

It better be Cole. He was supposed to take Cyclone to the abandoned copper mine to pull out some fallen timbers. She'd flatly refused to go anywhere near the decrepit mine, so he'd agreed to do it. It was the perfect chore for Cyclone. If the big horse wasn't given work to do at least every third day, he started breaking things. And she was the one who had to fix them.

Jumping onto the lower rail of the fencing, she waved her arm. "Cyclone! Come here, boy!" She just needed to break up his windup. From what she'd learned, he'd been well-named. The running in circles behavior was the precursor to major damage.

She tried again. "Cyclone!" Putting two fingers to her mouth, she let out a shrill whistle.

The Clydesdale slowed, bouncing his head once and looking at her.

"Come here, boy. I've got work for you."

As if he knew she lied, he started to pick up the pace.

"Well, crap." Jumping off the rail, she made a beeline for the barn. There had to be something in there for Cyclone to pull. Rounding the corner of the open barn doors, she grinned. "Perfect." Jumping onto the four-wheeler, she turned the key they always left in it and drove out of the barn and straight for the corral.

A truck with a horse trailer pulled to a stop in front of the house. Hoping Manuel could handle the new horse and whatever its issues were until she could get Cyclone settled, she stopped the ATV and jumped off.

Unfortunately, Cyclone had stopped, too.

"No, Cyclone!" She brought her fingers to her lips once again, but she was too late. The big horse's back legs lifted and he smashed the top rail of the corral. Wood flew everywhere, and she ducked. Then before the horse could gear-up for another kick, she climbed up on the fence post closest to him and jumped.

Grasping his mane, she cooed as he walked sideways. "Come on boy, I've got some work for—"

A strong arm grabbed her around the waist from behind and pulled her off to the side.

Not expecting that, she lost her grip on Cyclone and her full weight fell onto the person beneath her. They both went toppling to the ground inside the enclosure.

She rolled out of his grasp and jumped to her feet, more worried about the horse than the stranger lying on the ground inside the corral. Spotting Cyclone starting his circle run again, she brushed off her jeans before glaring at the cowboy now rising to his feet. "What the hell do you think you're doing?"

Striding past him, she climbed over the corral fence and hopped back on the four-wheeler.

"What am I doing? I'm saving your neck."

She barely spared him a glance as he picked up his cowboy hat and ran for the fence himself as Cyclone headed directly for him.

"If you want to help go get the collar harness hanging on the hook inside the barn while I keep him from jumping the fence."

Not caring if the dark-haired stranger bothered to listen to her or not, she turned the machine on and drove it parallel to the broken fence to fill the gap. The last thing she needed was a runaway Cyclone.

Not sure what the horse would do next, she jumped off and watched as he approached. He trotted by as if the four-wheeler was another part of the corral.

Figuring she had about thirty seconds before Cyclone came around again, she turned her attention to the cowboy who approached, harness in hand. She pointed to the horse trailer. "Is the horse in there okay for a few more minutes?"

At his nod, she waved toward the ATV. "Good. Do you think you can hook that up to the ATV?"

His brow furrowed. "I just saw you drive it. Why would you need to tow it?"

Cyclone was coming around again. Either she needed to get back on his back or let him out. Otherwise, there'd be two fence rails to repair. "Just tell me, can you do it?" Irritation colored her tone, but she didn't have time for pleasantries. Where the hell was Manny anyway?

The cowboy threw her a scowl before moving to the ATV.

She climbed on the fence. Maybe if she could interrupt the big horse's stride, it might take him a bit to build up steam again.

Jumping to the ground, she ran out in front of him, waving her arms. "Whoa, Cyclone!"

The Clydesdale swerved in midstride, cutting short his circle.

Just great. Turning back to the cowboy, she found him staring at her his eyes appearing almost silver. For shit's sake. "Is it hooked?"

"Are you trying to get yourself killed?" He dropped the harness and stalked to the fence.

She met him there. "No, I'm trying to keep this big boy from destroying the corral." She climbed over the fence and picked up the harness then dropped it on the handle bars of the machine. "Open the gate." She didn't wait to see if he would help. She just put the ATV in gear.

Come on, Cyclone, skip the break in the fence and get to work.

The cowboy opened the gate, so she drove the machine into the corral. Turning off the engine, she jumped to the ground and rattled the harness just as Cyclone approached the opening with the broken rail.

His ears perked up as he slowed, coming to a stop next to her. "Good boy. You ready to work?"

The Clydesdale's big brown eyes followed her as she started to lift the heavy harness onto him. When the weight was lessened, she nodded to the cowboy who lifted the other half onto the big brute. Once she had Cyclone hitched, she strode to the ATV and sat in the seat, hoping the harness would hold. Leaving the engine off, she shifted the machine into neutral. "Okay, Cyclone. Let's bring this baby to Cole's house." Clicking her tongue, she grabbed the handles wrapped in reins and the horse started to walk.

When the horse exited the corral, towing the ATV with her on it, she finally gave the cowboy her attention as he closed the gate behind her. Nice ass, not uncommon among the cowboys she'd worked with. He was clean shaven, broad at the shoulders and slender at the hips. He wore a long sleeve shirt, which she'd find stifling in the dry heat, though many landscapers did that. She assumed it was to avoid burning from the brutal Arizona sun.

He came up next to her as Cyclone plodded along. "So, what's this? Some kind of therapy?"

His eyes were actually a blue-grey and at the moment filled with curiosity as opposed to censure, which is what she would have expected from a stranger watching her over the last twenty minutes. Now that she had a good look at him, he reminded her of some of her military buddies before they'd all headed to the Middle East and changed. He had less swagger than the typical cowboy and a more commanding presence, but he was just as handsome as the rest at Last Chance. What was it, a prerequisite to work there?

She forced her attention back to his question. "Not exactly therapy. Cyclone likes to work, which means he likes to pull heavy objects. If he's left to his own devices for more than three days, he lives up to his name." She hooked her thumb over her shoulder. "And I'm the one left with the repairs."

He glanced back toward the broken fence of the corral before facing forward again. "Cole told me when he offered me the job that there would be some odd personalities." He chuckled. "I thought he meant the ranch hands."

She smothered a smirk. There were definitely some interesting human personalities on Last Chance, but the horses beat them out. "Where's Manuel?"

The cowboy grinned, and when he did his straight white teeth showed, making him appear very relaxed. "Grandson due any day and his daughter offered him and his wife to move onto their ranch in New Mexico. Nothing stronger than family ties."

Right. Family ties. In her family, those ties had been as likely to hang her as help her. "I'm Riley O'Hare. I do a bit of everything around here. To look at this place right now, you'd never know there are actually eight others involved with this rescue operation."

He reached over as he walked along next to her. "I'm Garrett Walker. I'll be the one bringing you horses."

She shook, his grip firm, not crushing, but the rough texture of the skin on the back of his right hand told her he had some serious scars. "Speaking of horses, what's the story with that one?" She nodded toward the trailer in front of them before she directed Cyclone to turn right down the dirt road that would take them to Cole's house.

"Just old. If you can stop Cyclone here for a moment, I'll take her out and walk with you. She'd probably like to stretch her legs."

She pulled on the reins for her answer.

Garrett strode over to the trailer and unlocked the back. Yup, definitely a more military bearing. That had to be why she felt comfortable with him. She hadn't been with fellow veterans in two years. On one hand, getting together with her former unit members was like old home week, but it always brought back bad memories, so she'd avoided the last two "get-togethers."

She watched the new hauler's moves. He was confident in his actions and comfortable around the horse. Probably grew up with horses. Yet when he'd leaned in to shake hands, she caught a scent of aftershave with an almost clove-like scent. Most of the cowboy's she'd run to when all cleaned up smelled more like soap or fresh linen. She liked the richer smell Garrett wore.

He walked a pretty buckskin quarter horse out of the trailer toward her. Yeah, totally confident and seriously had the face of an actor, more of a Captain America look than a GI Joe.

At the new horse's presence, Cyclone's head swiveled bringing her focus back to him. "Give her a nice welcome, boy, but don't be getting any ideas." Not that she needed to worry. Cyclone had the weirdest crush on Tiny Dancer, who was the frailest mare on the ranch.

He brought the horse over and allowed Cyclone and her to get acquainted.

"What's her name?"

"Lady, though I was told the old man who owned her started calling her Old Lady about seven years ago."

Old Lady? "Was that because Lady is getting older or because the owner was from the seventies?"

Garrett chuckled.

The sound reminded her of the rest of the men on Last Chance. They were always in a good mood. She found that seriously strange. Garrett was also just as good-looking and appeared to have the typical cowboy manners. Not bad overall.

"It was because Lady here is twenty-two, but from what I've seen, she's in very good health for her age."

From what she could see, she agreed, but she'd have Dr. Jenna come over and do her usual "welcome to Last Chance" physical.

Garrett clicked his tongue and Lady started to walk.

She didn't need to encourage Cyclone. The big horse started pulling her as soon as Lady moved beyond him. Typical male. Just couldn't stand to walk a few paces behind a woman. She squelched her attitude. "So why is Lady here?"

"Her owner died." Garrett spoke over his shoulder because Lady was determined to remain in the lead.

"The family doesn't want to keep her or sell her?" It was

rare that they received horses who were simply old. To her, they didn't really qualify as rescues. Most of the horses that came to Last Chance were like Nizhoni and Phoenix, the ones she'd been able to get away from her boss at the time.

Cyclone was moving along at a good clip now, determined to keep abreast of Lady. Garrett walked next to the ATV. "There's two more coming. I'll be bringing them by in another day or two. No one in the family has the property to take them on, which from what I saw would have been their first choice. They seem to care for these horses as much as their grandfather. In fact, one of them will be coming here to stay for a few days to make sure this is the right place for them to live out their lives."

Now that was a first. "I would think knowing this is a rescue ranch would be enough."

Garrett lost his easy-going smile. "It should be, but the youngest grandson was the closest to the old man and is very particular about how they're cared for. I think it's his way of dealing with his grief. He actually made me read a two-page write-up on how to transport them."

She groaned. She'd had by-the-book men under her command, and they just didn't realize that sometimes the "book" went up in flames. There was no way this would be good. "Are you saying this young man is coming here to make us all read policies and procedures on how to care for these horses?"

If that was the case, she would make herself scarce for a couple days. No young punk was going to tell her how to care for horses. She'd grown up with horses, even sleeping with them in the barn she worked in when she couldn't stand to be home.

"I'm not sure what he has planned. I feel for him. It's hard losing someone you're close to."

At his serious tone, she glanced at him. Had he experienced

what she had? The idea brought both sympathy and defenses. The only reason she was functioning normally now was because she wasn't around others who'd had her experience.

Also by Lexi Post

Contemporary Cowboy Romance

Cowboys Never Fold
(Poker Flat Series: Book 1)
Cowboy's Match
(Poker Flat Series: Book 2)
Cowboy's Best Shot
(Poker Flat Series: Book 3)
Cowboy's Break
(Poker Flat Series: Book 4)
Wedding at Poker Flat
(Poker Flat Series: Book 5)

Christmas with Angel
(Poker Flat Series Book 2.5, Last Chance Series: Book 1)
Trace's Trouble
(Last Chance Series: Book 2)
Fletcher's Flame
(Last Chance Series: Book 3)
Logan's Luck
(Last Chance Series: Book 4)

Dillon's Dare
(Last Chance Series: Book 5)
Riley's Rescue
(Last Chance Series: Book 6)

Aloha Cowboy
(Island Cowboy Series: Book 1)

Military Romance

When Love Chimes
(Broken Valor Series: Book 1)
Poisoned Honor
(Broken Valor Series: Book 2)

Paranormal Romance

Masque
Passion's Poison
Passion of Sleepy Hollow
Heart of Frankenstein

Pleasures of Christmas Past
(A Christmas Carol Series: Book 1)
Desires of Christmas Present
(A Christmas Carol Series: Book 2)
Temptations of Christmas Future
(A Christmas Carol: Book 3)
One of A Kind Christmas
(A Christmas Carol Series: Book 4)

On Highland Time
(Time Weavers, Inc.: Book 1)
A Pocket in Time
(Time Weavers, Inc. Book 2) *Coming in 2020*

Sci-fi Romance

Cruise into Eden
(The Eden Series: Book 1)
Unexpected Eden
(The Eden Series: Book 2)
Eden Discovered
(The Eden Series: Book 3)
Eden Revealed
(The Eden Series: Book 4)
Avenging Eden
(The Eden Series: Book 5)
Beast of Eden
(Eden Series: Book 6)
Bound by Eden
(The Eden Series: Book 7) *Coming Soon*

About Lexi Post

Lexi Post is a New York Times and USA Today best-selling author of romance inspired by the classics. She spent years in higher education taking and teaching courses about the classical literature she loved. From Edgar Allan Poe's short story "The Masque of the Red Death" to Tolstoy's *War and Peace*, she's read, studied, and taught wonderful classics.

But Lexi's first love is romance novels. In an effort to marry her two first loves, she started writing romance inspired by the classics and found she loved it. From hot paranormals to sizzling cowboys to hunks from out of this world, Lexi provides a sensuous experience with a "whole lotta story."

Lexi is living her own happily ever after with her husband and her cat in Florida. She makes her own ice cream every weekend, loves bright colors, and you will never see her without a hat.

www.lexipostbooks.com

Printed in Great Britain
by Amazon